Death in the
Dolomites

Books by David P. Wagner

The Rick Montoya Italian Mysteries
Cold Tuscan Stone
Death in the Dolomites

Death in the Dolomites

A Rick Montoya Italian Mystery

David P. Wagner

Poisoned Pen Press

Copyright © 2014 by David P. Wagner

First Edition 2014

10 9 8 7 6 5 4 3 2 1

Library of Congress Catalog Card Number: 2014938556

ISBN: 9781464202704   Hardcover
      9781464202728   Trade Paperback

Poisoned Pen Press
6962 E. First Ave., Ste. 103
Scottsdale, AZ 85251
www.poisonedpenpress.com
info@poisonedpenpress.com

Printed in the United States of America

This one's for Max, who could navigate
the *pista della morte* with his eyes closed.

Chapter One

It had snowed most of the day, but a new and stronger system had begun blowing over the mountain from the north, diving into the valley. Snow was always welcome in a ski town, especially the clumped flakes that now cast ever-larger shadows on the ground under the streetlamps. The cement of the sidewalk and the parking lot, barely visible an hour before, was now covered. Bad news for Campiglio's street crews but not for the skiers who had left Milan the previous afternoon to climb into the Dolomites, skis snapped to racks on the roofs of their cars. They had been rewarded with an excellent day of skiing, and with this snow, tomorrow would be even better. If it kept up through the night, the base could last for weeks. The local merchants were likely standing outside their shops right now, letting the flakes fall on their grinning faces.

At this moment the man's interest was not in tourists, but in the stained canvas duffel at his feet. He pulled his wool cap down over his ears and adjusted a small backpack before looking once more around the large lot. It was deserted save for a few cars of the remaining employees at the far side. His eyes moved to the bulky building and the thick cables that ran out of one side toward the mountain. On its top, the last weak rays of late afternoon sun, long gone from the valley below, outlined the station at the high end of the cable line.

It was time.

With a grunt he wrapped the strap of the duffel around his gloved hand and began to drag it toward the building. His burden slid easily through the accumulating snow and occasional patches of ice, like an injured skier on a ski-patrol sled. The last few meters would be inside on the loading platform, but the snow sticking to the bag would help it slide. This would be even easier than he'd planned. Halfway he stopped to catch his breath, pulling up his jacket sleeve to check his watch. Perfect, he thought. There would be one more run of the gondola before its cables stopped for the night, and he would be on it.

On the mountain the cleaning crew was finishing its duties. Given the number of skiers who had passed through the snack bar on their way to the *piste* during the day, the workload was heavy. The floor was now clean of slush and mud, and four black garbage bags, almost as tall as the women who handled them, had been loaded into the waiting gondola. It would be the same story the next night, especially with the snow now falling. One of the workers—a woman who had been doing the late afternoon shift for more years than she would admit—put down her mop, walked to the window, and peered out at the falling snow. She shook her head and returned to her job. A few moments later the crew stood in a silent clump near the door while the supervisor made a final check of the room. The woman closest to the door slid it open, letting in a light gust of wind and snow. The others, now in parkas and wool coats, instinctively pulled them around their necks in anticipation of the cold. The supervisor finally nodded and the group began to file onto the platform to the waiting gondola, snow already covering its roof and the windows on one side. When they were all inside, the supervisor closed the latch on the door and took a silent head count before picking up the black phone hanging near the door.

"Guido, *siamo pronti*," she said.

Below, the man in the control room hung up his phone while keeping his eyes on the last sentences of a story in *Gazzetta dello Sport*. Guido knew it was not going to be a good year for his team, and again wondered why last season's star player had been sold. To make it worse, the bastard would now play for their biggest rival. He folded the paper in disgust and pulled the long wooden lever, never glancing at the platform below. The huge dynamo came slowly to life and the cable above the long window shuddered and began to move.

The man was crouched on the floor of the gondola, well below its ski-scratched windows, when it swung slowly and lurched upward. Neither he nor the sack were visible from above, even if Guido had taken his eyes off the newspaper and looked down from his seat in the control room. As the huge metal box was dragged from the dim light of the lower station into the darkness, the man inside it heard the snow slapping softly against the glass windows above his head. He slowly got to his feet and looked down at the base station, now fading quickly as the cable picked up speed. In a few minutes its lights would be hard to distinguish from those of the other buildings at the northern edge of Campiglio.

The route was a steep shot straight to the top of the mountain, suspended over a forest of tall pines. The only breaks in the thick covering of trees were the clearings around the pylons or a few spots where the stone core of the mountain had pushed itself through the dirt. The ski trails, in contrast, returned to Campiglio over a tamer terrain. They took their time to work through the softer hills of the mountain's other side, carrying skiers to a choice of bases along the east side of town.

He walked to the other end of the gondola cabin and looked upward. In the swirling wind and snow he could not make out his gondola's twin, but he knew it was rushing toward him and would be passing soon. He dragged the duffel toward the door and checked to see that the latch had not slipped closed. It had not. According to his calculations the best time would be after passing the second pylon, and just at that moment the cable carrying his gondola slipped over the first one. He flexed his knees as the floor bounced slowly while continuing its climb. Suddenly the other gondola appeared out of the storm and the man dropped to his knees to get out of sight. Through the howling wind he heard a laugh from one of the workers as the two gondolas passed each other. Seconds later the only sound was once more the hum of the cable and the increasing patter of the snow. He reached over and slowly slid the door open with his right hand. As the snow swirled inside he sat back on the floor, the sack between him and the opening.

When the next pylon passed he waited until the swinging stopped and firmly pushed the sack out the door with both feet. As he got up to slide the door closed he heard the crack of a tree branch and then the soft thump as the sack hit the snow below. The sound meant that it had sunk in, and with the new snow it would be well covered. Once the door was closed he slipped the latch into place. Safety first.

A few minutes later the other gondola bumped slowly into its berth at the edge of the town, where it would stay until it took the morning crew up on the first run of the day. The workers pushed out, waving at Guido in the control room while they pulled the plastic garbage bags behind them. Guido nodded to the group leader but kept his eyes on the young body of one of the newer members of the crew. When they had all shuffled through the door below him, he switched off the motors and gathered his belongings—the newspaper and a thermos. He was always sure to straighten up so the morning shift would have no complaints. He turned out the lights and locked the door behind him. As he walked down the stairs to the streets he wondered what his wife would be serving for dinner. She had not made lasagna in a while, perhaps this was the night. After pulling on a wide-brimmed hat, Guido buttoned his leather coat and walked into the storm.

High above, the man stepped out of the gondola and slid the door shut. On the platform the footprints of the cleaning crew were already covered, as his own would be in a matter of minutes. He turned and looked down at the valley, its lights blending together through the prisms of the falling flakes. After a moment of reflection he adjusted his backpack and walked on the deck that ran along the outside of the building.

Its tables and chairs had been stacked and pushed against the windows under the overhanging eaves, but the protection was not enough. The morning work crew would need their shovels. Two steps led from the deck down to where the wide trail began, a relatively benign incline for the skiers to start their runs, but still often littered with fallen beginners. He could barely make out the trail, but it didn't really matter, he could get down the mountain blindfolded.

He cleared away a patch of snow at the edge of the deck with his foot and put down his backpack before stepping off and walking around to the far side of building to a small storage shed. After bending over, he used his gloved hands to scrape away the snow under the shed's door, revealing a small opening from which he pulled a pair of dark skis and poles. Even though the falling snow would do the job for him, he carefully brushed the snow back with his foot before hoisting the equipment over his shoulder and returning to where he had left the backpack. From it he took out a pair of ski boots whose dark plastic matched the skis. After the usual grunts he had the ski boots on his feet and the snow boots secured in the pack. He also had a pair of ski goggles over his cap. It took him only a few seconds to snap into the skis and strap the poles around his wrists. It was snowing even more heavily now. The clear yellow plastic brightened the view slightly as he pulled the goggles down over his eyes and squeezed the rubber grips of the poles. He straightened up, pulling back the sleeve of his parka to check his watch again in the little light that was left in the day. Yes, the ski patrol would already be at the bottom after their final run to catch any stragglers. He pushed off slowly and began to work his way left and right through the fresh powder, his boots always touching as he flexed his knees for each turn. The flakes swirled around his bare cheeks, but he did not feel the cold. He knew that by the time he reached the valley, his tracks, as well as everything else on the mountain, would be shrouded in snow.

Chapter Two

Rick Montoya came to a stop on a small ledge, leaned on his ski poles, and surveyed Campiglio. Rays of midday sunlight cut diagonally through the falling snow, reflecting off chalet roofs for a few seconds before disappearing under more waves of white flakes. Like so many towns in the Dolomites, Campiglio could thank the post-war economic boom and the growth of skiing for its prosperity. It had once been an isolated mountain village whose economy was based on sheep and goats. Today it swarmed with flatlanders from both sides of the border, eager to spend their euros in the thin Alpine air. And when the skiers left, the locals barely had time to enjoy a glass of wine before the hikers rolled in. Business was good, though that never kept them from complaining.

The town nestled in a narrow valley surrounded on three sides by the Dolomites. Each side had its own sets of cabled machinery to transport the skiers from the town to the trails; only at the southern end did the mountains open. That was the only direction that Campiglio could grow, wedged in as it was by the peaks which gave it its livelihood. It was to the south, along the road to Trento, where the newest of the chalets and apartments were being built. The center that Rick surveyed had maintained its small-town feel. He looked down on an irregular carpet of roofs, some broken by chimneys emitting wisps of smoke. It was completely different from many of the resorts he'd skied in the Rockies, where high-rise hotels came right up to the trail bases. Above all, it was the quiet here that was most relaxing. The occasional call of one skier to another, or the scrape of a ski, was quickly muffled by an all-consuming silence.

A few hundred meters below Rick was the end of the trail, open and treeless, where ski classes formed up in the morning and families found each other at the end of a run. He could hear the clanking of the chairlifts as they swung around before silently following the cable back up the hill. It was lunch time, so the lift would not be getting much business until later in the afternoon. Two skiers shushed past him on the way to the bottom where they would slip out of their skis and clomp into town for the best meal of the day.

Rick knew that a steaming bowl of pasta tastes even better, if that's possible, after a morning of skiing. And he had known all morning what he was about to be treated to in the hotel dining room: *fettuccine* with a mushroom cream sauce. Both he and Flavio had chosen it over the bowl of broth when the girl had appeared at their breakfast table to get their lunch preferences. A bowl of broth after a morning on the slopes? Not on your life.

From his vantage point he could see the roof of their hotel and managed to convince himself that he could smell the mushrooms simmering in the sauce. Flavio's choice of a hotel had been a good one, but that would be expected from someone who grew up in the town. In addition to the food, the bonus was location, tucked quietly above the more congested parts of Campiglio, yet a short walk down to the action. And the family that owned it was so relaxed and informal they would have fit in perfectly in Rick's native New Mexico. Well, perhaps native wasn't the right word, since he was born in Rome, but Rick Montoya's family roots were planted deeply on both sides of the Atlantic. He looked over the housetops of Campiglio and was reminded again how far he was from the American Southwest—in more ways than distance. Too many deep thoughts, he decided; this is a vacation. And it is lunch time.

◇◇◇

After stowing his ski equipment in the storage room Rick climbed the stairs to the lobby in his loafers, found no messages, and walked into the wood-paneled dining room. There were about thirty tables, a few more than the number of rooms, a third of them now filled with hotel guests in ski pants and sweaters. Flavio was already at his place at their assigned table along the windows at the far side of the room. The table location was one of the advantages of knowing the owners, as Flavio had pointed out when they took their first meal. Rick was surprised to see another man sitting with him. The surprise was not that there was someone with Flavio, since his friend seemed to know half the people in Campiglio. It was the way the man was dressed. In contrast with Flavio's ski outfit, the stranger wore a dark suit with a white shirt and striped tie—the first suit Rick had seen since driving into the ski resort three days earlier. The man looked as out of place here as Rick would have looked wearing ski clothes in a restaurant near his apartment in Rome.

A few years older than Rick and Flavio, probably in his late thirties, the man had a round face and a smile guaranteed to put anyone at ease. Rick remembered the game he played with his Uncle Piero, the policeman, when they had their weekly lunches in Rome. Each would guess the profession of someone at a neighboring table, stating the reasons. His uncle used his years of experience dealing with criminals and the general public, as well as a few detective techniques, to make his guesses. Rick used intuition and studied body language. Rick now guessed this man was either an insurance salesman or a mortician. Flavio looked up and waved Rick to the table with a characteristic scooping motion of the hand.

"Rick," he said, "a good friend from Trento has just appeared and will be staying in our hotel. Meet Luca Albani. Luca, this is my American-Roman friend Riccardo Montoya." The two shook hands and Rick took a seat.

"Luca, I hope you're not planning on skiing in that suit," said Rick, as Flavio poured him some red wine.

The man smiled, but his face was anything but carefree. "Unfortunately, my new American friend, I am here on business. And I have never worn skis in my life. Is that how you say it, Flavio, 'wear skis'?"

"Close enough."

Rick remembered his guessing game. "And what business brings you to Campiglio?"

"An unfortunate situation. A visitor to the town has been reported missing. Because the sub-station here is small, I have been sent to investigate." He noticed Rick's perplexed look. "You see, Riccardo, I am a policeman." The smile returned.

So much for guessing professions, thought Rick. He would not mention this to Uncle Piero.

"Luca is fighting a losing battle against crime in the region," said Flavio before taking a drink of his wine. "Despite his efforts we will eventually be overrun with criminal elements like the rest of Italy."

It was classic Flavio. Rick looked at the policeman and noted his grin. "You appear to know Flavio as well as I do, Luca. At the university he was known as Glass Half-Empty Flavio." This got a smile even from Flavio. "But you are not from Trento," Rick continued. "You sound more Roman. How long have you been up here in the north?"

The answer was delayed by the arrival of their *primi*, three dishes of fresh pasta in a creamy mushroom sauce, just as Rick had pictured it all morning. They passed the cheese bowl, wished each other *buon appetito*, picked up their forks, and began to eat. After a few bites Luca replied.

"It has been, let's see, a little more than two years, hasn't it, Flavio?" Flavio nodded as he ate. "Flavio and I remember it well, Riccardo, since my first case when I arrived in Trento involved the accountant in Flavio's wine export business who was embezzling funds. I hope you don't mind me mentioning that, Flavio." Flavio shrugged and continued working on his *fettuccine*. "It has been a fascinating two years," the policeman said. "There is so much to see up here, so much to learn." Rick noticed Flavio rolling his eyes. "But tell me about how you two met, it must be an interesting story. Flavio told me it was at the university in America?"

Rick sprinkled more cheese on his *fettuccine*. "It was. Our friend here came to my university on a skiing scholarship, and our paths crossed. When he found out my mother was Italian and I spoke the language, I couldn't get rid of him. His English, I'm sorry to say, was atrocious."

"Was not," mumbled Flavio through a mouthful of pasta.

Rick continued as if Flavio had said nothing. "Since I was studying languages, I was able to help him. And he managed eventually to get his business degree. Though a lot of good it did him if now he goes around hiring embezzlers to work in his company."

"This is a wonderful story." Luca beamed. "I must hear all the details of your studies in America. I am fascinated by other cultures."

Flavio pushed back his empty dish. "Luca is fascinated with everything, Rick. Sometimes it makes me tired to be around him."

Luca grinned. It was the default facial feature of the man. "Flavio told me your uncle is a policeman in Rome. Perhaps I would know him?"

"Commissario Piero Fontana."

"Commissario Fontana, of course. One of our best detectives. He sometimes teaches at the academy. And have you ever thought about entering the profession, Rick?"

"Funny you should say that." Rick took a piece of crusty bread from the basket on the table. "My uncle has asked me that question more than once. But I have a translation business which is now well established in Rome, so I'm satisfied with my present work. And my mother would not be pleased if I became involved in criminal activity, even if it were on the correct side of the law."

The waitress appeared and removed their empty plates. Flavio wordlessly pointed to the empty wine bottle and she nodded before heading into the kitchen.

The policeman's face turned pensive. "You know, Rick, you being a translator, and American, perhaps you could be of some help to me in this case." Puzzled looks spread over both Rick and Flavio's faces. "But without getting you in trouble with your mother."

Rick took a sip of the wine. "Tell me more."

Luca brushed some crumbs from his suit jacket and checked to be sure that no mushroom sauce had dropped on his tie. "Well, the person who has gone missing is one of your compatriots, a man named Cameron Taylor who works for an American bank in Milan. He is here on holiday with his sister who is visiting from America. It was she who reported him missing, and I am going to talk with her this afternoon. I studied English at the *liceo*, but…"

"I understand," said Rick. "Of course, if I can be of assistance, it would be my pleasure."

"What about our skiing in the afternoon?" asked Flavio. "I don't want to ski by myself."

"*Caro* Flavio," answered Rick patiently, "first of all, I spent the morning watching you ski out of sight as I made my way leisurely down the mountain. Second, the only times I caught up with you were when you stopped to chat with people you knew, which was often. So I doubt if you will be lonely out there. And finally, it is my civic duty to help our police."

"I liked the last part," said Luca. "And spoken by an American, yet."

"He's got dual citizenship, Luca. Italian mother."

The waitress arrived with another bottle of the wine and showed the label to Flavio. "I think," he said to his tablemates, "that perhaps we should switch from this Casteller, which was perfect with the cream sauce, to something more substantial to go with our cutlets. Do you agree?"

"Whatever you say, Flavio," said Luca.

"You're the wine guy," Rick added.

"Fine." Flavio turned to the waitress. "I think Giulio has a few bottles of Teroldego Rotaliano. Bring us one of them if you would." She walked back into the kitchen through the swinging door, clutching the rejected bottle. "Since I supply them their stock, I know what's on the wine list. You'll like this one, it is produced just east of here, and—"

"Don't start the wine-speak on us, Flavio," said Rick. Luca enjoyed the comment while Flavio scowled. The contrast between the two men was striking, and Rick wondered how they could have become friends. Probably the same way he and Flavio had hit it off ten years earlier in Albuquerque.

When Flavio Caldaro had arrived on the campus of the University of New Mexico, the only person he knew was the assistant ski coach who had recruited him during a trip to Europe the previous year. The university was known for its foreign student athletes, especially in soccer and basketball, but one from Italy was out of the ordinary. The change from Alps to high desert was tough on the Italian, not to mention getting used to taking classes in English and the total absence of decent Italian food. He was determined to stick it out, at least for one year, but at the end of one semester he was ready to pack it in and head back to the Dolomites. Enter Rick Montoya, son of an American diplomat father and a Roman mother. Rick was already fluent in English and Italian, and his Spanish was pretty good thanks to visits to his grandparents in northern New Mexico, so languages had been the logical, and easy, choice for a course of study. When one of his professors told him an Italian foreign student needed some tutoring, he volunteered to help. Do one for the *patria*, Rick had thought. After spending about half his life in Italy and half in the States, a sub-theme of Rick's college years was the issue of his own national identity. Nobody was pushing him to choose between the two countries, but it was something he thought about. Not obsessively—Rick's main obsession was enjoying college life—but he did think about it. So he welcomed the chance to help a fellow Italian. At first they didn't get along very well. In fact, after a few weeks of tutoring, Rick went to the professor to say it just wasn't working. The guy is too negative, Rick told him, I get depressed just being around him. Fortunately the professor convinced him to stick with it.

The waitress returned, opened the new bottle, and poured an inch into a fresh glass in front of Flavio. He tasted it and gave her a nod, after which she filled the other two glasses before returning to his.

"Did you ever think that it might be hard to send it back," asked Rick, "since they bought it from you?"

"I don't test every bottle, Rick."

"Your time is better spent supervising your accountants, I suppose."

The policeman listened to the exchange and asked: "Are you two always like this?"

Rick stood in front of the mirror and used the hair dryer that came with the room, remembering his mother's admonition never to go out in the winter with a wet head. He also contemplated the word Italians used for hair dryer: *föhn*. There was a literal translation, *asciuga capelli*, but most Italians seemed to use the German word which came from a brand of hair dryer, in turn derived from a warming Alpine wind. As Rick mused that such etymological trivia was the curse and delight of the professional translator, he heard the call of his cell phone. Its ring, the Lobo Fight Song, managed to cut through the sound of the dryer. He walked out to the dresser, checked the number, and smiled.

"Commissario Piero Fontana, I am honored." It was the standard greeting he used when his Uncle Piero called.

"Riccardo, my favorite nephew." The reply was also traditional, both knowing that Rick was the man's only nephew. "I trust you are enjoying your ski holiday. Here in Rome it rains without ceasing."

"That makes me enjoy my holiday even more, *Zio*. If you called to find out the weather in the Dolomites, it is perfect. A light snow has been falling since I arrived, making ideal powder for skiing. I'm not sure which group is happier here in Campiglio, the merchants and ski lift operators, or the tourists."

"I was not calling for a meteorological update, Riccardo, but I'm pleased to hear it. The purpose of my call was something else." Rick waited, hoping that there was not a problem, though the tone of his uncle's voice indicated all was well in Rome. Except the weather. "Word has reached my office that there is a police investigation going on in Campiglio, and it has occurred to me that you could be of some assistance."

Once again the commissario was trying to get Rick into police work, even if it had to be through the back door. Thanks to Piero's efforts, Rick was already on the books of the *Polizia dello Stato* as an informal consultant. Ostensibly it would be for cases involving cross-cultural problems or translations, but as far as Piero was concerned, it could be for anything interesting that might pop up.

"I'm already on it, *Zio*, you needn't have called." Rick grinned as he waited for a reply, which did not come immediately. Piero had been caught off guard, and that didn't happen very often.

"The missing American?"

"Exactly. I am about to head into town with Inspector Luca—"

"Albani, Inspector Luca Albani. Yes, he's the one. But how could you…?"

Rick was tempted to have some more fun with his uncle, but opted instead to tell him the story of meeting the policeman in the hotel and being asked to help with translation. In such a small town, such things happen, he said.

"Well, Riccardo, I am pleased that you were so willing to help one of my colleagues, though I don't think I have ever met the man. It means you won't be displeased to hear that I had called Trento to suggest that you be brought into the investigation."

Rick shook his head as he held the phone to his ear. This was typical of Uncle Piero. "I doubt if I can be of much help, except to do some translating for the inspector."

"You never know, Riccardo." There was a pause. "I should tell you that Inspector Albani has a good reputation."

Rick grinned. It was just the kind of thing his uncle would have checked on before getting his nephew involved.

"There's something else, though," Piero added. "Inspector Albani is also known to have some quirks."

I'd already sensed that, Rick thought.

They exchanged family pleasantries for a while longer before Rick hung up and finished getting dressed. He was pleased and flattered that his uncle had gotten semi-official support for his assisting in the disappearance investigation. This could allow him to get more into things than simply translating for Luca with the sister of the missing man. He wondered how the inspector would take having an amateur forced on him.

Chapter Three

The main square of Campiglio was getting another dusting of light snow. Earlier a Zamboni-like machine had pushed the night's accumulation into high piles on two sides of the *piazza*, allowing the pensioners out for their morning exercise to stroll across it without trouble. The afternoon crowd was different, more mothers with carriages and small children, and even some tourists who for some reason had skipped the afternoon session on the slopes. The shops were open, but would not be doing much business until the late afternoon and evening when the mountain closed. Luca gestured Rick to stop, pointing to three little boys who had climbed to the top of one of the snowbanks. They were pushing chunks of snow off their little hill and watching them splatter over the pavement.

"Look at the reactions of those men on the bench," said Luca. Four men in their seventies sat watching the boys' antics. "The two on the left, who are frowning, they don't have any grandchildren. But not the other two men, they are loving it."

Rick studied the bench. "Perhaps the two grumpy ones are relatives of the men who sweep the *piazza*. Or maybe they had the job themselves before they retired."

"When I retire, I will prefer watching children."

"You're too young to be thinking about retirement, aren't you Luca?" They walked out of the square onto Campiglio's main street, following the directions given them at the local police station. Luca had politely turned down the offer of the sergeant to accompany them to the apartment of the missing man's sister.

"It is never too early to think about choices in life, my American friend, no matter how distant they may seem to be. Life is like riding in a car on the autostrada. You vaguely make out something very far off, and before you realize it…zoom, it is past you. You must always be watching, enjoying what is around you, asking questions. Like that balcony up there." Most of the buildings on the main street had shops at street level, apartments in the upper stories, most with balconies. Inspector Albani was looking at one whose flower boxes, despite the season, were filled with healthy red geraniums. "The person living in that apartment has taken loving care of those flowers, perhaps covering them at night to avoid freezing or even bringing them inside. The contrast with the other apartments on the floor is striking. What would cause someone to go to such trouble? The desire to show up the neighbors? Or something more noble, like a vow to continue to care for the flowers after the death of a spouse who in life took great joy in them? There is a story there, either an uplifting one or something more banal."

Rick was starting to understand what Flavio meant about getting tired around Luca.

"I am curious, Riccardo, about you and Flavio, the chance meeting at the university which has turned into a strong friendship. He was immersed in a foreign culture, struggled, but was thrown a lifeline by someone who by chance had lived in two cultures himself. The story fascinates me."

"Everything seems to fascinate you, Luca."

The policeman laughed. "You are right. But you two are so different. You seem very relaxed and cheerful. Flavio, he's…"

"He's not relaxed and cheerful. True. But now it's my turn for the analysis, Luca. I think you know very well how we could have become friends, since you went through the same process after you two met during that embezzlement investigation. He came to trust you, and you eventually got through Flavio's armor and found that he could be a loyal friend. You learned that he would, as we say in America, give you the shirt off his back. And now you want to see if my experience was the same as yours. Am I right?"

Luca's grin almost ran the width of his round face. "I am impressed by your intuition, Riccardo. You will be of great help in this investigation, and not just by allowing me to bounce my theories off a fellow Roman." Rick threw up his hands defensively. "Yes, yes," responded Luca, "you are not a *Romano* in the usual sense. But regardless, your uncle is right in trying to get you into police work full time rather than occasionally helping out policemen like me." He brushed snow off his thick black hair.

"Won't happen, Luca. Where's your hat?"

"How embarrassing. I left Trento this morning in such a rush I forgot to pack it. Mine would not be as stylish as yours, though."

Rick touched his fingers to the brim of his Borsalino. He'd admired it in the window of a hat shop near Piazza Navona for weeks before the cooler weather in Rome finally provided a justification for the purchase. "Unless you can find this guy quickly, Luca, you'll have to get one here. You don't want to be catching a head cold."

"You sound like my wife." He looked at a piece of paper he'd pulled from his coat. "The building should be just ahead. There it is, number 381. Apartment 4A."

The entrance to the residential floors was centered between two shops. A shoe store was on the left, its *vetrina* shelves filled with thick-soled boots and furry after-ski footwear. Sweet smells escaped through the glass doors of the bakery on the other side. Cookies and small cakes were artistically stacked to lure the passing public, but after his hearty lunch at the hotel, Rick was not tempted. The door to the apartment entrance was open and the two men walked into a small hallway that was decorated with marble and glass. Not luxurious, but certainly not shabby. They got into the elevator and took it to the top floor where they found apartment A and rang the bell.

Money was what came to mind when Rick saw the woman who answered the door. Who was it who said you can never be too rich or too thin? Catherine Taylor's outfit was casual but chic: black corduroy slacks over brown leather boots, a white cashmere sweater, a single pearl hanging from a gold pendant around her neck. The blond hair was pulled back and held in place with a thin wine-colored scarf, revealing small gold hoops in her ears. Makeup was minimal, but she didn't need much after what nature had bestowed. Despite her age, which Rick guessed to be about twenty-five, she did not appear to be awed by the presence of the police. Whether she had summoned them or been stopped by them in the past remained to be seen. What she did show on her face was surprise that the policeman—and it was clear from Luca's suit and overcoat who was the policeman—was accompanied by someone in the more informal attire of the town, including—strangely enough—cowboy boots. And that person was only a few years older than she was, and good-looking.

"I was expecting only one person."

Luca extended his hand to the woman and stepped slowly into English. "I am Inspector Albani, from Trento. My English, it is not good. I have brought Signor Montoya who will give a help." He grinned at her and then at Rick.

"I'm Rick Montoya, Miss Taylor."

"Montoya. That sounds Mexican." She concentrated on Rick as if the policeman, after making his initial speech, had suddenly disappeared.

"*New* Mexican, actually." Rick wondered what other warm and welcoming phrases would emerge from this lovely mouth. "Montoyas have been living there for about three hundred years. May we come in?" Luca continued to smile, not getting any of what Rick had said.

"Oh, of course. Sorry." She stood back and gestured toward the room which opened off the small entranceway, giving Rick a whiff of a perfume that smelled vaguely familiar. The living room had the kind of furniture expected in a Dolomite ski resort rental: wood and more wood. Had it been Montana, there would have been a few antlers hanging somewhere, but here the wall decorations were local tourism posters. On a table in one corner sat a large wood carving of a deer or elk, he wasn't sure which. Rick's eyes were drawn to the large window and its view of the eastern side of the valley. He could see a few rays of sun hitting the *piste* where he would have been had he gone skiing with Flavio. Getting a tan was one of the primary reasons Italians went to the mountains, so the east-slope trails were popular with the afternoon skiers.

Without being asked, the two men pulled off their overcoats and folded them over a lone wooden chair near the door. Catherine Taylor took a seat in a cushioned chair with arms of roughly hewn logs, and motioned her visitors to the matching sofa that faced her.

The policeman took a notebook and pen from his suit pocket and spoke in Italian. "Riccardo, if you could ask her about the circumstances of her brother's disappearance? When it was, what he did in the days before, that kind of thing."

"Miss Taylor," said Rick in English, "could you—"

"Please call me Cat, everyone does."

So the snow queen wants to melt, he thought. "Fine, Cat. And please call me Rick. If you could tell us exactly what happened, on a time line, to get things started. I will give the inspector a running translation as you talk." He inclined his head toward the policeman who sat with pen poised, and when she started to speak, Rick translated in a low voice, as he had done countless times in his work.

"My brother and I have been here for five days. That is, here in Campiglio. I was in Milan for one night before we came up here. He rents this apartment from someone he knows. Well, we both know him, from Milan."

"So you have been to Italy before." Rick translated his question for the policeman before turning back to her.

"Oh, yes. Cam—nobody calls him Cameron except our parents—Cam has been living in Milan for almost two years, and I've visited him a few times."

Cam and Cat, thought Rick. Cute. "It sounds like you are very close to your brother."

Her answer was not what he expected. "I don't think you could characterize our relationship as close. Saying that my older brother has always bullied me would be too strong, but he has tried always to order me around, like he knows what's best for me." Luca looked up from his pad for the first time to see that the look on her face matched her comment.

"My older sister used to treat me like that," said Rick, hoping to lighten things up.

"This was more than the usual brother-sister rivalry, Rick."

"Yet you came here for various visits."

She leaned back in the chair and carefully crossed her legs, the slacks tightening over her knee. "He's my brother," she said, as if that explained everything. "And, I just went through a difficult divorce, so what better way to get away from problems than jump on a plane for Italy? Cam had told me not to marry the guy in the first place, but at least he's been decent enough not to keep reminding me."

"And what has been your routine since you got to Campiglio?"

"What you would expect on a ski holiday, though for Cam it's been a combination of business and pleasure."

"How so?"

"Cam was meeting with someone involved in real estate regarding a possible loan from the bank where he works." This got another look from the policeman. "He didn't give me any details, of course."

"Well," said Rick, "it's a good way to write off some of the expenses for the trip."

For the first time Cat Taylor laughed, and it was not endearing. "Let me tell you something about my brother, Rick. He attended parochial school and then went on to fulfill his dream of graduating from Notre Dame. He stayed on in South Bend to study international business. One of the basic precepts that was drummed into his head in business school was the importance of ethics. He takes the morality of business dealings very seriously. So, in response to what you said, I know for certain that he would never go on a ski trip and write it off as business expense because of some short meeting with someone. Even if the bank allowed it."

Rick was impressed. "He sounds like a very—"

She raised her hand to interrupt. "Ah, but unfortunately this high moral posturing only counts in his work. His personal life is a different story."

By now the policeman was concentrating on her face. His pen rested on the pad.

"Are you talking about the way he treats you?" Rick asked.

"The way he treats me is of no real importance. I've been able to defend myself since I was in grade school." The two men continued to stare at her, waiting. "Let me put it this way. When this job in his bank's Milan office came up, he jumped at it. After all, he had done a semester abroad in Rome as an undergraduate at Notre Dame and spoke passable Italian. But the real reason he was so enthusiastic was that it would get him out of town, way out of town, far from not just one but two women." She laid her right arm carefully over the back of the chair and smirked.

Rick was intrigued. Why is this woman talking this way about her missing brother? Apparently Luca had the same thought, and he spoke softly into the ear of his trusted interpreter who listened and then turned back to Catherine Taylor.

"Cat, we seem to have gotten off track. Can we get into the details of what your brother did since you arrived here? He's the one the inspector is here to find."

"Of course." She gazed at the ceiling to gather her thoughts and Luca once again readied his pen and pad. "We drove up Wednesday from Milan after lunch and got here just as it was getting dark. There was no food in the apartment so we went out to a restaurant for dinner."

"Just the two of you?"

"Yes. I wasn't very hungry, and was still tired from the flight since I'd arrived that morning. I'm not very good with jet lag.

I'm still not sleeping through the night and need a nap in the late afternoon. Cam naturally tries to keep me going all day, says it's the only way to beat it."

Rick tried to keep her on topic. "The next day?"

"Thursday we skied in the morning and had some lunch on the mountain. After eating we skied down, I stayed in, and Cam went to his meeting. Before you came I was trying to recall the man's name since I knew you'd ask, and all I can remember is that Cam said his name meant pomegranate."

"Melograno."

"That's it. Funny that people would be called pomegranate. Although I had a friend at boarding school whose last name was Pear." She stopped and looked at Rick. "You didn't translate what I just said for the inspector?"

"No I didn't. What about Thursday night?"

"Cam had picked up some food after his meeting in the afternoon so we ate here. Then he went out and I read a book and went to sleep early. Of course I woke up in the middle of the night. I told you I have a problem—"

"With jet lag. Yes you did. Do you know where your brother went that night?"

"He went to a bar, but I don't know which one. Since he's spent a lot of time up here in the last year he's become familiar with the nightlife, such as it is, in this town."

"Did he mention who he talked to, or anything about what happened in the bar?"

A satisfied smile came to her face. "Normally he wouldn't tell me anything, but the next morning I found out that he'd met a woman in the bar, and they'd hit it off quite well."

Rick was about to ask if the woman was in the apartment when Cam woke up, but decided against it. "How was it you found out?"

"When we went skiing we ran into her. Or she spotted Cam and ran into us. I don't understand Italian, of course, but I could tell by her tone of voice, and his, that there was something there. When he introduced me to her he said they'd been together the night before."

"What was her name?"

"That, I remember. Gina Cortese. The name fits her."

Rick wasn't sure what she meant by the comment, and from Luca's expression he didn't either, despite a good translation. "So he picked up this Gina Cortese in the bar."

"No, I didn't mean to give that impression. He already knew her from previous visits here. In fact he said he'd met her the first summer he came up to Campiglio for the hiking, a year and a half ago. That was when he decided to rent a place. I doubt if Cam's latest girlfriend in Milan knows about her, but that's typical of my brother."

"Do you know if this woman is from here or only comes for holiday?"

"She's from here, she has to be."

"Why do you say that?"

"She's a ski instructor, complete with the blue ski coat they all wear, with the round patch. I took some lessons last year and my instructor wore the same outfit. Her class was waiting while she and Cam made goo-goo eyes at each other."

It took Rick a couple seconds to come up with an Italian equivalent for "goo-goo eyes," but Luca didn't appear to notice the delay. "So you skied again that morning. And the rest of Friday?"

"I stayed in for the afternoon, after eating lunch here, and Cam went back up. That night he had dinner with Miss Cortese."

"You ate here in the apartment?"

"I thought you were only interested in my brother's movements?" Rick shrugged. "Well," Catherine continued, "I went to a restaurant with Daniele. Daniele Lotti, he owns this apartment and the one across the hall, and he arrived in town Friday afternoon. Cam knows him from Milan, which is how he came to rent this apartment."

"So a friend from Milan. Also a banker?"

"No, he works for a drug company, Cam met him through the American Chamber of Commerce. Daniele studied in the States."

"Notre Dame business school?"

She rolled her eyes. "No, thank goodness."

"So you'd met him before this trip."

"Yes, in Milan and up here. Shouldn't we get back to talking about my brother?"

Rick and Luca noted her tone. "Certainly," said Rick. "Did you see your brother that night?"

"Yes, I was still up when he came in. He asked me if I was going to ski the next morning and I said I would pass and see him at lunch. I needed a morning off. "

"So he went out skiing the next morning."

"I have to assume so. His ski clothes are gone from his closet, and his skis, boots, and poles are not in the building's storage room in the basement. But his scuffs, which he wears down the elevator, are in his boot locker down there. So he put on his ski boots and walked out to the street carrying his skis, like we always do."

Luca said something to Rick while she watched. He translated. "The inspector wonders why you waited until Sunday afternoon to notify the authorities."

"I expected you to ask that," she said, shifting in her chair. "I thought my brother had run into that woman again and they'd decided to spend the day together. And when it got late in the evening I assumed one thing had led to another." Rick nodded and Luca kept his eyes on the small pad, filling its pages with notes. "But when I got up Sunday morning and he wasn't here, I began to get worried. In the afternoon I called the embassy in Milan."

"Consulate," Rick corrected. It was a pet peeve.

"Whatever. Cam had given me their number on my first trip to Milan last year, in case I needed it in an emergency. Since it's the weekend, I got the duty officer, and he called the police." She glanced at Luca. "And now you are here."

"Please tell her, Riccardo, that—" Rick held up his hand and leaned forward toward Cat, indicating that he was going to be translating in the other direction. "—tell her that we ordered a search of the mountain by the ski patrol. They had not found anyone yesterday evening on their final run, so they did another one this morning, with special care, and came up with nothing.

If she can provide me a photograph of her brother, I will give it to the local policemen, who will be glad to be doing something other than issue parking citations. We will attempt to find someone who remembers seeing him yesterday morning."

She listened to Rick's translation and spoke. "You must find my brother," she said with more passion than she'd shown since their arrival. Luca noticed it, but she didn't see the faint smile on the policeman's face, since her attention was on Rick alone. "Let me get you a photograph. I have one from my last trip here." She jumped to her feet. "It's perfect since he's wearing the same ski clothes he had on yesterday morning."

She walked quickly out of the room and Rick noticed again that her slacks were a perfect fit. He looked at Luca whose smile had widened. Rick was about to speak when Cat returned with a picture inside a cardboard frame and passed it to Rick. Luca leaned to get a look while she returned to her chair.

The photograph was taken by one of the commercial photographers who stationed themselves on the mountain at places with the most picturesque backgrounds. It showed Cat and her brother leaning on their ski poles, a whitened peak behind them. He wore black ski pants and black boots, a light-blue ski coat, and a dark-blue baseball cap with the gold letters ND on the front. Sunglasses hung from leashes, covering the top of a red sweater visible above the zipper of the coat. Around his neck a blue print bandana was tied, almost in the style of the Old West. Cat wore a one-piece puffy suit, blue with a matching belt, and white ski boots. Her goggles were pushed up to the front of a knit cap that covered most of her blond hair. The resemblance was more than clear. The siblings had the same cheekbones and nose, and they wore similar smiles, no doubt perfected by posing for countless family albums and school yearbooks.

"I can't make out your brother's hair," Rick asked. "Is he blond like you?"

"His hair is darker, almost brown."

It was Luca's turn to ask a question. "His skis, they look silver, but is that just the snow on them?"

"They are silver," she answered after Rick translated. "He special-ordered them from the Kolmartz factory in Austria. Those skis and the Notre Dame cap are his most prized possessions."

"Do you have Kolmartz skis too?"

"Heavens no. I always rent skis with Bruno, his shop is just across the street."

"I think that's the place where I rented my skis," said Rick.

"Did her brother have his cell phone with him?" Rick translated the question.

"He usually carries it when he skies, even though much of the mountain is a dead zone. Just habit. The phone is not here in the apartment, so I assume he has it with him. Of course he hasn't answered it when I've tried to call."

"But he could have called you," said the policeman through Rick.

She turned to Rick. "Doesn't the inspector understand that Cam not calling just could be one reason I notified the consulate? Is he understanding what's going on here?"

Rick decided not to translate, instead asking his own question. "Did he always ski on the same trails in the morning?"

"When I'm not with him he usually gets on the chairlift right behind the apartment, since the runs up there are too difficult for me. He's a very good skier. When I'm with him we walk to the gondola just up the hill from here. The trails there are more my speed."

Luca said something in Rick's ear while she watched. When finished, Rick asked, "Cat, do you have his office phone, and the name of his supervisor at the bank?"

"Didn't I give you that? I think there are some of his cards in this desk." She went to a desk set against one wall, bare save for a laptop computer and a small lamp. From the drawer she pulled out a card which she passed to Rick before sitting down again. "I don't know anyone who works there. Cam has decided I'm not important enough to be introduced to his fellow bankers."

"Thank you, Cat," Rick said, for lack of any other way to react to her comment.

Rick glanced at Luca, silently asking if there were more questions. The policeman shook his head. "We will talk with her again, Rick. For now we have what we want." Rick noticed the use of "we" instead of "I."

They got to their feet. "Cat," said Rick, "thanks for your time. I can assure you that the inspector will let you know as soon as he has something about your brother."

She looked up at them for a few moments before rising from the chair. "I'm glad that you are helping him, Rick." It was a strange thing to say, Rick thought. "Can you give me your cell phone in case I hear anything myself? I can't call *him* since he doesn't speak English." She said it without looking at Luca.

"Of course." Rick pulled out his wallet and passed her a business card. "My cell is on there."

She studied the card and looked at Rick, smiling. "Translation services. And in Rome. I thought you lived up here."

"No, I'm here on holiday and got roped into helping the inspector. Which I was glad to do, of course."

She stuffed the card into her front pants pocket and took Rick's arm. "Let me see you to the door." Luca remained invisible until the two men had slipped on their coats and she was obliged to shake the policeman's hand. "Thank you, Inspector," she said before turning back to Rick. "I know you will find my brother, Rick. The inspector has my number, call me."

Rick waited for her to add "when you find my brother," but she didn't.

Chapter Four

In the elevator Rick studied Cameron Taylor's business card. He was a vice president, but Rick had learned once that almost everyone in a bank except the cleaning crew had such titles. The name of the bank rang a bell in his head.

"Luca, I think I know the guy who runs this bank. I did a simultaneous interpreting job at an economic conference last year in Milan and he was a panelist."

"You know him well enough to call him about this case?"

"Sure. I had a long chat with him at the reception. Since he was new and didn't speak Italian, he didn't mix much with the other participants."

"All the more reason for you to make the call, Riccardo."

"He's probably fairly fluent by now, Luca, that was months ago. He had a tutor."

"I'm sure the language abilities of most of your compatriots are similar to mine."

When they got to the street, the snow was falling more steadily, enough so that some of the passing cars had turned on their wipers, though not their lights. The strong scent of bakery goods hit their nostrils through the cold air.

"Shall we have a coffee, Riccardo?"

"And perhaps a pastry with it?"

"If you don't tell my wife."

"My lips are sealed, Luca."

As in most pastry shops in Italy, a small bar ran half the width of the store, behind which stood a gleaming silver espresso machine. The other half was devoted to the pastries, the full collection rather than just the tempters in the window. The various categories—brioches, cakes, cookies, strudel, éclairs—were separated on the glass shelves by colorful sprigs of artificial flowers. As always in Italy, style was paramount.

A bell had rung when they came in, and a red-faced woman appeared from a door behind the glass display cases. She wiped her hands on a flour-spotted apron as she appeared. From her shape Rick guessed that the pastries behind the counter did not get thrown away when they became stale.

"*Desidera?*"

"*Si, grazie,*" Luca answered. "*Due espressi, per favore.*" He moved to the glass case and turned to Rick. "How about this *mille foglie?*" He was pointing at square layers alternating tissue-thin pastry with a white filling, and topped with powdered sugar. Rick nodded, and the woman took time from her coffee-making duties to put two on a plate and place it between the two customers. After getting their coffees and taking the first sips, Rick spoke.

"Well, Luca, what do you think of our American visitor?"

"A fascinating young woman, Riccardo, who clearly has a very strange relationship with her brother. Not unlike siblings in many Italian families, I should add. Two of my cousins, the children of my Zia Beppa, for example, have been fighting since they were children. Beppa thought that once past childhood they would outgrow it and be close, but they're my age and still bicker at each other about the silliest things. My aunt has given up. But Signora Taylor and her brother appear to have something more complicated going than do my two cousins. Did I understand correctly that he is called Cam and she Cat? Doesn't Cat mean *gatto?*"

"In her case, *gatta*, but yes, you're right on both counts, Luca. So what comes next?"

The policeman bit into the pastry, sprinkling powdered sugar down the front of his coat. "Well, I will have copies made of this photograph and the local police can take it around to the ski lift operators and throughout the town. And there are the two men who must be interviewed." After an attempt to brush off the sugar he pulled his notebook from his suit jacket and flipped through some pages. "A certain signor Melograno, who met with our missing man about a loan, and Daniele Lotti, who lives across the hall from our two siblings. And of course, Signora Cortese, the ski instructor."

Rick bit more carefully into his pastry, and had a small napkin ready. It was excellent, with just a hint of almond paste. "Melograno shouldn't be hard to find. They probably will know him at the police station."

Luca winked and turned to the woman, who was washing cups in a small sink. "Signora, do you know a Signor Melograno, involved in real estate here in Campiglio?"

"Of course, Inspector," she answered brightly. "Dottor Umberto Melograno, he often buys cakes here. His office is on this street, about a hundred meters up on the left, just as the hill starts."

"Thank you. And how did you—?"

"My neighbor has a cousin who works in the police station. Have you found the American?"

"Not yet, Signora." He pulled out some bills to pay for the coffee and waved away Rick's protests. "You just helped me a great deal, Riccardo, and I know you will continue to do so. You must allow me to buy you a simple cup of coffee." He paid, thanked the woman, and they left the shop.

"I would have liked to have stayed longer in that warmth and wonderful bakery smell, but our friend there was trying to catch everything we said. She already knows the three people we're going to interview."

Rick adjusted his hat and looked up at the falling snow. "We, Luca?"

"It is too late to join Flavio at this hour, you might as well keep me company. And as I said earlier, I would rather test my theories on the nephew of a prominent policeman than with the local police force." He held up his index finger and tapped it gently on the side of his nose. "And, my American friend, it helps that my colleagues in Rome agree with me. They have given the okay to have you assist."

Rick knew very well which "colleagues in Rome" were behind it.

Luca put on a mock face of sadness. "In the American western movies, of which I am very fond, the sheriff pins a badge on the man who is being deputized. Alas, I have no such badge for you."

"I appreciate that, Luca, but we can keep this informal."

"Excellent. Now, back to my theories that are in need of testing."

"Test away, Luca." They set off in the direction of Melograno's office.

"Well, *caro* Riccardo, did you notice how Signora Taylor reacted when it was revealed that she had dinner with Lotti, the man who lives across the hall and owns their rental apartment? I found that intriguing. But that said, I wouldn't think that her dinner arrangements with Signor Lotti would have anything to do with her brother going missing. No, it is more likely that this Melograno, or the ski instructor, could lead us to some answers. But we will have to talk to Lotti too. What were your impressions?"

The hatless detective walked on the building side of the sidewalk, keeping himself under the occasional storefront portico that protected him from the snow. Rick noticed him ducking out of the weather, but refrained from mentioning the headcover issue again.

"Yes, Luca, I too noticed her reaction to bringing up her dinner companion, but also saw the way she perked up when mentioning Bruno, the ski rental guy. I met him a few days ago when Flavio took me there to rent my skis." He pointed across the street. "That's his shop there, by the way. You know," Rick added with a grin, "I think he sells hats."

The policeman considered the idea. "Okay, let's make a detour. But allow me to make a quick call to the station so that we can learn where to find this ski instructor." He pulled out his phone, dialed, and told the person on the other end what he needed. "They'll call me back." They crossed the streets, dodging a few cars which were fortunately not going very fast. A thin, gray slush covered the pavement, streaked by the tracks of tires. Luca shook the snow off his hair before they entered the shop.

Only a few customers wandered through the store, and they didn't appear to be serious buyers, but this was not the busy time of day for Campiglio merchants. On one side of the large room, men's clothing was stacked on tables or hung on racks: sweaters, ski coats, pants, and even hats. On the other side was the women's clothing, similarly arranged on tables, and along the rear wall ranged skis, boots, and poles, for both purchase and rental. At a bench, a boy of about ten was trying on a pair of red ski boots, his mother and a saleswoman looking on. The boy stood up and clomped around the carpet, happiness covering his face. Rick and Luca watched him and then turned to a shelf holding various styles of hats. As they looked, a man with thick dark hair and matching goatee approached them. He was dressed in the uniform of Campiglio locals: a light cashmere sweater, elegant slacks, and thick-soled shoes.

"Can I help you find something?" he asked.

Rick turned and smiled. "*Salve*, Bruno. We met a few days ago when I came in with Flavio to rent skis. Riccardo Montoya."

Bruno nodded and smiled. "Yes, of course, Riccardo. The skis are serving you well, I trust?"

"They are, thank you. I'm here with a friend who arrived in Campiglio without a hat. Perhaps he can find one here."

Luca turned around to reveal the suit and tie under his coat. He extended his hand and smiled. "Luca Albani. *Piacere*."

Bauer took a moment to react as he reciprocated the policeman's handshake. "Bruno Bauer, *piacere mio*. We have some more hats over here if you don't see what you want on this shelf. Will you, uh, be in Campiglio long?"

"That depends, that depends." Luca held up a plaid wool hat that to Rick looked suspiciously like something Sherlock Holmes would wear. "I don't really ski, so perhaps something other than the knit ones would be what I'll need."

Again Bruno did not answer immediately, looking at Luca with a blank expression. "Take your time, and if you need any help please let me know. Riccardo, nice to see you. If you'll excuse me…" He strode off toward the back of the store as Luca looked at himself in a mirror on the wall, the deerstalker hat on his head. He didn't seem to notice that the store owner had left them.

"I kind of like this one, Riccardo, not just because it will keep my head warm, but the herringbone pattern of the cloth is very handsome. And it's on sale."

"I can see why it's on sale. You're not really considering buying that, are you Luca?"

"And why not? Look, the back brim will keep the snow off my neck, and if it gets really cold, the flaps come down over my ears." He demonstrated; untying the ribbons from the top and letting the sides flop down. "*Ecco*. I'll take it."

"*Sei pazzo*."

"You won't call me crazy when your ears are frozen and mine are like bread from the oven. You'll wish you'd bought one of these instead of that out-of-fashion hat you're wearing."

"This is a Borsalino."

"I rest my case. I'll pay for this and we'll be off to see Signor Melograno."

When they got to the street Rick looked at Luca in his new hat and shook his head in wonder. "Luca, did you even take notice of Bruno Bauer?"

"Of course I did." He turned to admire himself in the glass of the store window. "He obviously knew who I was, I might just as well have been wearing a sign on my back. And he could not have gotten away from me faster. Very curious."

"I had the same impression. And after the way Cat spoke about him, I looked him over in a different light than when I was in there with Flavio a few days ago."

"Your conclusion?"

"That she may be interested in more than his rental skis."

"I would concur." In contrast to when he was hatless, Luca now grabbed the place close to the curb, the snow settling softly on his new hat. He pulled out his cell phone and punched some buttons. "Sergeant? Inspector Albani. Any word on where to find Gina Cortese?…Excellent." He wedged the phone against his ear and made some notes. "Thank you, we'll do that later this afternoon. We've talked with the American woman and now we're off to interview a certain Signor Umberto Melograno. What can you tell me about him?"

They found the office of Agenzia Immobiliare Melograno S.A. just up the hill from the town's main square. The building was a new construction, but in the chalet-style that dominated Campiglio. Rick surmised the design came under municipal building ordinances like the pueblo revival or territorial style required in Santa Fe. The covered porch allowed window-shoppers to peer at the merchandise of two stores on the ground floor. Next to the door leading to the second floor, a glass case with pictures of apartments and houses invited those interested to visit the real estate office. Luca and Rick shook the snow off their hats and shoulders and accepted the invitation.

They opened the door at the top of the stairwell and found that the office took up the entire second floor. Directly in front of them was a reception area divided into two sections, each with two sofas facing each other and low tables between them. Magazines were fanned in neat arrangements on both tables. From their covers, Rick guessed them to be tourist and ski publications. Behind the seating area, on the far wall, Rick counted three doors, all closed. Along the left side of the room, glass walls enclosed a long wooden table and chairs where four people were meeting, their voices muffled by the glass. The right side of the office had three cubicles, two of which were unoccupied. In the third cubicle, a woman rose from her desk when she noticed the two new arrivals.

"May I help you?"

"We would like to talk with Signor Melograno, please. I am Inspector Albani and this is Signor Montoya."

The woman's eyes darted from one to the other before settling on the policeman. "Signor Melograno is in a meeting at the moment." She motioned toward the meeting room. "Is this about the missing American?"

Luca gave her his best smile. "Yes it is."

"I'll tell Signor Melograno you're here."

They sat on one of the sofas while she walked to the door of the conference room and tapped on its glass door. The man at the head of the table looked up in annoyance. She opened the door, went to Melograno and whispered in his ear. As she talked he leaned forward to take stock of the two men sitting in the waiting area, giving them a stilted smile and nod. After hearing his reply she closed the door and came back to the two visitors. "Signor Melograno will be with you as soon as he finishes his meeting. May I bring you some coffee or something else to drink?"

"Thank you, no need to trouble you, we'll just wait," said Luca, answering for both of them. She returned to her cubicle and the policeman twirled his new hat on his knee before joining Rick in studying the man in the glass room. The only real estate agents Rick had known were in Albuquerque, and they had mostly been smiling middle-aged women with ample hair, usually blond. Melograno was a large man with a jowl bordering on a double chin, his head topped with thick, dark hair that fell slightly over the back of his collar. Rick was struck by the man's resemblance to a former governor of New Mexico. Had Melograno's shirt not been a clean, starched tattersall, he could almost have been described as unkempt. The nearly sloppy image was reinforced when he stood up—his belt was only partially visible and the shirt buttons strained under pressure. The other three people were standing as the meeting broke up. Two of them left the room after pulling on coats and went directly out the door to the stairway. The other listened to Melograno without speaking, then left the room herself and walked past Rick and

Luca to one of the two unoccupied cubicles. Melograno walked to the chairs and the two visitors rose. His handshake was strong, almost intimidating. Luca introduced Rick without any explanation of his presence. If Melograno was curious, he didn't show it.

"Inspector, I am at your disposal. A strange business, that of Mister Taylor."

"It is indeed. I hope you can be of some assistance."

"I shall do my best. Perhaps it would be better if we went to my office. Let me lead the way."

Melograno walked to one of the doors at the back of the room, and they followed with hats and coats in hand. He opened it and stood aside to let them enter. "Please make yourselves comfortable." He gestured at a set of thick leather chairs at one side of the room. The other side held a large desk, behind which stretched a low shelf with a few magazines stacked on it, and a standard filing cabinet. Except for a telephone and a small laptop computer, the desk was bare. The most striking feature of the room was its picture window. Its view extended vertically from the base where skiers finished their runs, all the way to the peak of the mountain. The only competition with the window was a roughly carved wooden bear, almost the size of Melograno himself. The beast stood on its back legs, its bared claws and fangs guarding a side door that Rick guessed led to the executive washroom. A few meters to one side of it was another door, probably leading to a back stairway, which would be required in a building of this size. Between the two doors, on the wall, three colorful pheasants perched proudly. Each stood on its own small shelf, looking as lifelike as the day it had been dropped from the air. The two visitors settled into the chairs, coats and hats over their laps, and their host took a seat opposite them.

"The real estate business is going well?" Luca's question was a normal way to start a conversation with a real estate agent and nothing more. Even though the man knew his visitors didn't work for the tax police, it wouldn't be the kind of information a businessman would volunteer.

Melograno shrugged. "Not my best year, not my worst."

"But the snow must help business," said Rick.

Melograno looked at Rick, as if debating with himself whether to ask why he was there. "Snow is always welcome in a ski resort town. The last few days have been especially helpful. Weekends are usually a busy time for real estate, when tourists arrive from Lombardy and the Veneto, and that has been the case yesterday and today." He turned to the policeman. "But you are here about the disappearance of Signor Taylor."

Luca flipped open his notebook. "Signor Taylor's sister told us that you met with him on Thursday. Tell us about that."

Melograno put the tips of his fingers together in a praying gesture and tapped them against his chin. After a few moments of thought he answered. "The meeting was business-related, of course, and though I can't go into detail because of proprietary information, it is not a secret that I have applied for a loan from his bank. It isn't a large loan from their point of view, but for me it will be extremely helpful."

"May I ask what the loan will finance?"

"That too is not a secret, since almost nothing in this town is. I want to purchase and develop a plot of land. Vacation apartments."

"I wish you luck on that." Melograno nodded, and Luca continued. "You had met with Signor Taylor before, I assume?"

"In addition to business? Our paths had crossed. He comes up to Campiglio frequently to ski."

"And how was his manner this time, in comparison with the other times you had met? Did he seem different? Preoccupied?"

Melograno rubbed his chin and thick neck with his right hand to help him remember. "I wouldn't say so. He is always very serious, very correct, when talking business. Not that I have seen him in any social occasions. That was the way he was on Thursday. Very correct."

And that matches the way his sister had described his business dealings, thought Rick. "Did you notice anything which could be a clue to his disappearance? Did he mention anything he was planning to do while in Campiglio?"

He looked at Rick for a few seconds before answering. "We only talked about the loan."

"Your meeting was here?" Luca asked.

"Yes, Inspector, he sat where you are sitting."

"So the meeting was cordial and businesslike?" Melograno did not answer, but nodded slowly, as if running out of patience with the questions. "And you haven't talked to Signor Taylor since that meeting?"

This time he spoke. "No, no, of course not. Otherwise I would have told the police."

Luca flipped his notebook closed. "Naturally you would have. You don't want to have problems with the police." Melograno's eyes narrowed but he remained silent.

◇◇◇

"What was that last comment about?" asked Rick when they had descended the stairs and emerged into the cold air.

"The local sergeant told me that our friend Melograno was involved in a bribery scandal last year. Something involving a regional politician. It never made it out of the investigation stage since someone obviously stepped in to quash it. Melograno didn't seem very happy when I made what he deduced was a very indirect reference to that case. Correctly deduced, I might add." Luca's face became even happier when he carefully placed his new hat over his head of thick dark hair and turned to catch his image in the glass of the shop window. "I'd better check in with the station. Perhaps Taylor has turned up."

The phone call lasted several minutes and involved a few gestures that indicated he was not pleased with what he heard. As Luca was speaking, Rick looked at the merchandise in the shop window—hand-knitted children's clothing. He tried to calculate what size his two nephews back in Albuquerque would be, but without success since he hadn't seen them in almost a year. A wool sweater from Italy would be a nice gift, since their birthdays were coming up soon. As least he thought it was soon. He made a mental note to email his mother to find out.

Luca snapped the phone closed. "The mayor of Campiglio wants to see me. He just called the station."

"Does he have some ideas to help your investigation?" They had walked to the edge of the porch and flakes began falling on their hats and clothing.

"A logical question for an American to ask. No, my friend, the *sindaco* is worried about how all this will affect tourism. The sergeant thinks the man wishes to make his concerns known to the investigative officer. That's me. We will call immediately on Mayor Grandi at his shop on the *piazza*. Perhaps you could assure him, as a tourist, and even better, an American tourist, that missing countrymen play no part in your euro spending decisions. Then we will get back to our work and interview Gina Cortese."

Rick chuckled as they stepped off the porch. It seemed that he was now Luca's permanent sidekick. They reached the main square five minutes later and Luca marveled again at what a tiny gem of urban architecture it was, framed by the mountains. Rick pulled out his phone and checked the time. "This might be a good time to call the bank, Luca. It shouldn't take long."

"Go right ahead, I'll check out the wares of this shop." He walked toward a window filled with chocolate. Rick smiled and opened his phone.

It was surprisingly easy to get through to the banker. Only two secretaries, the first Italian and the second American, blocked the way. Apparently Rick had made some kind of positive impression. The man's voice boomed so loudly Rick pulled the phone from his ear.

"Rick, so good to hear from you."

"My pleasure, Mr. Fries."

"What's this Mr. Fries stuff? It's Mark."

"My pleasure, Mark. Though I would rather be calling under better circumstances. I'm up here in Campiglio, in the mountains, and the local police have pulled me in to help with a missing persons case."

"Some cloak and dagger work? I always suspected that you—"

"No, Mark, local police work, but the missing person is Cameron Taylor."

"Cam? What's happened to him?"

"That's what the police are trying to find out. His sister is here, which is why I was asked to help, since she doesn't speak Italian." He watched Luca enter the chocolate shop. "I can tell the police that you don't know where he might be? He wasn't called back to work?"

"No, absolutely not. He wasn't going to be back in the bank until Thursday at the earliest. Could he have been lost on some ski trail? I know he's a good skier, but—"

"They've searched the trails and found nothing. Mark, was there also some business he was doing up here?"

"Yes, that's right, I'd forgotten. It's a loan, but not a very large one for us." The banker voice intruded, like he didn't want to discuss private business. "Cam has complete discretion on such transactions."

It would be a big loan for me, Rick thought, and also for Melograno. "Is there anything else that might help us discover where he is? Anyone else who he might have gone to see?"

"He was going there to ski, as far as I know. And that loan, of course, but he was really taking some days off to spend with his sister. Have you met her?"

"Yes, about an hour ago. Do you know her?"

"No. She's been to Milan a few times, I think, but I've never had the pleasure."

That confirms what Cat said, Rick thought. "Well, if you think of anything, give me a call. You have my cell number?"

"My secretary has it in her Rolodex."

They exchanged pleasantries, with the usual promises to get together, and the call ended. Rick closed his phone and watched Luca emerge from the shop carrying a small bag. The smell of chocolate pushed out into the *piazza* before the door closed again.

"*Tartufo?*" Luca extended the open bag to Rick.

Rick couldn't resist. Mass-produced Baci were his favorites, but he had to admit that any handmade *cioccolatini*, just cooled, couldn't be rivaled. This truffle was filled with a smooth *gianduia* ganache. After enjoying one and fending off a second, Rick recounted his phone conversation with the banker.

"That doesn't help much," said Luca before popping another chocolate ball into his mouth.

Mayor Elio Grandi's shop sold wood objects of all shapes and sizes. Most of its wares were handmade and carved in clean natural pine, keeping alive the artisan traditions of a snowy mountain hamlet. Rick almost expected to see elves sitting at small benches in one corner, hard at work and chattering happily in Munchkin voices. Instead, one corner of the shop revealed someone who had to be Grandi himself, chipping away at a large block of wood, its eventual shape not yet recognizable. Rick remembered the sculptor who was asked how he did his work and replied, "If I'm sculpting a hippopotamus, I just chip away everything that doesn't look like a hippopotamus." Grandi, when he'd been told by his assistant that Inspector Albani was here to see him, said he'd be with him in a moment.

"He's the mayor, after all," Luca said to Rick while twirling his new hat in his hand. "He can make us wait. Mayors do that."

The two walked around the shop checking out all the wood—and a lot of it there was. The smell reminded Rick of the pine logs he used to split for his grandfather in northern New Mexico. Luca went to a section filled with carved figures, mostly animals. Rick's eye was caught by one corner near the window which had several shelves of wooden toys. Among them was a set of trucks and machines, including a crane and a steam shovel. He reached down to turn the crank on the crane, lowering a small wooden hook on the end of a string. As he did, he thought again of his nephews. It occurred to him that no little boy, after getting a toy for his birthday, had ever said he would have preferred a nice wool sweater instead. He checked the price. Wow.

"Inspector Albani? I am Elio Grandi." Rick turned to see the mayor shaking hands with Luca. "I regret," continued the mayor, "that you are here under these circumstances, but I welcome you to Campiglio no less warmly. I hope you will return in an unofficial capacity once this unfortunate business is resolved."

If Grandi wanted to foster the image of the little village wood-carver, he failed, looking instead like a football lineman Rick had known in college. He had taken off his long apron and hung it—on a wooden peg, of course—in the work area, revealing a pair of well-tailored jeans and a dark blue turtleneck. He was bald, though probably by choice using his own razor, giving his appearance even more authority, but also making him appear older than his what Rick estimated to be about forty years.

"And this must be Signor Montoya," Grandi said, turning with an outstretched hand. The word of Rick's presence was around town, no use even asking how he knew.

"My pleasure, Signor Sindaco."

"I have some chairs over here. Why don't we sit while we talk?" He gestured toward a round table surrounded by four chairs. The card on it read nine hundred euros for the set, but the decorative inlay on the tabletop, which matched the chair backs, may have justified the price. "Needless to say," Grandi said when they were seated, "I am very anxious that this business be cleared up as soon as possible." His eyes jumped from one face to the other as he spoke, a serious look on his own.

"I could not agree more," said Luca. "We all hope this is simply some terrible misunderstanding."

"The man is here with his sister, I understand? You've spoken to her already, I trust."

Rick had the sense that the mayor knew exactly who they'd seen. "She was the first person Inspector Albani interviewed."

Grandi nodded in approval. "Excellent. Do you have any leads? Any idea where the man could be?"

"Nothing yet, Signor Sindaco," said Luca. "We were just going around interviewing people who had seen Signor Taylor before his disappearance, when I got word from the station that you'd called." The policeman was smiling, but Rick hoped the mayor would get the message that there was work to be done if Cameron Taylor was to be found. Apparently he didn't.

"Yes, of course. No one has been able to help so far? Who else have you spoken to?

"Just Signor Melograno. He apparently had a meeting with the missing man."

"I'd heard that Umberto was looking for a loan, that's probably what the meeting was about." He looked at the policeman for a reaction but none came. "The missing man is a banker, is he not?" This time Luca nodded, but stayed silent. It seemed, at last, to work. "But I should not be keeping you from your investigation. I just wanted to emphasize how important for Campiglio it is that this man be found, our only industry here is tourism, and as you can appreciate—"

"I understand completely," said Luca, "and you can be assured that we are doing everything in our power to find him."

They got to their feet. "If there is anything I can do to help, anything the municipality of Campiglio can assist with, you will let me know." It sounded like an order.

"You can be sure of that, Signor Sindaco," Luca said, extending his hand.

◇◇◇

"That was a waste of time," said Rick as they adjusted their hats outside the store.

"I'm not sure I would say that, my friend." Luca looked around the street as if he were seeing it for the first time.

"I saw something interesting in Grandi's shop. Perhaps it is of no consequence, but interesting nonetheless." Rick waited for Luca to continue, and after adjusting the new cap, he did. "Among the carved animals for sale on one of the shelves was a bear. Not as large as the one in Melograno's office, but the resemblance was striking. Given the price on the one at the shop, I think Melograno must have paid quite a lot for the bigger model."

"Maybe Grandi sells a lot of bears. I noticed that one of them is on the coat of arms of Campiglio."

"True. And this is a small town. That was the other benefit of meeting the mayor, Riccardo. We were reminded how small this town is. And that, I dare say, could be the key to finding our missing man. Someone here knows something, and likely there are others who know that that someone knows something, so we just have to discover which someone that someone is. Did I explain that right?"

"I think I got it. Where to now?"

The policeman looked at his watch. "According to the sergeant, Signora Cortese should be finishing her classes right about now, and can be found in the bar at the bottom of the lift over…" He twisted his head around, getting his bearings, before pointing to the east. "Over there. He said we should be able to walk to it easily. But then everything is within easy walking distance here." He slapped Rick on the back. "This isn't Rome, is it?" They began to walk, and Luca continued to chatter. "There is something to be said for the small town, isn't there, Riccardo? I grew up in Rome, just outside the walls near San Giovanni in Laterano, and getting anywhere was problematic. Always buses, taxis, or the metro, if the metro happened to go somewhere you wanted to reach, which wasn't often. Look around us. Few cars, everyone walking, the air is fresh. I now wonder why our friend Flavio left here to move to Trento. True, Trento isn't very big, either, but this place, well, it's so—what's the phrase?—*misura di uomo*. That's it, human-sized."

They had left the center of the town, such as it was, and were walking along a sidewalk below the mountain. On their left the mountain rose steeply behind houses, its upper reaches visible through the trees as they walked. On the other side of the street a treeless park formed a white bowl in the center of the alpine valley, its curving paths cleared to give access to a small frozen lake. Three solitary skaters moved around the ice under the light snowfall, reminding Rick of a snow globe he had as a kid. Whatever happened to it? Could Mamma have given it away along with his Topolino comics?

On their left, past a few apartment buildings, a field opened up where two skiers took off their skis, hoisted them over their shoulders, and walked stiffly off in heavy ski boots. Beside the field rose a large structure concealing the machinery for the ski lift that served this part of the mountain. High above its roof the egg-shaped capsules descended from the mountaintop or rose toward it. Fortunately for Rick and Luca, who were without snow boots, there was a cleared stairway leading to the entrance.

The bar at the top of the stairs looked out over the end of a *pista*. It was an unpretentious establishment: scuffed cement floors, no wall decorations, and a dozen wooden tables and chairs served by a bored barman. On the snow outside the windows a few skiers, all of them young, pushed hard on their poles to reach the waiting line for another ride to the top. They knew it was getting late in the afternoon and the lifts would be closing soon. The trick was to come back down just before the line closed, get on one of the last *cabine* to the top, then make that final, relaxed run before the ski patrol did its sweep of the trails.

It was not difficult to spot Gina Cortese. The ski instructors sitting at a table in one corner of the bar were dressed the same, their matching ski coats sporting the round patch of the *Scuola Italiana di Sci*. All the faces were evenly tanned and all the bodies were athletic, but she was the only woman. A variety of drinks stood on the table, from coffee to mineral water, but in front of her was what appeared to be a small glass of grappa. As Rick and Luca watched, she ran her hand through her hair, then shook it out with a rapid snap of the head. Despite her efforts, and its relatively short length, the hair remained matted from a day spent under a knit cap. Rick stood back while Luca approached the group.

"Signora Cortese? I wonder if I could have a word with you?"

"If you need good skiing lessons, Signore, you should talk to one of the rest of us." The man's comments brought laughter from the group.

"Perhaps he needs lessons in something other than skiing," said the one sitting next to her.

She got to her feet, seeming to ignore the comment, but then lashed out an open hand against the back of the man's head. The man cowered, a look of anger on his face, while the group reacted with a roar. She picked up her glass in one hand and the jacket in the other. "Let's go over to that table. We can talk about when I could schedule you this week." She looked more closely at the policeman. "Or is it for some family member?"

"We can sit over here." Luca gestured toward the table where Rick was already standing. "In fact, Signora Cortese, I do not want to set up lessons, though I have never learned to ski. I am Inspector Luca Albani, and this is Riccardo Montoya." He flashed his police ID.

She took the seat offered by Rick and gave them a puzzled look. "Police? Why would you need to talk to me? I paid off that traffic ticket a month ago. Is that what this is about?"

Luca held up his hands defensively. "No, no, we are not interested in your traffic infractions, I can assure you. We would like to ask you about Signor Cameron Taylor. We understand you are a friend of his."

A half sneer crossed her lips as she took a sip from her drink. "Cam? He *was* a friend, until he stood me up last night." The smile disappeared. "Wait, has something happened to him?" Her eyes went from Luca to Rick and back.

"We don't know, Signora. He has been reported missing and we hoped you could help us find him. His sister said you were with him two nights ago."

"Yes, I was. Friday night, we had dinner."

"Could you give us more detail?" asked Rick.

She gave a worried glance back at her colleagues at the other table, but they were now deep in another conversation. "He picked me up at my apartment at about eight thirty, and we went to a restaurant near my place where they serve fondue. Then we went to a nightclub. Then he took me home."

"Did you see anyone else at those two places?"

She looked at Luca as if trying to figure out what was behind his question. "It's a small town, and I'm from here, so we saw some people I know. That always happens."

"Did you see him the next day?"

"Yesterday? I had classes all day starting at ten. Saturdays are always busy since people come up just for the weekend. Today too. I didn't see him on the mountain yesterday or today."

"You had run into him the day before," said Rick.

"Yes, that was a coincidence. He was with his sister, so I imagine she told you."

"And he was supposed to see you last night."

"That's right. Dinner again." She looked at them both, waiting for another question. Rick noticed that the skin around her eyes was paler than her cheeks and nose, the result of wearing snow goggles all day in the sun.

"Did you just meet Signor Taylor? We understand you saw him Thursday night. Was that the first time?"

She took a drink before answering, and not a small one. "No, we met about a year and a half ago." As the interview progressed her answers had become shorter. "Do you think something has happened to him?" she finally said. "I mean...something bad?"

"We don't really know," answered the detective. "Did he seem worried about anything when you last saw him? Did you notice something that could tell us where he might have gone?" She shook her head and remained silent. Luca looked at Rick and back at the woman. "If you think of anything else that may give a clue as to where Signor Taylor might be, please give me a call." He pushed a card across the table to her. "And if I could have your cell phone number in case I have any other questions?" She unzipped a pocket inside her coat and pulled out a card which was passed to Luca.

After thanking her, the two men walked to the door while buttoning their coats. Rick glanced back to see Gina Cortese walking slowly back to the other table, her eyes on Luca's card, her ski boots scuffing along the cement floor.

"Either Signora Cortese is a very good actor or she was surprised to hear about Taylor's disappearance," said Luca when the door closed behind them. "Did you see the way she batted that guy? Impressive." He happily placed his new hat on his head and looked at the sky. It was starting to get dark, but there was enough light to see the snow falling. "Should I use my ear flaps?"

"Not cold enough yet, Luca." Rick did not relish the idea of walking beside him with the flaps down. "Wait until it gets really cold." They started down the path to the sidewalk. "I had the same impression," Rick continued, "that she didn't know about Taylor going missing. News seems to travel fast in this town, but I guess if you spend the day on the mountain you don't keep up with things."

"Like the mayor does. Very true."

The sidewalk was filling up with skiers who had finished their runs for the day, skis over their shoulders. They passed a woman changing into snow boots as she sat in the open back of a large Toyota SUV, while a man snapped their skis onto the roof rack and locked it with a small key. Rick noticed the Milan plates. It seemed to him that every other vehicle in the town that wasn't local was either from Milan or Verona. He looked back at the policeman and noticed a smile on his face.

"What are you thinking, Luca?"

"I was remembering our meeting with Mayor Grandi and thinking how coincidental it was that the next person we talked to was Gina Cortese."

"Okay, Luca, explain."

"Well, my American friend, the sergeant told me that our esteemed mayor, up until recently, was married. The divorce came through a few short months ago." He pulled his collar up and Rick wondered if the gesture was an attempt to justify bringing down the ear flaps.

"And his former wife is…"

"Exactly. The lovely Signora Cortese."

"And curiously, she has known Cam Taylor for more than a year."

"Riccardo, you must promise me that you will listen more carefully to your uncle when he advises you to go into police work."

Chapter Five

On the steep northern mountainside above Campiglio, four teenage boys on snowboards went from one small clearing in the trees to another. They were dressed in the standard uniform of the shredder: baggy pants, jackets that looked at least two sizes too large, and stretched knit caps that could have come from a charity shop. Each time they stopped, they looked down at the town before deciding on the next opening to continue their descent. There was little agreement over the best route.

"We never should have gotten off the trail. We'll never find our way back to it now. And it's starting to get dark." The boy's voice held a slight edge of fear. Through the waving trees, far below, they could make out the first few lights that had come on in the town.

"Relax. As long as we keep going down, we get there. So just don't go up."

The other two found that funny, laughing as they flipped their boards over with a loud flop and started to cut between the trees again. After twenty minutes and numerous pauses they could see one of the towers of the *funivia*, rising from the trees like a giant steel insect. Its thick cables were so high above them to be invisible in the darkening sky. There was a slight hum coming from the wires, as if messages were being transmitted along them.

"There may be some clearings under the *cabine*," said one of the boys, "let's get over there under the cables and we should be able to get down faster."

"I hope so. If I get home much after dark my mother will kill me."

Ten minutes later the foursome broke into a strip of clearing underneath the cables, its trees cut down years earlier when the towers had been erected and the cables strung in place. New trees were starting to sprout up, and there were uneven sections where boulders jutted from the snow, but the relative open area would be considerably faster going than the thick forest. A light snow, which had been falling all afternoon, swirled in the gusts in the center of the clearing. As the boys slid down the hill, they cut through the deep drifts built by winds crossing from one valley to the next, the same winds which had cut bare spots around boulders. They moved deftly to stay on the snow, threading between the obstacles.

"This is way better than the main trail, and—Lando, are you okay? Did you catch a rock?"

Behind him the second boy in the line had fallen hard. He pushed himself to his feet with a groan, snapped his boots out of the board and rubbed his leg. "After I fell I hit this rock, but it wasn't a rock that made me fall. I ran over something." He trudged back to where he had taken his spill and scraped his boot over the snow. A piece of dirty white canvas appeared. "There's something under here."

"Forget it, let's keep moving." It was the boy who had worried of his mother's tendency toward infanticide. The other boy bent down and pushed away the snow with his gloves, revealing more of the thick materials, and then a zipper.

"It looks like a sack." He looked up at the others. "It could be full of Nazi gold, hidden here by the Mafia." Two of the others laughed, kicked off their boards, and joined in the dig until the top of the bag was completely uncovered. One of them pulled off his glove and reached for the zipper.

"Wait a minute, shouldn't we tell the police or the ski patrol?"

"Then they'll pull our ski passes for being *fuori pista*. Let's just look to see what's inside, then we can decide what to do." He reached over an pulled on the zipper. It was either frozen or rusted from being under the snow, but after some harder tugs it finally opened with a low growl.

"*Cazzo!*"

The square had begun to fill with the late afternoon crowd, many still wearing ski outfits but shuffling about in soft, puffy boots or sturdy street shoes. The tall streetlamps had come to life, their yellow light picking up the flakes as they fell to the ground. The old men that Rick and Luca had seen earlier were gone, replaced by clumps of teenagers who talked loudly and kept their eyes moving about the square to see if anyone of interest had appeared. Except for their clothing, they could have been standing in any *piazza* in Italy.

"It is very comical, Riccardo."

Rick looked at the policeman. "And what is that?"

"I was just thinking. If this snow were coming down in Rome, the city would be in chaos. Buses would not run, traffic would be snarled, everything would come to a halt. I have been there when the snow came, and it was not enjoyable. But here, look at everyone in the *piazza*. There is a smile on each face." Rick was about to respond when Luca continued. "Do your towns in America have squares like this, Riccardo?"

Rick instinctively glanced around before answering. "Where my father comes from, in the Southwest, we do have them, but they are usually square or rectangular, and at the center of a grid. The Spaniards liked geometric street plans. It was something they picked up from the Romans, I think."

Luca smiled as he adjusted his hat, which was serving its purpose to keep the falling snow off his head. "There's no getting away from us Romans. Despite our inability to deal with snow." He checked his watch. "I think we have time to call on the last person on our list before dinner. This should be a good time to find Signor Lotti at his apartment, and we already know the way."

By the time they reached the apartment, darkness had fully covered the valley. The streets were full of cars leaving the town center, skis strapped to racks on roofs, starting their descent to the Po Valley or beyond. They were watched from the sidewalks by those fortunate enough to be starting their holiday week. Unlike the rest of Italy where shops were closed, Sunday evening was a busy time in Campiglio. Tourists who weren't shopping or strolling the streets sat in bars sipping a hot chocolate or something more potent. Rick and Luca worked their way through the people to reach the apartment. The policeman found the nameplate and pushed the button.

A man's voice crackled from the intercom. "Who is it?"

"Signor Lotti?"

"Yes. Who is it?"

"Inspector Albani."

They waited, and when Luca was about to push the button again the voice returned. "Apartment 4B." The door buzzed open, they walked into the lobby and pressed for the elevator. When they reached the top floor and emerged, they saw a man peering out from the door.

Daniele Lotti's appearance was not what Rick expected. Would an elegant and beautiful woman like Cat Taylor be dating—if that was the right term for their relationship—someone like this guy? He was tall with red curly hair, immediately reminding Rick of a basketball player at UNM who only got to play when the game was clearly won or lost. Lotti stared at the two men, his ping-pong ball eyes darting from one to the other.

"Is this about Cam Taylor?"

"Yes, it is, Signor Lotti," said Luca, "may we come in?"

"Certainly, certainly." He stepped aside and Rick could see that the apartment was the mirror image of the one across the hall. The furnishings were also the same. Lotti, it appeared, had saved money by purchasing everything in sets to cover all the rooms in the two apartments on the floor. They walked to the living room and took seats in the same wooden furniture as in the Taylor apartment. Even the view out of the picture window was the same, though now almost covered with darkness.

"When did you see Signor Taylor last?" asked Luca once he had introduced Rick, and all three were settled in their seats.

Lotti sat with his arms folded tightly across his chest. It looked like a show of defiance, but Rick guessed it was more that he didn't know what to do with his arms. He wore a bright red cotton turtleneck which clashed with his hair, its collar stretched out so that it accentuated a long neck. His legs splayed out in front of the chair like they were glad to have the space. Rick guessed at least a size twelve for the loafers, maybe thirteen. Lotti stared at the ceiling as he framed an answer.

"The last time I saw Cam? Last week. On Tuesday. We had lunch in Milan."

"You haven't seen him here in Campiglio?"

Lotti did not seem bothered by Rick asking a question. "No, I arrived Friday night. Later than expected since the *carabinieri* were stopping everyone at Dimaro and requiring chains. It was the first time I'd put mine on, so it took a while. I expected to see him yesterday, but he wasn't there. As you know. His sister told me he was missing."

"Do you know Signor Taylor well?" asked Luca.

"Fairly well, I suppose, though we are not close friends. We met at one of the monthly luncheons of the American Chamber of Commerce in Milan. I did my graduate studies in the States, so my company has me attend the chamber meetings. They're mostly conducted in English."

"Did he say anything at the lunch that could give a clue as to why he's disappeared? Was he worried about anything?"

"Not really. We chatted about the usual topics, business gossip. Or perhaps you could call it networking." The last word was in English, and he grinned briefly at Rick as he said it, the first time he had shown anything but seriousness. "He was looking forward to the week of skiing, I do remember that."

"And to the arrival of his sister?" asked Luca.

Lotti's face froze. "Uh, yes, of course," he finally answered.

"Do you know Gina Cortese?"

Lotti did not appear surprised by the question. He shrugged. "Met her once. Cam talked about her, but he likes to brag about all his exploits." His face froze as he realized what he'd said about his friend to two strangers, but he quickly snapped out of it. "Do you have any idea what's happened to him, Inspector?"

Luca studied the man's face and shook his head. "If you think of anything, please give me a call." He passed his card to Lotti and stood up, followed by Rick. Lotti stared at them before getting to his feet.

"That's all? I mean, yes, certainly, Inspector, I'll call you if anything comes to mind."

"Not what I expected," said Luca as they emerged onto the street and he placed his cap back on his head.

Rick adjusted his Borsalino and looked at the darkened sky. The snowflakes, now getting larger, burst into view as they reached the light of streetlamps. "Not what I expected either, Luca." The word "doofus" came to mind, but Rick wasn't sure how to translate it. "Did you notice something in his apartment?"

"The furniture? Yes, it was like—"

"No, Luca, not the furniture, something in the air, literally."

"*Non capisco,* Riccardo."

"Cat Taylor's perfume. And strong enough to indicate that she had just been in Lotti's apartment."

Luca nodded and grinned. "She was there when we rang the door buzzer, which is why it took him a few seconds to answer. Very good, Riccardo. Perhaps I am coming down with a cold and my nose didn't pick it up."

"You won't get a cold now that you have that hat."

Luca touched his recent purchase and flashed a smile as wide as its brim. They walked slowly along the crowded sidewalk. Ahead of them, three pre-teen boys followed three girls of similar age. The girls talked in low voices, glancing back toward the boys from time to time and giggling. When they turned around, the boys quickly moved their attention to the store windows. Rick was trying to decide if the two trios actually knew each other, when Luca spoke. His serious mood had returned.

"I've had a few missing persons cases, Riccardo, and usually that person disappears because they want to. Once you've asked everyone if the person seemed nervous or upset or depressed, and the answers are negative, it's hard to know what to do next. I wouldn't say that to the man's sister, but with you…"

"Thanks for confiding, Luca. There doesn't seem to be any reason for this guy to take off on his own. He's here for a holiday, the ski conditions are ideal, he's got the beautiful ski instructor for when he's not on the slopes. What's there to make him leave town?"

"Exactly, Riccardo." He stared at the slushy sidewalk as they approached the square once again. "That's why I'm worried."

At the moment they stepped into the hotel, Luca's cell phone rang.

"I'll meet you in the bar," he said to Rick, and walked into a corner of the lobby, putting the phone to his ear with one hand and shaking the snow off his hat with the other.

Rick walked into the bar and spotted Flavio sitting with a man and a woman in their late thirties whom Rick immediately pegged as Americans. The man was muscular and wore his hair very short. The woman had looks which in some circles would be characterized as perky, with a pleasant smile and hair styled to be practical rather than alluring. They did not wear matching sweaters, but looked like the type of couple who would. Flavio spotted Rick and waved him over.

"Rick, I'd like you to meet John and Mary Smith," he said in English. "They just checked in."

The man noticed Rick's look as he shook hands. "Yeah, I know. The names. We get that reaction a lot. Nice to meet you Rick."

"Flavio tells us you are an American." Mary Smith shook Rick's hand. "And that you met at school in New Mexico." She had a genuine smile, without all the nuances that often came with Italian women.

"That's right. And you two are on vacation from the States? It's a long way to come to ski."

"John's in the Army, and we've been at the base in Vicenza since September. This is the first chance we've had to ski so we're looking forward to spending the week here."

Rick knew about Caserma Ederle, outside the city of Vicenza in the upper Po Valley, but had never met anyone who was stationed there. "Thank you for your service." His words were meant for both of them and they smiled in appreciation. "Where are you from?" he added. It was the standard question for expats of any country when meeting, especially Americans.

"We're both from Colorado, and met at CSU."

"I reminded them," said Flavio, "that our ski team never lost to Colorado State when I was there."

"But you didn't mention that our football team never beat them."

"I do not concern myself with the minor sports, Rick, you know that."

"I feel like I'm back in the Rocky Mountains," John Smith said as he stood up. "We have to get our skis rented before dinner, so we'd better be on our way. Flavio, thanks for the suggestion of a rental place, we'll be sure to ask for Bruno. Rick, nice to meet you."

"The pleasure is mine, I look forward to chatting with you again."

They all shook hands again and the couple hurried out of the room.

"Nice people," said Flavio, returning to Italian. "Now I want to know everything you two detectives have been up to. Where's Luca?"

"He took a call when we walked in—here he is."

Luca's normal smile was gone, replaced by a dark look that Rick had not seen the entire afternoon. The policeman tossed his coat and hat on a bench and slid into the booth where his friends sat. "A body has been found wearing a light blue ski jacket, dark pants, and a blue bandana. Almost certainly it is that of Signor Taylor. The crime scene team is on its way from Trento, and when it arrives I will accompany them to where the body was found, which unfortunately is halfway up the mountain under the gondola cables."

"Could he have fallen from the gondola?" asked Flavio.

"He almost certainly fell from the gondola, but since the body is inside a sack, I must conclude that he was already dead when he was pushed out. The crime scene people and the medical examiner will determine it, but it's hard to think of another scenario. I doubt if he was dragged to where he was found. The boys who found him were almost lost, they were so far off the trails."

Luca looked at the bar, as if deciding whether to have something to drink. Reading his mind, Rick said: "Perhaps a shot of brandy is called for. It will be cold on the mountain."

The suggestion drew a weak nod from the policeman. "I'd better not, but you're right about the cold. Good thing I have my new hat. The sergeant told me they'll have snow boots and a suit ready for me. It will be my first ride on a snowmobile." He looked at Rick and sighed deeply. "So, my American friend, our investigation has turned from missing person to homicide."

And there is no lack of suspects, thought Rick. Luca rose to his feet and turned to pick up his coat. "Riccardo, I must ask a favor since my English is not good. I can see from your face that you know what it will be."

"If you'd like me to go with you to tell Cat Taylor, of course I will."

"*Grazie*," said Luca as he picked up his coat and hat and walked into the lobby toward the door.

Flavio's eyes followed the policeman. "This is a tragedy, Rick, and it will bring back some painful memories for the people of Campiglio." He took a couple breaths before continuing. "Five years ago, right about this time, a local girl—I remember her name was Fiametta—disappeared. A few days later her body was found. She had taken her own life. The reason, as the police were able to piece it together from her parents, was that a year before, she had undergone an abortion. Its anniversary had plunged her into deep despair. Enough to…"

They remained silent for a few moments before Rick spoke. "How sadly appropriate was her name, Fiametta. A 'little flame' whose light disappeared too soon."

Flavio nodded his head slowly. "That time we went from a disappearance to a suicide. Now, five years later, Campiglio goes from a disappearance to a murder."

Flavio leaned back in his chair and studied his friend's face. They were almost finished with a second bottle of wine—a rich, dark Bardolino from the hills along Lake Garda. Rick had recounted the various interviews of the afternoon over the first two courses of asparagus risotto and veal with lemon sauce. Flavio let him talk, sensing that it was having a therapeutic effect on Rick, and knowing that his friend was dreading his second meeting with the dead man's sister.

"So the interviews were fine as far as they went, but of course, when we did them, Luca was investigating a disappearance. Now that we're into homicide, everything changes."

"Riccardo, I know Luca appreciates your help, and not just the translations."

Rick shrugged, took another drink from his wineglass, and glanced out the window. There was just enough light from inside to see that the snow had stopped falling. That, he thought, was at least some good news for Luca.

Flavio waved to the Smiths, who were leaving their table at the other side of the room and walking toward the door of the dining room. That left about four other tables still occupied, including the one where Rick and Flavio sat. The wait staff moved around the room, clearing the tables and setting them for breakfast. "Here's Luca."

The policeman spoke with one of the waitresses who nodded and hurried into the kitchen. "They kept a meal for me," he said as he slipped into his seat. "God knows I can use it." Rick filled the new arrival's glass with the Bardolino and waited for him to continue. After a long swig of the wine he did. "It's definitely Signor Taylor, not that I had any doubt. His ski pass, with name and photograph, was hanging around his neck." Luca noticed the bread basket, pulled out a packet of bread sticks, and tore open the top. "After checking the site, it is clear that he was dropped from the gondola, so they are bringing the body down now. They'll put it in a local mortuary, where the autopsy can be performed tomorrow." The change in Luca was noticeable, from relaxed and smiling to businesslike. He snapped off a piece of bread stick with his teeth and thanked the waitress when a plate was put in front of him.

"I told Flavio about all our meetings today, Luca. I didn't think it mattered, but now that the case is homicide…"

"No, no, Riccardo, it's perfectly all right. Flavio may be our secret weapon in the investigation, since he knows so many people in this town." Luca's familiar grin returned. "This *vitello* is excellent. And once again Flavio has chosen an excellent wine."

Rick was not thinking of the meal. "Luca, she'll have to identify the body, won't she?"

"Yes, Riccardo," he answered quietly, "first thing in the morning. I don't know how long it will take to bring the body down, and there are photographs that must be taken before they do."

Rick looked at the wine in his half-filled glass, swirling it slowly. He looked up at the other two men. "It's time to start talking about suspects, don't you think?"

"I'm sure each of us, in his thoughts, already has," said Luca as he pushed his empty plate to one side, took his notebook from his pocket, and laid it in front of him, unopened. "We must begin by reconstructing the crime. While the formal autopsy will have to confirm it, it appears that he was killed by a blow to the head, probably sometime yesterday morning. And of course somewhere other than where he was found. So he was already dead when the body, inside a canvas sack, was dropped from the gondola. My local colleagues tell me that there was only one time when the body could have been dropped, and that was on the last run up the mountain. The work crew comes down on that run, passing the empty gondola going up. Apparently on this occasion it wasn't completely empty."

"So the murderer would have been familiar with the schedule of the gondola," said Rick. "Which would seem to rule out Cat

Taylor. Not to mention that she would have trouble hauling a dead body onto the gondola."

"Assuming," said Flavio," that there was only one person involved."

"You're both correct," said Luca. "But getting back to the reconstruction…the drop was either yesterday evening or Saturday evening, the day he disappeared. The local police who went up there with me were sure it was Saturday, given the amount of snow covering the sack. The snow-cover also rules out this evening, and the discovery by the boys was too close to today's last gondola run, anyway. So we'll assume Saturday. Unfortunately that means thousands of skiers got on that gondola since the drop, all but obliterating any trace of evidence from when the body was taken up."

They thought about that for a moment before Flavio spoke. "Whoever dumped the body had to ski down once he reached the top. So he had skis as well as the body on board. And boots."

"I am not a skier," said Luca," but that seems like a lot to bring along when you're dealing with a body."

"Snowshoes?"

"No, Rick," said Flavio, shaking his head. "It would have taken forever to get back to town. Had to be skis. I could make that run almost blindfolded, but so could just about anyone who grew up in Campiglio."

"Where would the trail end, Flavio?"

"Almost anyplace on the north and east sides of town, Luca. If you know the mountain you can come out almost anywhere, including at your own back door if you live near a trail." He tapped a finger on the window. "One ends about a hundred meters from here." The eyes of Rick and Luca moved toward the glass, but beyond the few flakes visible from the room's light, it was only blackness.

Rick looked at his empty wineglass and decided not to fill it. He was already starting to fade after what he'd consumed so far. It had been a long day and with another visit to Cat to come, it wasn't over. "So we know from the crime scene that the murder took place sometime Saturday between the early morning when Cam left the apartment and when his body was dropped in the late afternoon. That time frame will be important for establishing alibis." Luca and Flavio nodded in agreement. "What about motive?"

"Not robbery," said Luca before taking a sip from his glass, "unless they wanted his expensive Kolmartz skis and poles, which I suppose is possible. He didn't have his boots on, but they would have made the sack much heavier. He also didn't have his hat. Everything else was on the body including his wallet with about a hundred euros inside, and his cell phone. So the motive was likely something other than robbery." He glanced at the faces of the other two, and got no reaction. "For suspects, we have to begin with his sister."

"But we agreed," Rick said, "that she couldn't have taken the body on the gondola and skied down."

The other two men noticed Rick's quick reaction. "Rick," said Flavio slowly, "she could have been in on it with someone else."

Rick reached for the bottle of wine and then pulled back. "That's true. And her main motive could well be an inheritance. My first strong impression of Cat Taylor was that she comes from money and is used to having it. Likely there are aging parents—aging and wealthy parents—and only two siblings to inherit. She will get it all. But who would have helped her?"

"The guy across the hall, Lotti," said Flavio. "She doesn't know anyone else in town."

"She knows Bruno. She told Luca and me that she rents her skis from him. And their relationship could go beyond ski-fitting."

"What's important is we can't rule her out," said Luca, taking charge of the discussion. "The next logical suspect would be the real estate developer, Melograno. He was trying to get a loan to develop that property. Taylor may have turned him down when they met the previous day. Not usually the motive for a murder, but it's possible, I suppose."

"Umberto has the reputation of using any means, but usually money, to get what he wants," said Flavio. "There was something last year about him trying to bribe a regional official, but I don't remember the details."

Luca nodded. "The local police mentioned that to me. Nothing came of it."

Flavio chuckled. "Hmm. I wonder why nothing came of it? But it's quite a jump from bribery to homicide. Umberto's always been a bully, but murdering someone…I don't know about that."

"Riccardo and I saw one of the mayor's wood sculptures in his office. Coincidence?"

Flavio thought a moment before answering. "Probably. Many people have bought Elio's work. He's the best wood-carver in town. But more important than having one of his carvings is that Umberto is Elio's main political backer, and the next election is coming up in a few weeks. It doesn't hurt to have the mayor in your pocket if you're a real estate developer."

"And if we're talking about suspects, what about the mayor?" asked Rick. "His ex-wife was dating the victim, and possibly was doing it even before the marriage formally ended. Could be a motive there."

Flavio's frowned and shook his head slowly. "This is turning into a South American novella."

"My wife watches them all the time," said Luca.

"But you don't?" asked Flavio.

"Of course not. Everyone want coffee?" They nodded and Luca asked the waitress to bring it, checking the wine bottle before she left. There was still a glass or two in it, so it was left on the table. "Now, before moving to the rest of the inhabitants of Campiglio, there is Gina Cortese. No real motive for murder that I can think of. How about you?"

Flavio shrugged. "She found out about his girlfriend in Milan?"

"Weak," said Luca. "Possible, but weak."

Their coffee arrived and they each stirred varying amounts of sugar into their small cups while staring at the dark liquid.

"Perhaps something will come to one of us during the evening," said Flavio, though his voice indicated he considered the prospect unlikely. "I forgot to mention a related development, something that will interest you, Riccardo."

"I can't imagine what," said Rick as he drained his small cup.

"Since the dead man and his sister are Americans, your consulate in Milan is sending up a vice consul to assist Signora Taylor. A nice touch, but I hope he doesn't get in the way of the investigation."

"It's the basic consular function, helping American citizens far from home who are in trouble," Rick explained. "My father did it for many years before he moved up in the ranks. It's mostly with Americans who've lost passports or been victims of pickpockets, but it can be more serious, like this case."

"Do we have that for Italians, Flavio?"

"I suppose if I'd gotten into trouble in Albuquerque I could have asked the Italian consul to bail me out. The nearest one was in Los Angeles."

"Flavio," said Rick, "you know very well who would have saved your ass if you'd gotten into legal trouble in the States, and it wouldn't have been the Italian consul."

Luca turned to Flavio and waited for his answer. He was enjoying getting his mind off the case, even for a moment.

"I never got into any trouble, Rick, as you well know. If I remember correctly, it was *you* who—"

Rick held up his hand. "Luca isn't interested in frivolous stories of American university life."

"Well," muttered Luca, "in truth, I wouldn't mind—"

"See, Flavio? So, Luca, when is this American consul arriving in Campiglio?"

"Not sure. Probably early tomorrow morning. If I could ask you another favor, Riccardo?"

"If he's a consular officer, Luca, he'll speak Italian. You don't need—"

"No, no, it's not that. The problem is that tomorrow I have to write and fax a report to the prosecuting attorney, now that it's a homicide At least she hasn't insisted on coming up here to get in my hair. But also I have to deal with some reporters tomorrow morning, two from Milano and one from Trento."

"Who from Trento?" asked Flavio. "Not Sandri, I hope."

"I'm afraid so." He picked up his coffee cup, saw that there was not even a drop left, and set it back in the saucer. The two Italians shook their heads sadly.

Rick was tempted to ask about this Sandri, but his mind was on Cat Taylor. "I'll be glad to deal with the vice consul for you tomorrow, Luca."

"I was so hoping that…" Cat's voice trailed off.

She sat with her hands clasped and stared at Rick without seeing his face. Once again she treated the policeman as if he were invisible, even though Luca had carefully stated the facts for her. As Rick translated he marveled at how Luca was dealing with the situation. There was a combination of patience and empathy in the policeman's words which Rick tried to convey when he put them into English.

"I'll start making a list of things to be done. Perhaps it's best to immerse myself in details, to keep my mind off the reality of his death." Her eyes moved to the wood beams on the ceiling and back to Rick. "That doesn't make sense, does it?"

"Whatever works for you, Cat."

Her hair was not brushed, and she was without makeup. A heavy, wine-colored robe covered most of her body, but below it and at the neck he could see flannel pajamas decorated with tiny brown bears. On her feet were furry slippers that covered her ankles. It was sleepwear a twelve-year-old would wear, Rick thought, but perhaps it gave her comfort. It was also likely that she was not expecting to see Lotti this evening. And she'd hoped not to have this visit.

Luca tapped Rick on the shoulder. "I think I've done what I've had to," he whispered. "Perhaps it would be easier for her if I left. I know you can do better at comforting than I."

Rick nodded. "Sure, Luca. You've done well. I'll do what I

can." They rose to their feet. "Cat, the inspector has to get back to the station. I'll stay for a while if you'd like."

"I would, Rick." She got to her feet and thanked the policeman. Luca shook her hand and made hand gestures to indicate that he could see himself out. When the door shut quietly, Rick and Cat took seats opposite each other.

"I called home, and Maria reminded me that my parents are on their annual cruise in the Caribbean. I forgot it was this week." She took a sip from a glass next to the sofa. It looked like Scotch, but since he hadn't been offered anything, it was only a guess. Rick also guessed that Maria was someone on the Taylor homestead staff, but he didn't ask for clarification. "They won't be back in port for a week," she continued. "And it's not worth getting them off the ship. What can they do at this point?"

Rick wondered how he would have reacted to the news that his sister had been murdered. Both sides of his family, New Mexican and Italian, would be vying with the other to give him support and share his sadness. In that way, his two cultures were not all that different. "Do you have any other family you should be in touch with, Cat? Aunts? Uncles?"

She appeared to find the question strange. "I have an uncle," she said finally, "but he's old and lives in a nursing home in Florida. I haven't seen him in years. He wasn't even invited to my wedding. There's nobody else, really."

Rick silently thanked his good fortune of being born into a large, extended family.

"Inspector Albani told me that someone from the consulate will be here tomorrow to help you. I'll bring him over when he arrives." She nodded mechanically. "There's something else, Cat. As the inspector said, tomorrow morning you'll have to identify your brother's body. It's a formality that has to be done. I'll go with you if you'd like."

Her blank look made him wonder if she was understanding anything he'd said. After nodding her head slowly she responded. "Of course. I understand. It's kind of you to go with me." She looked down at the glass as if it had just appeared on the table, picked it up, and took a long pull. Rick was now sure it was some kind of whiskey.

He rose to his feet. "Cat, I'd better go. Try to get some sleep. I'll call you in the morning."

She made no attempt to get up, but looked at him with a weak smile. "Thank you, Rick."

"You have my cell phone number, if you need anything before that."

"Yes. Thank you. I'll be okay."

Her eyes turned toward the window where the lights of the town gave the darkness a faintly yellow glow. She pulled up her knees, held them together with her arms, and rocked slowly in the chair. Rick silently let himself out.

Heavy snow swirled into the hallway when Rick opened the door to step out on the sidewalk in front of Cat's building. He tightened his hat and pulled up the collar of his coat. It covered only the bottom half of his ears, but was better than leaving them completely exposed. The snow and the hour had pushed people into the warmth of the buildings. Only an occasional car made its way tentatively along the street, its headlights carving a wedge of speckled, moving light through the darkness. Rick kept his head down, watching his cowboy boots scuff through the accumulating snow.

Doubts ran through his mind. Could he have done something more to comfort her? Should he have stayed longer? It was not a situation he had experienced before, giving that kind of news to someone. Even though it was Luca who had delivered the words officially, Rick felt responsible. She had heard it from him. The girl is alone in a foreign country, he thought, and all I did was give her the terrible news, say a few kind words, and leave. He shook his head, stopped and looked back up at the windows of Cat's apartment, its faint light just visible through the snow. After a few moments of thought he started back toward the door. After taking two steps he heard a muffled cry behind him.

He turned and squinted through the swirling flakes, barely making out two figures. One lay on the sidewalk, the other stood defiantly above him before landing a sharp kick and running in the opposite direction, disappearing almost instantly into the storm. Rick's first thought was that the two men had taken a bar argument outside to settle, something he was all too familiar with from his time in Albuquerque. Forgetting about Cat, he jogged toward the fallen man and reached him within seconds.

If this was a bar fight, it was a nasty one.

The man lay on his back in the snow, eyes half closed, his head bent to one side. A dark stain of blood spread steadily from a wound on the neck and his arms twitched slightly. The snow was starting to cover the hat which had landed top-down on the sidewalk next to him. Rick looked around for help and saw that a car had come to a stop, its driver out and running up to him. Rick knelt down and pressed a gloved hand against the victim's neck in an attempt to stop the bleeding.

"Call an ambulance," Rick said, but then looked up to see the man staring, his face frozen. "*Subito!*" The driver pulled out his cell phone and began frantically punching in numbers. Rick took out his own phone with his free hand and scrolled down to the number he wanted. Pressing the neck seemed to slow the bleeding, but there was more blood than he'd ever seen.

"Luca? I'm on the street outside the apartment. Some guy's been stabbed. What? No, I'm okay. You'd better get over here." He got a curt reply and snapped his phone closed.

The police car carrying Luca arrived almost simultaneously with the ambulance. The flashing lights and sirens of the two vehicles assured that the small group of people already gathered around the body would grow to a large crowd. Other eyes came from the buildings on the street—shutters began banging open one by one, allowing faces behind the windows to take in the drama below. The two uniformed policemen with Luca had sprung from the car to push back the gawkers, making room for the emergency crew who now knelt by the victim. Rick rose to his feet and stood back, removing the bloody glove. He glanced at Luca who was looking down at the body while talking with one of the other cops. Luca caught Rick's eyes and walked over to him.

"Tell me what happened, Riccardo."

"I had just come out of the apartment, and heard a cry. When I looked up I could see this guy on the ground. A man was standing above him. He gave him a kick and ran off." He pointed. "In that direction. But I lost sight of him almost immediately in the snow." They both looked at the sky. Rick realized that Luca was wearing his new hat, and had to admit to himself that it was perfect for the present conditions, even with the flaps still tied at the top. "I didn't even think of chasing the guy."

"And a good thing." He turned back to the man on the ground, almost hidden by the team working on him. "You may have kept him from bleeding to death. Could you see the weapon? I doubt if he did this kind of damage with his bare hands."

"No, didn't see any weapon. And I didn't even see the violence, except for the kick, and that seemed like more of an afterthought."

Luca called over two policeman who had just arrived on the scene and pointed in the direction the assailant had fled. He ordered them to look for any footprints, find anyone who might have seen something or someone, and look for a discarded weapon. "I don't hold out much hope of finding a weapon, but you never know," he said to Rick as the men hurried off. "And the late hour, as well as this snow, won't work in favor of finding any witnesses."

They both watched as the man was placed on a stretcher. His leather coat had been removed, replaced by a blanket covering him up to the now-bandaged neck. Standing above the stretcher, one of the team held a plastic sack attached to a tube that ran under the blanket to some part of the body. On a signal the stretcher was heaved up and carried to the open ambulance. Someone picked up the hat, brushed off the snow, and took it with the coat to the ambulance. Within seconds of the doors slamming, it drove off under the looping wail of its siren.

"I wonder who the guy is," said Rick after the ambulance disappeared in the distance.

"The sergeant just told me. Name's Guido Pittini. He works for the corporation that runs the ski lifts and trails. Has a reputation as a womanizer."

"So the attack was from a jealous husband?"

"That's a possibility, I suppose. He was also active in the mayor's re-election campaign, the main organizer for Grandi inside the ski-lift workers union." Luca noticed Rick's face and nodded. "Your mind is working quickly, Riccardo, despite just witnessing a violent crime. Yes, I suppose it could be political. But I'd rather start with his day job. The sergeant tells me that Pittini is one of the gondola operators."

Rick had been staring at the dark blotch in the snow, now almost covered with white. His face snapped up. "He was running the gondola when Taylor's body was dropped?"

"We'll find that out soon, but there couldn't be that many shifts." He looked at Rick's hand, which still clung to the bloody glove. "That's ruined. You'll have to get yourself another pair."

Rick nodded and noticed a trash can a few feet away. He walked over and threw the glove away, turned to walk back, then pulled off the other and tossed it in too. He stuffed his bare hands in the pockets of his shearling coat and came back to Luca. "Let's assume that this man was in on the dumping of the body. He could have been part of the murder itself, but let's only assume he was merely abetting the crime."

"Go ahead, Riccardo."

"You show up, Luca. Then the body is found, something the murderer didn't expect. And now there's someone who knows about the drop who could go to the police. This poor guy might not have even known that it was a body being dumped. He even could have thought someone was just getting a ride on the gondola so he could ski down without paying."

"Could be."

"And now that everyone knows what really happened, the murderer needs to eliminate a key witness."

"But he may not have succeeded. Pittini is still alive, thanks to your quick action. Let's hope he pulls through and can tell me something that will explain the attack." Luca noticed Rick looking up at Cat's window. "Are you going back up to see her?"

Rick shook his head. "Not now. She should be asleep, if the sirens didn't keep her up. And I don't want to tell her about this. She's upset enough. I'll just go back to the hotel."

Luca nodded in agreement. "I'd ask to meet you in the bar later, but the crime scene here could take a while." He showed a small grin. "You'll likely have this crime solved by the time you reach the hotel. But you can tell me in the morning."

Rick nodded silently. He was exhausted both mentally and physically. As he began walking toward the hotel, Luca's voice stopped him.

"Riccardo, something else. A possibility you may not have considered. Did you notice that Pittini's coat and hat were very similar to yours, and he's about your height? Be careful."

Chapter Six

"Yes, that's my brother."

The funeral director pulled the sheet back over Cam Taylor's face and stepped away from the others standing around the body. Rick instinctively put his arm around Cat's shoulder and she pushed her head against his chest. There were no tears. Luca inclined his head toward the door, a silent message for Rick, and the three walked out into the waiting area where the warm air contrasted with the chill of the other room. Cat separated herself from Rick and massaged her face and eyes with both hands.

"I'd like to go back to the apartment."

Of course, Cat." Rick looked at the policeman who nodded.

"We'll talk later," Luca said in Italian.

They had spoken just a few words as they walked along the streets of Campiglio. Cat stared at the sidewalk, only occasionally glancing at the sky, with her hands pushed deep into the pockets of her ski coat. The snow was taking a break. A few rays of sunlight knifed through the cloud cover over the eastern mountain, casting shadows that had been rarely seen the past few days. The sun would bring joy to the skiers who passed Rick and Cat on their way to the *piste*.

"Why don't you come up, Rick. I'll make us coffee."

"That would be good."

Cat pulled a key chain from her pocket when they emerged from the elevator. As she slipped one of the keys into the door they heard a noise behind them and both turned to see the long face of Daniele Lotti staring at them. Rick saw that he still wore the red turtleneck. Perhaps he slept in it.

"Daniele," said Cat. It was an acknowledgment of his presence, nothing more. She glanced at Rick and turned back to Lotti. "This is—"

"Yes, Cat, I met him and the other policeman yesterday."

Rick was about to correct him when Cat spoke. "I'll talk to you later, Daniele."

Lotti's eyes darted from her face to Rick's and back. "But I thought we—"

"I said I'll talk to you later, Daniele."

◇◇◇

"Does he know what's happened?" asked Rick. They were in the small kitchen of the apartment. Water in the bottom of a small espresso pot was beginning to boil, pushing up through the tube to packed coffee above it. The aroma spread through the room.

"Yes, I told him this morning before you came. Sometimes I wonder why I ever paid any attention to him in the first place." She leaned against the counter while Rick sat on one of the stools. "He was one of the few men I met who spoke English. Not the best of reasons to start a relationship."

"Probably as good as any, Cat." The gurgling of the pot had stopped, and Rick got up from the stool and turned off the fire under it. Using a dish towel to keep from burning his fingers, he took it from the stove and poured the steaming, black liquid into the two cups. "Sugar?"

"Just one."

He put a spoonful of sugar into her cup and two into his. They both picked up the saucers, stirred the cups, and smelled the brew before taking tentative sips.

"Do you always wear cowboy boots, Rick?"

"They're comfortable."

"That's what a friend in college always said. I thought she was trying to make a statement about being from Oklahoma."

"Nothing wrong with being proud of where you're from."

"I suppose not. Tell me about where you're from, Rick."

She was trying to get her mind off her brother, and he was glad to help, even if it meant talking about himself. Or to himself—her eyes were hollow.

"I'm from various places. Spent a lot of time in Italy, since my mother's Italian, but also much of my life in New Mexico, where my father is from. I went to high school in Rome but college in New Mexico. Piles of relatives in both countries. Dad's a diplomat, so we moved around. A couple times we lived in Washington when I was in grade school. And then South America. Washington was the hardship posting—no live-in help." It was a joke, but her face showed that she didn't get it. Of course, he thought; growing up she'd always had Maria or someone else to pick up after her.

"That must have been very…interesting."

"I guess you could say that." And people often did say just that, Rick thought. Foreign service life was something most Americans couldn't get their head around. Next she'll say something about traveling a lot.

"You must like traveling." She had taken a seat on one of the stools.

"Actually, Cat, I hate plane rides. Most times my family stayed put where we were living. Our vacations were by car to someplace close by. You probably did more traveling when you were a kid than I did."

She took the last sip from her cup and walked it to the sink. "Well, we skied in Vail every winter and there was also the trip to the Bahamas. Summers, it was Maine."

Poor thing, he thought. "I rest my case."

"Do you think this policeman is competent? He didn't say much when he was here with you yesterday, and the same this morning."

"Cat, he doesn't speak English, so he's not going to be chatty with you. But to answer your question, I think he knows what he's doing. I can say that now, after being with him for a full day." He took his cup to the sink and ran some water in it, considering her question in his own mind. True, Luca was somewhat eccentric, if for nothing other than his taste in hats, but he appeared to know his business. And if the guy had a poor reputation in the ranks of the police, Uncle Piero would have called to warn him rather than encouraging his nephew to assist.

"I hope you're right, Rick." She rubbed her eyes, red from lack of sleep and tears. "I really have to get some rest. I shouldn't have had that coffee."

"Espresso doesn't keep you awake, it's all the water in American coffee that brings out the caffeine. Scientific fact."

"Really?"

"Really. Go lie down, you'll drop off quickly."

She wandered to the one small window of the kitchen. It looked out over the roof of the building behind and beyond to the evergreens of the mountain. A sliver of trail was visible through the trees, its whiteness outlining a red snowcat that was finishing its morning grooming chores. Soon the first skiers would cut smooth grooves into the lines left by the machine. When the snowcat disappeared behind the trees she turned to Rick.

"I'm supposed to be devastated, grieving, falling to pieces, but all I feel is exhaustion. I guess that's because I never really got along that well with my brother. We went through the motions. He was supposed to be protective, like big brothers are, and I was supposed to appreciate it. We played that game well, especially around my parents, but there was no substance to it. We didn't dislike each other, Rick, we just never were friends. Maybe someday I'll feel some regret that we never were close, but right now I don't. Is that wrong?"

Rick thought about his own sister. With all the moves they'd made growing up there was a bond between them, something unique to foreign service families, and that bond remained. Except for the pictures on the walls, home had changed every three years. Home was wherever he and his sister found themselves, and they'd made the best of it. Rick knew that his early years were very different from Cat's, but he still had trouble fathoming her feelings toward her brother.

"It's not wrong," he said. "Everyone is different. Perhaps it's better that you feel that way. It will help you get through this."

"Thanks, Rick. That helps a lot."

As he let himself out he realized he hadn't told her about the previous night's violence on the street down from her building. And she had not said anything about the sirens, or if she'd heard them, didn't think much of it. Probably a good thing. She had enough to think about without adding something else. Something which likely had nothing to do with her.

Rick walked the few short blocks to the police station, dodging skis swinging from the shoulders of those heading for the mountain. The sergeant on duty waved him past the front desk and pointed toward a door which was half open. Taped to it was a handwritten sign: "Inspector Albani." He pushed the door open and heard Luca's voice.

"Come in, Riccardo, welcome to my mountain empire. Please make yourself comfortable, if that is possible in these chairs. The body of Signor Taylor is on its way to Trento for the autopsy, so I have been going over what we know about the case. It's not a lot." He tapped his hand on a file. "And now we have a second crime."

Rick looked around the room and took a seat at one end of the long conference table that served as Luca's temporary desk. The walls were bare except for a calendar whose pages had not been flipped to the present month, and a local tourism poster that showed a busty blond skier. One of the poster's bottom corners had come loose from its thumbtack and curled up to cover the tips of the girl's skis. The room had no windows.

The inspector's shirtsleeves were rolled up to his elbows, exposing dark arm hair that matched the hair on his head. The suit jacket draped the chair next to him, the overcoat lay on the next chair, but his new hat had a place of honor at the end of the table. He put his hands behind his head and leaned back, surrounded by files, papers, and a few empty paper cups.

It appeared that Luca was not especially neat, which somehow did not surprise Rick.

"Thanks to your quick reaction last night, Riccardo, Guido Pittini is probably going to survive the attack. But he is in critical condition and has not regained consciousness. The wound was from a small knife, according to the attending doctor. He was attacked from behind and stabbed in the neck over the shoulder. But you know where he was stabbed. Ironically it may turn out that the blow to his head on the cement will be the more critical of Pittini's injuries…that is what is keeping him unconscious. If the snow had not cushioned him slightly, he could have been killed."

"Did your men find anything last night?"

"*Un bel niente.* There wasn't anyone around at that hour to question, and any footprints along the sidewalk were already covered. You remember how hard it was snowing."

"And no bloody knives lying in the snow."

"Not a one." Luca twirled a pencil between his fingers as if it were a weapon. "I talked to his wife."

"And?"

"She was shocked, as you would expect she would be, and had no idea who would want to harm her husband. She said he had gone out, but he didn't tell her where."

"No doubt working on the campaign. Stuffing envelopes, perhaps."

Rick's attempt at humor fell flat. Perhaps it didn't make it through translation. "I'll ask the mayor if he was doing some campaign work, but somehow I doubt it at that hour. I have some men checking the nightspots to see if he was seen anywhere. There aren't that many of them in a town this size. If he was in a public place with a woman, we'll likely find out soon."

"We can rule out one woman, at least."

A puzzled look showed on the policeman's face, but then he got it. "Tell me how it went with Signora Taylor. As well as could be expected?"

Rick briefly described his conversation with Cat at the apartment, leaving out that he'd told her something of his own background to help get her mind off the death.

"So, my American friend, from what you said I sense that Signora Taylor is not suffering in her grief."

Rick shrugged. "Not yet, Luca, but it all may not have sunk in yet."

"What was her reaction to the excitement of last night?"

"I didn't bring it up, and she didn't either. Her apartment must be soundproof if she didn't hear all the sirens."

Luca gave that some thought. "And you say you had a brief encounter with her neighbor, Signor Lotti?"

"There wasn't much to it. She was annoyed and snapped at him, and he took it. He was a bit shocked, first at seeing me and then by her reaction. I found it strange that he thought I was a policeman."

Luca grinned. "Well, we never actually explained your presence when we visited him yesterday. You should take it as a compliment, of course." He stood up and reached for his jacket. "I need a good coffee, the stuff from the machine here is terrible."

"I just had one with Cat, but I'll go with you. This room is starting to close in on me."

"And you've only been sitting here for five minutes."

They left the room, nodded to the sergeant, and walked outside. The sunlight that had started to peek through the clouds was now out in full. It would be a good morning on the trails. A parking lot spread out in front of the entrance to the police station was surrounded by hotels and businesses. Luca pointed out a bar at the opposite end and they began to walk between the parked cars to reach it. Ahead of them four young men were getting out of a muddy SUV, slipping on their coats and stretching their limbs. One checked the skis on the roof while the others looked around the square and up at the mountains surrounding Campiglio. Once the vehicle was secured, they began walking toward a hotel at the far end of the square, talking loudly. Rick watched them and suddenly grabbed Luca's coat.

"Riccardo, what—"

"That kid, Luca, we've got to get him."

Rick began running toward the group, followed by a bewildered Luca. The lot was full, and they darted between cars, sometimes having to double-back where there was no space. Rick kept his eye on one of the group, who he estimated was in his early twenties. When Rick was about twenty meters from him, the boy looked around and saw the two men running toward him. A look of panic came over his face and he started to run while his three friends stopped and stared. Rick and Luca brushed past the three and continued the pursuit.

"Stop, police!" yelled Luca as he gasped the thin air.

The boy tripped and fell against the hood of a car, his hat flying to the ground. Rick was on him immediately, forcing the boy's chest and face against the front of the car like he'd seen cops in Albuquerque do on various occasions.

"I didn't do anything." The boy's words were muffled by the metal of the hood.

Luca finally reached the car, breathing heavily. "What… is going on…Riccardo?"

Rick kept one hand against the boy's back and pointed to the ground with the other. "There, Luca, look there."

The policeman reached down and picked up the cap. It was dark blue, and the gold letters ND were intertwined on the front. On the back, also in gold, was the word IRISH.

◇◇◇

The boy sat at one end of the long table, a tape recorder directly in front of him. A uniformed policeman with a pad and pen sat to his left, Luca to his right. Rick leaned against a side wall, wishing there were windows in the room.

"Go over it again, Lorenzo, to be sure I understand."

The boy looked up at Rick, as if he could somehow avoid repeating the story. Rick shrugged.

"We were just coming to the edge of town. We'd left Verona before dawn, stopping only to have a cappuccino and a roll at a bar in some small town on the road. We knew it would be a while before we could check into the hotel, and we, well, after the coffee, we needed to…"

"You had to take a leak," said Luca. "I don't need the specifics. Go on."

The boy took a sip from the cup in front of him. "We pulled off the road into a clearing. No trees, but covered with snow, of course. We could see the trails off in the distance where people were coming down off the mountain, and the chairlift to take them back up. After we, uh—"

"Yes, took care of your bodily needs. Go on."

"I saw something blue sticking out of the snow, walked over and pulled it out. It was mostly covered, but after I shook off the snow I saw it was a nice cap. It wasn't like it was anything that valuable. If it had been, I would have turned it in when we got to town."

"I'm sure you would have," said Luca. "You didn't see anything else lying around?"

"No, sir, just the cap."

"Then what?"

"We got back into Gino's car and drove into Campiglio. It took us a while to find a place to park, but luckily we got that space near our hotel when somebody was pulling out. That's when you grabbed me." He frowned and looked up at Rick who grinned back.

"And you think you can find this place?"

"Sure. I'm good with directions. It's right outside town."

"Good. Sergeant, take him out and make copies of his documents. And let him use the bathroom if he needs to, we don't want him up there contaminating the crime scene any more than he has already."

Lorenzo and the sergeant left the room. Before the door closed, another policeman stuck his head through the doorway. "Two journalists are here, Inspector. They say they have an appointment with you. I asked them to wait."

"Thank you, Corporal. I'll be with them in a moment."

Rick was pushing down the corner of the old ski poster on the wall when Luca gestured for him to take a seat at the table. "The newspapers can wait. What did you think of our little hat thief?"

"It sounded to me like he was telling the truth," Rick said as he eased into one of the chairs.

"I'm sure he is. And it's very possible that we have found where the murder actually took place." Luca looked at the blue cap, sealed inside a clear plastic evidence bag. It sat in the middle of the table. "Explain something to me, Riccardo." He picked up the bag.

"If I can, Luca."

"Notre Dame, the name of this university. That is French, is it not?"

"It is indeed."

Luca turned the bag in his hands. "And the word on the back, 'Irish.' That means *irlandese*, if I am not mistaken?"

"Yes, Luca, Irish are people from Ireland."

The policeman nodded slowly, his face serious. "So we have an American university with a French name whose students are from Ireland?"

"That's close enough."

"I will never understand your country, Riccardo."

"Don't even try, Luca. It's easier to solve murders."

So much for the sun. As Rick walked up the hill from the police station to the hotel, the clouds closed ranks to eliminate the last patch of open sky. And it had begun to snow again. He looked at his watch and wondered if Flavio had already headed for the mountain. Not that he'd blame him if he had. Just because Rick had become involved in the investigation didn't mean Flavio had to stay in the hotel.

He pushed his hands into his coat pockets, reminding himself that he had to get another pair of gloves, and felt his phone vibrating. When he checked the number it was a 2 area code. Milano.

"Montoya."

"Rick, this is Mark Fries."

"I thought it might be you, Mark. I suppose you heard the news."

"Yes, the police came to the bank today. This is terrible. How is his sister taking it?"

"As well as can be expected. The consulate is sending someone up to help her out."

"I know. I called the consul general and he told me. I said that the bank is ready to help in any way we can."

Rick brushed the snow off his phone. "What did the police ask you?"

"Pretty much the same things you asked when you called, and I gave them the same answers. Well, they also asked about possible enemies, arguments he may have had with someone, that sort of thing. Nobody here could think of anyone with a motive to…to take Cam's life."

"I suppose they asked you to contact them if anyone recalled anything that could help the investigation."

"They did. I suppose that's standard procedure."

"I think so. But if someone does remember something, since I'm helping out the inspector here who's running the investigation, it might speed things if you called me, and I can pass it immediately on to him."

"Certainly. I'll be glad to do that, Rick. I've asked my assistant to check on that loan. Perhaps there's something there that could be of help. I'll let you know."

They said their good-byes and Rick tucked his phone back in his coat pocket before continuing up the road. He wondered if the Milanese police would be annoyed that he'd cut them out of the loop. Probably not, and Luca was the lead investigator who had likely instructed them to question the workers at the bank in the first place.

He pushed open the door of the hotel and walked into the lobby. Flavio was standing near the front desk, dressed in his ski pants and sweater, talking with a woman whose back was to Rick. She wore a dark pantsuit and had short hair, instantly reminding him, even without seeing the face, of one of his college classmates, Linda Chavez, who got a job with an Albuquerque bank on graduation. Flavio noticed Rick and said something to the woman. She immediately turned on her heel and began striding toward him. She even walks like Linda, he thought, but is much better looking. She stuck out her hand.

"I am Lori Shafer, from the American Consulate General in Milan. Signor Caldaro told me that you know how I can get in contact with Catherine Taylor." She spoke in relatively correct but somewhat accented Italian, like she was reading from a practice dialogue in language class.

Rick glanced at Flavio's grin and toyed for an instant with the idea of continuing in Italian, but decided against it. "You can speak English with me, Ms. Shafer. Pleased to meet you, I am Rick Montoya."

"But I…" She looked back to Flavio, who did a theatrical shrug, and then returned her glare to Rick. "He didn't tell me you spoke English."

"He probably didn't tell you that he speaks English himself." Flavio was now at her side, and Rick added: "Though not very well."

"I was so impressed by your Italian, Signorina," said Flavio, "that I did not want to expose my limited English."

Rick shook his head. It was Flavio's Latin Lover persona that Rick had not seen since they'd frequented the bars on Route 66 those many years ago. The vice consul would have none of it.

"I really must contact Ms. Taylor immediately. If you could *please* give me her address?"

Her demeanor, which was so common in young American professionals, was something that drove Rick crazy. And it was why he'd had only one date with Linda Chavez.

"This is Italy, Ms. Shafer, and we go through certain niceties before charging into business. Call it Old World, if you'd like, but that's the way Italians are. Apart from that, Catherine Taylor is resting now after a very difficult morning, and she shouldn't be disturbed."

Flavio watched the two, fascinated by the exchange. His grin was wider than ever.

"I don't think you understand the function of United States consular officers, *Signor* Montoya."

Rick took a deep breath. "My father is the American Consul General in Rio, Ms. Shafer. He's told me about his work over the years."

Her mouth dropped open. "He's…Wait a minute, there was a Mr. Montoya who lectured in my Italian area studies course. Was—"

"He's done some lecturing at the Foreign Service Institute."

"So you…you're American."

"*Brava*. So why don't you relax, call me Rick, and call this guy Flavio. And we'll call you Lori. We'll get you over to see Catherine Taylor in good time. She goes by Cat, by the way."

For the first time Lori Shafer's frown somewhat softened. "Thank you, Rick. And Flavio. I guess I was a little short. I just want to be sure to do the right thing for this poor woman. Milan is my first overseas assignment."

"Somehow I guessed that," said Rick.

Her face was returning to normal from the previous blush. She checked her watch. "Since there's no rush I'll get settled in my room. Will you be here when I get back?"

"Yes, I will be in the bar," said Flavio quickly.

She took the handle of her bag and rolled it toward the elevator while the two men watched.

"She's a fire biscuit, isn't she?" Flavio, without realizing it, was still stuck in English.

"The expression is 'firecracker,' Flavio, and let's get back into Italian." He glanced at his friend's attire. "Aren't you going skiing?"

"Not now, Rick."

Inspector Albani stepped out of the police car, adjusted his hat, and looked across the field. The area was just as Lorenzo had described it, surrounded by trees, but open and flat. He pushed away the snow with his boot to reveal dormant grass. The regular clanking of a distant ski lift's chairs was barely audible. He looked toward the sound, and through a break in the trees could see skiers coming down off the mountain into a large valley. In the summer, the driver had told him, it was a nine-hole golf course. Luca Albani was neither a skier nor a golfer.

The tire tracks made by the boys' car were still visible. Little snow had fallen in the hours since they had made their pit stop, but it was starting again. The same for their footprints, now small but regular dips in the snow. They were the only indentations in the blanket of white that covered the field. Luca sighed, confirming that any marks made by the vehicle that brought Taylor and his murderer to this spot had long since disappeared. Was this where the violence had taken place?

"Come out here, Lorenzo." The boy squeezed his body from the backseat and zipped up his ski coat. "Now, take me through what happened." Luca looked toward the driver, and the occupants of a second police car. "Listen to what he's saying," he said as they got out of the car.

The boy looked around, getting his bearings. "We parked there. You can still see some of the tire marks. Then the four of us walked over to the edge and pissed near those trees. I was on the end, and when we were walking back I noticed something blue sticking out of the snow. You can just see the tracks from where I walked over and got the cap. It was right over there." The others looked where he was pointing. "I brushed the snow off it and walked back to the car to join the others. We drove back out to the road and into town. That's all."

Luca rubbed his chin and tried to picture the murder scene. It was unlikely that the wind had blown the hat from somewhere else, given the protection of the surrounding trees. Equally unlikely was that someone had come up here to dispose of the hat after Taylor had been killed. More probably, Taylor and his assailant had driven here, and it was in this field that the murder took place. In the struggle the hat had fallen to the ground and the murderer had not noticed. Or he did notice and either didn't care or was too busy figuring out what to do with the body. Where exactly had the struggle taken place? Near, but not next to where the hat was found? If they drove into the middle of the field, rather than stopping at the edge where the boys had, then their vehicle could have had four-wheel drive to get through the snow. And they would not have walked very far from it. He turned to the driver of the second car, a sergeant.

"You've got the shovels, right?"

"Yes, sir, they're in the back."

"Start from over there, where he said he found the cap. Dig through the snow to see if you can find anything else. Like skis and poles. Or some object that could have been used to crack the victim's skull. Or any sign of struggle. Work out from that point until you've covered the whole area."

They began the search and something was found almost immediately. It was not the murder weapon, but potentially almost as useful.

"Sir, you'd better come look at this." The policeman stood stiffly, pointing toward his feet, not wanting to disturb what he'd found. The snow came up to his ankles. The inspector slogged toward the man, his borrowed boots at least a size too large. He reached him and peered at the spot. After a moment he removed a plastic evidence bag from his pocket, opened it completely and brushed snow into it.

"Good work. It could just be mud, but since the ground is frozen, it's more likely to be blood." He held up the bag and they looked at the dark brown stain inside the clump of white. "We'll send it to the lab. Keep looking, we could find the murder weapon."

After more than an hour of searching, the only objects found had been in the area for a long time and did not appear to be related to the crime. It was what would be expected for a spot which the youth of Campiglio had used for activities that were either immoral, illegal, or both. Luca left one group of men to continue the search and sent another to check the road back into town and farther up the mountain. The murder weapon could have been thrown from the killer's vehicle. While they worked, he drove back into town, dropping off Lorenzo in the same square where he had been accosted earlier in the day. Lorenzo got out of the police car and shot off like a trout released in a stream.

Chapter Seven

"You weren't supposed to work, Rick. You needed a break, especially after what you witnessed last night. Helping Luca with the man's sister, catching the hat thief, I'll let that pass. But working on translations the rest of the morning, well, that's unacceptable. Do you see me calling my office?"

The chairlift was approaching the highest point of Campiglio's hundreds of kilometers of ski trails, a full 2,500 meters above sea level. The wide trail below ran between two jagged escarpments, its location above the tree line giving it a barren, moon-like quality. Rick and Flavio looked down at the skiers on the two sides of the lift. The trail on the left was wider, attracting the snowboarders and the faster skiers. Several ski school groups made their way slowly down on the right, led by instructors exaggerating their lifts and dips as they encouraged the students to do the same. Rick thought he recognized Gina Cortese, but it was impossible to be sure with the hat and goggles.

"Your office would call you if there was a problem, Flavio. I've got no staff, not even a secretary, so I have to keep on top of things myself. And it was just a short translation, I did it without a dictionary. Even you could have done it. With a good dictionary, of course."

They sat in silence for a few minutes, enjoying the view. The only sound was the call of the ski instructors. *Appoggiare—SU—giu. Appoggiare—SU—giu.* The students dutifully dug in their poles and flexed their legs up and down, trying—mostly without success—to mirror the movements of the instructor.

"And if the lovely vice consul had not gone off to assist Cat, you might have skipped the afternoon skiing yourself, Flavio. Admit it."

"That is certainly possible." Flavio grinned and slapped his gloves together. "Speaking of lovelies, Rick, when I talked with you a few months ago you said you were dating someone. An art history professor, as I remember. You haven't mentioned her since you arrived."

"And you haven't brought her up."

"Have I touched a nerve, my friend?"

Rick chuckled. "No, Flavio, you have not. Erica is in the States at the moment, teaching a seminar on Italian Mannerism at a major university."

"The University of New Mexico?"

"Another major university. On the East Coast."

"They have universities on the East Coast?"

"A few. But when she left, our relationship was up in the air. I'm not sure if it's going anywhere."

"So you have no qualms about dating this Taylor woman."

"I do not think, *caro* Flavio, that my comforting a fellow American in her time of grief could be categorized as dating."

"Whatever you say, Rick." They watched a snowboarder crash and burn on their left. "Did Erica use the *S* word before she departed for America?"

"The *S* word?"

"*Spazio*. Did she say she needed space?"

"No, I don't remember her saying that."

"I got the space thing a month ago from a girl. Lives in Bolzano and works for a vineyard we do business with. Beautiful dark eyes to go with her hair. Speaks Italian with a sexy German accent."

"Everybody in Bolzano has a German accent."

"Not like Inga."

They pushed up the safety bar and leveled their skis in preparation for the dismount. When they came to a small snow hill they slid gently off. The empty chair continued ahead for a few meters before whipping around to start its empty descent. Having skied the wider run twice already, they decided to take the other, less crowded run. Once again Rick marveled at his friend's style, taking each bump, large or small, like it wasn't there. The upper part of his body barely moved as his arms reached out to place the pole at just the right spot before starting a smooth turn around it. Rick tried his best to copy. He was certainly not a bad skier, but still found himself fighting the mountain. Flavio had become part of the mountain.

Halfway down the lift they stopped, allowing Rick to lean on his poles and catch his breath. Below, the trail split into three smaller routes that made their way back to the Campiglio, but all that was visible from this point were white peaks. Somewhere between the peaks lay the town, waiting for the afternoon's skiers to descend for the evening.

Rick was ready to start off again when a man wearing the uniform of a ski instructor shot past him, his skis slapping the snow. He was followed by a skier about half as tall, then another, until about ten kids had whizzed past. The skiers, each about eleven or twelve, all wore the same yellow bibs with matching yellow helmets, some trailing ponytails. Bees on skis. They kept close to the ground, not that they were that far from it anyway, given their height, and they were having no trouble staying with the instructor. As quickly as they had appeared, they were gone. Rick looked up and saw Flavio grinning.

"That was me twenty years ago, Rick. They pick the best kids in the town and train them after school in the winter. Every ski town on both sides of the Alps does the same thing." He looked in the direction the line of kids had taken. "You never know, there might be a future Lobo among them."

"I doubt it," Rick said. "UNM learned its lesson when they gave you a scholarship." Flavio didn't hear the comment. He had shot down the hill after the kids, as if by catching them he could catch some part of his youth.

Rick's wide turns brought him down to the flat area near the entrance to the chairlift, the meeting point for ski classes. As he approached, he noticed Flavio standing with one of the instructors, who was calling out to her class.

"As you ski down to Campiglio, remember what I told you. Take the turns wide and shift your weight as you do. *A domani.*" Rick recognized the voice. The class returned her *a domani* and pushed off down the hill as he slid up next to Flavio.

"I think you two have already met," Flavio said.

Gina Cortese studied Rick for a few moments and said: "The policeman."

"I'm actually not a policeman, but I am helping the inspector with this case." Rick wasn't sure if that was the best way to characterize his role, but it was what came to mind.

"Are you involved in the investigation too, Flavio?"

Flavio shrugged, lifting his ski poles by his wrist straps. "Not really. I know Luca, the inspector, from Trento. And I know Riccardo here from our college days in America."

Gina looked from one face to the other. "Is everybody involved in this investigation? Reinforcements, since it's now a murder?" The two men remained silent. "Well, you can cross me off the list of suspects. I was teaching classes all day Saturday. And when I was done I went home and had a hot bath, and then—"

She suddenly began sobbing uncontrollably. Flavio shuffled next to her and put his arm over her shoulder. She pressed her head against his chest.

"It's all right, Gina."

"I waited for him. Then I was so mad at him for standing me up. So mad. And he was dead, Flavio. I got mad at him and he was dead. I didn't know, I didn't know."

"You had no way of knowing," Flavio said softly. "It was a natural reaction when he didn't appear."

Slowly she regained control and separated herself from Flavio's arm. She ripped at the zipper of her ski coat and extracted a tissue before pressing it against one eye and then the other. "I have to go, I have another class. It was nice to see you, Flavio. And…"

"Riccardo," Flavio helped.

She pushed off across the snow, cross-country style, as she adjusted her goggles. Two people, a man and a woman, waved at her as she approached them.

"I didn't know Gina that well. She's a few years older than me," Flavio said as they watched her talking with her students. "But that's the way I remember her."

"You mean emotional like that? First she's mad at us, then she's mad at herself. I couldn't help wondering if it wasn't—"

"An act, Rick? With Italian women it's sometimes difficult to know the difference between what's real and what's an act, they often don't even know themselves."

"Those are the most profound words I've ever heard you say, Flavio." They continued to watch Gina, who now moved toward the ski lift line with her two new students. Rick broke their trance. "Do I remember passing a chalet partway down this trail where liquid refreshment is served?"

"Your memory is correct, Rick. A fine idea."

Their lengthening shadows were growing faint as a gauzy cloud attempted to block the late afternoon sun. Other skiers were also opting to head down rather than get on the chairlift again. In another hour the lifts would close and those left on the mountain would converge on the lower trails. It was the time of day, thanks to tired skiers and lower visibility, when the most accidents happened, especially on crowded weekends. Rick and Flavio skied slowly, dropping from the open expanses of the higher elevations into the woods where trails were cut through the trees. They came down into a valley where a four-seat chairlift took them up to their destination. It would be their last lift of the day; from there it would be all downhill.

Inspector Albani looked out through the glass wall into the main office of the Melograno Real Estate Agency. The chair was the most comfortable he had sat in since coming to Campiglio, certainly a lot easier to sit in than the one he used at the police station. When he'd been shown into the small conference room by Melograno's receptionist he almost took the seat at the head of the table. It had a slightly higher back and, unlike the other chairs, armrests. Melograno would take the place of honor. The policeman looked out the glass around the large room, which seemed busier than it had been during his and Montoya's previous visit, despite it being a weekday. All three of the cubicles on the opposite side of the room were filled today—one by the woman who had escorted him to the conference room, the same one who had greeted them the previous visit. In the other two sat a woman talking on her phone and a younger man working diligently at his computer screen. Was there a physical similarity between this man and Melograno? Luca decided there was not.

Melograno's door opened and the policeman watched Mayor Grandi emerge, followed by the real estate developer. Interesting, thought Luca. The woman had called Melograno to tell him that the inspector was waiting, so Melograno must have told the mayor. Would there be any reason for the mayor to have slipped out the back? Not really. Melograno did not know he was going to get a visit from the police, so the mayor being there was just a coincidence. Unless someone at the police station had alerted the mayor. As Luca turned this over in his mind, the mayor glanced over to him and turned to Melograno. They exchanged a few words and Grandi strode toward the glass room. Luca arose from his seat and opened the door as the mayor reached it.

"Inspector," he said, as if there was a need to confirm the policeman's existence. No handshake was offered. "This business with the American has become especially troubling. And now the stabbing of Guido Pittini. Please come to see me so you can explain what you are doing to resolve them. I'll be at my shop."

Luca was given no chance to reply; the man turned on his heel and walked to where Melograno was waiting. The mayor said something into Melograno's ear while keeping his eyes on the policeman, then moved toward the door. One of the women rushed up to him with his coat and he took it without acknowledgment before pulling open the door and disappearing.

Melograno, in contrast, was polite, like the two were playing good-suspect bad-suspect roles. He shook hands with Luca and asked him if he'd like a coffee or something else to drink. When his guest politely declined, the door was closed and they took seats at the table. As expected, Melograno sat at the head, in the taller chair.

From the moment Melograno had emerged from his office with the mayor, Luca had noticed a change in the man's body language since they'd met the previous day. To begin with, he seemed even more unkempt. The eyes looked like they needed sleep, just as the face begged for a razor and the hair a comb. The annoyed demeanor was still there, but it was not as convincing. This time he was going through the motions. As Melograno talked, the policeman's instincts were confirmed.

"The mayor is correct, this incident has turned nasty, very nasty indeed. I knew Signor Taylor as well as anyone here, so the news of his death has been a great shock to me. Do you have any suspicions as to who could have done this?"

He didn't know Taylor as well as the mayor's ex-wife, thought Luca. "I am just beginning the investigation," he said, deflecting the question. "Could you tell me again about your meeting with him? Perhaps you have remembered some detail that could be helpful." Melograno frowned as the policeman's pad and pen appeared.

"I don't know what else I can say." More of the previous bravado appeared. "You do remember what I said then, don't you?" When no answer was forthcoming, he gave a theatrical shrug and continued. "All right. Our meeting was relatively brief. I asked him about the loan I had requested from his bank. He said it was still pending but there were some questions. I asked what were the questions. He told me. I answered the questions, or at least I believe I answered them."

"If you don't mind me asking, Signor Melograno, what were the questions? Bear in mind that I know very little about banking."

Melograno looked at him as if trying to decide if the last comment was intended to be sarcastic. "They were financial issues. Collateral, my company's income, that sort of thing. I hardly think—"

"Nor do I, Signore. And he did not appear to be upset, pre-occupied, worried about anything?"

"He was as he always was. All business. That's the way Americans are."

Luca tapped his pen on the pad and studied what he had written, which was very little. "That meeting was Thursday afternoon. You didn't see him on Friday?"

"No, I was working here all day."

"And on Saturday?"

"I didn't see him after our meeting on Thursday. I thought I made that clear."

"You were also working here on Saturday?" He was making small squares in the top corners of the paper, then carefully filling them in with crosses. Melograno watched.

"Yes, I came in early and worked in my office the whole day, except for a break for lunch. My assistant was here working, if you are looking for an alibi. He will tell you." He glanced at the young man working in the cubicle.

The policeman looked up from his notes and acknowledged the other man. "His name?"

"Alberto Zoff." He watched as Luca wrote down the name.

"What time did you leave the office?"

"About five o'clock. I stopped for a coffee at the bar a few doors up, like I always do at the end of the workday. Then I went home."

"Do you live far?"

"My apartment is on the top floor of this building. I own it. The whole building, I mean."

"Very convenient. You can walk everywhere. That is something delightful that I have noticed about your town. Do you even have a car?"

"I do, Inspector, I have a Mercedes SUV. I need it to show real estate that is outside the city center. Unfortunately it is in the shop. A problem with the electrical system."

"That's surprising, the German cars are usually quite reliable. Not that I would know…my office always issues me a Fiat." Luca closed his notebook and put it and his pen in his coat pocket. "Tell me something, Signor Melograno. Do you ski?"

From the look on Melograno's face, he might have been asked if he knew how to read. "I was born and raised in Campiglio, Inspector. Here we all ski."

Once outside, Luca adjusted his hat in the glass of the store at street level, barely noticing what was displayed inside. He was thinking that Melograno had not mentioned the stabbing of the previous night. Then again, neither had he.

After sticking their skis and poles into the snow at the edge of the porch, Rick and Flavio clomped across the wooden planks toward the door. A few people sat outside, taking in the view with drinks in their gloved hands. Though the sun was low in the horizon, and mostly behind clouds, the porch was bright compared with the interior of the bar. It took the two men a few moments for their eyes to adjust to the dim ambiance. There was a lone person at the bar, a tall man with a ski cap pulled around his ears. He was drinking a beer and checking his cell phone for messages. Apparently this spot on the mountain had a signal.

"How about a hot VOV, Rick?" They both peeled off their ski gloves and placed them on the bar.

"I haven't had VOV in years. Great idea."

The order was given to the bar man, who pulled a white, ceramic bottle off the shelf and poured a thick, equally white liquid into two small glasses. He stepped to the espresso machine and gave each of the glasses a long shot of steam until the liqueur was covered with a light froth. The drinks were placed on saucers and set in front of the two men. They carefully picked up the hot glasses, clinked them together, and took sips.

"Much better than eggnog," said Rick. "And my grandfather makes a great eggnog."

"It's the strong *zabaglione* flavor that does it, and strangely enough, I don't like it in *gelato*. It's a flavor that needs to be served hot."

Rick was about to continue the discussion of liqueurs and gelato when he heard a voice on his right. It was the man who had been at the other end of the bar.

"Aren't you…?"

Rick glanced up and saw who it was. "Daniele, I didn't recognize you with the ski cap. Yes, it's me, Rick Montoya. This is my friend Flavio Caldaro."

Lotti extended his hand. "Daniele Lotti, *piacere*." He turned back to Rick. "And I wasn't sure I recognized you either. Ski gear does that."

"Out for an afternoon ski by yourself?" asked Rick, immediately regretting the way it was said.

Lotti didn't seem to notice. "I was going to ski with Cat, but she's tied up with the vice consul."

"I imagine they have a lot to deal with."

Lotti nodded. Rick noticed that the man didn't look as gawky or as skinny as when he'd seen him at the apartment. It must be the bulkiness of the ski coat, or the fact that his red hair was now covered. Red hair somehow added to gawkiness. His face looked raw, perhaps from the icy wind of the trails. Or the sun, though there hadn't been much sun that afternoon.

"You're from Milan, I assume," Flavio said.

"And from your accent, I trust you live around here."

"Correct. Trento. But I grew up right here in Campiglio."

"But you're not a policeman."

"Flavio has a wine business, Daniele, and as you know I'm not a policeman either. I hope you don't mind me calling you Daniele."

Lotti responded with a shrug. He took a sip from his beer glass. "Have you found the murderer yet? Even though you're not a policeman?"

"It was only last night that the body was found."

"Has your policeman friend found out where he was actually killed?"

Rick thought for a moment about whether he should answer and decided that word would be around the town by now. "A field north of town that overlooks the golf course."

"You're kidding."

Rick gave Lotti a surprised frown. "Why do you say that?"

The man sneered and took another swig of beer. "He's dead now, so he won't mind me saying. Cam liked to brag about his exploits with women, and I remember him telling me that he took a girl up to a field north of town that first summer he was here. I'll bet that was the place. How ironic."

"Did he mention the name of the girl?"

"If he did I don't remember. I think he said she was a ski instructor."

Rick and Flavio exchanged glances, but Lotti kept his eyes on his beer and didn't notice.

"Do you have any thoughts on who could have done it?"

The man's head snapped up and his eyes bore in on Rick's face. "How would I know? I just came up here for a few days of skiing. Now a friend is dead and his sister can't even give me the time of day. I might as well drive to Milan and go back to work at the office."

"You must know some other people in Campiglio," Flavio said. Rick could tell from his voice that his friend was not warming to the man from Milan.

"A few," was the curt answer.

"How long have you owned your apartment?"

"Apartments," corrected Lotti, "I own two. I've had them a couple of years. It seemed like a good investment, as well as having a place to stay when I wanted to ski. Yesterday I ran into the guy who sold it to me, and he said it's increased in value by at least ten percent." For the first time a slight smile crossed the man's face.

Flavio glanced at Rick, then asked, "Somebody local sold it to you, or someone from Milan?"

"A guy in my office recommended a real estate office here. You're not also in real estate, are you?"

"No," answered Flavio, "just wine."

"Well, the skiing has been good," said Rick. "I trust you've done a lot since you got here Friday. If I remember right it was late Friday afternoon when you drove up from Milan."

The suspicious look returned to Lotti face. "All it's done is snow since I arrived, and all I've done is ski." He glanced out the one small window behind the bar. "It looks like it's starting again. I think I'll be heading down. *Ciao.*" He drained the last of his beer and walked to the door, his ski boots scuffing the floor.

"Charming fellow," Flavio said as he picked up his glass and looked at it. "My VOV's getting cold."

"We could have him heat it up again."

"Not worth it." Flavio opened his mouth and tossed down the liqueur with a quick jerk of his hand. "Rick, he bought his apartments from Umberto."

"Melograno? Aren't there any other real estate offices in Campiglio?"

"A few, but Umberto is the best known, and he sells a lot of apartments. I'd bet on it."

Luca looked at the sky and touched the front brim of his hat, noting how well it kept the snow from his face. One of his better purchases, no doubt about it. Would his wife's opinion of the hat be the same as Riccardo's? Didn't matter; he loved it. And he'd bring her back something from the chocolate shop next to the mayor's store so she'd know he'd been thinking of her. He stopped and looked in the window at the rows of chocolate stacked elegantly. Handmade inside, of course, in various flavors and shapes, light and dark. It all looked good. There must have been some kind of hidden exhaust fan, since the aroma of chocolate brushed his nostrils. He sighed and walked a few steps to the entrance to the mayor's shop. A bell over the door rang when he entered.

The mayor was nowhere to be seen. An older couple was looking at a table full of wooden Pinocchios, some as tall as the grandchild they likely were shopping for. A salesgirl who was hovering over them looked up at the policeman with an "I'll be with you in a moment" smile, so he shook the snow off his hat and began wandering around the shop. It was, he decided, exactly what one would expect to find in an alpine town anywhere. What better souvenir could you bring back from the Dolomites than something carved out of wood? The image that came to mind was the goatherd, locked in his wooden hut, carving away in front of the fire while the goats bleeted in the cellar below and the wind howled outside. Man and goat, waiting for spring when they would climb the mountain again to find succulent grass peeking from the melting snow. So while the winter held on, there was the old man, working away, turning a rough block of wood into a tiny work of art. Must have been some movie he'd seen as a kid. Luca was turning a tiny carved goat in his hand when he heard Grandi's voice.

"Inspector, I hope you have some news for me. There are already stories in the papers that will not be helpful to tourism in Campiglio." The head seemed even balder than it had been in Melograno's office. It could have been the lighting, or its pink contrasted just enough with all the natural wood around the shop.

"We are just beginning to gather evidence, Signor Sindaco."

"And where is that evidence pointing?"

They were still standing, and Luca glanced at the couple nearby, who were now looking at cuckoo clocks. Grandi got the message. "Ah, yes. Why don't we sit over there?" He motioned to the table where they had talked previously, out of earshot of the others. When they were seated, Luca spoke in a lowered voice.

"My sense is that the criminal is a local, or at least someone who knows the town well." He was trying to give the mayor the impression that he was sharing confidential information, though everyone in town must have come to the same conclusion. It seemed to work. Grandi looked over at the other people and then leaned toward Luca.

"Is that so?" His voice was also almost a whisper. "But who could it be? I know everyone in town, and I can't for the life of me think who would have murdered the man."

"Had you known Signor Taylor?"

"Me? Why, no. I don't make a point of meeting every tourist that comes to Campiglio. Though some people here would say that I try." From Grandi's smile, Luca sensed this was an attempt at humor. He waited for the man to continue. "Inspector, you've talked to the people he saw before he was killed, I know that. What have you concluded?"

The mayor knows exactly who I've interviewed since setting foot in his little town, Luca thought. He probably knows what I had for dinner last night. Is this the time to bring up the issue of his ex-wife? Why not?

"How is your relationship with Gina Cortese, Signor Sindaco?"

He must have been expecting the question. "I don't see her very often now that our divorce is final. There were no children. It's a small town, so we can't avoid occasionally running into each other, but we've both moved on."

"I assume you know that she was seeing Signor Taylor?"

Grandi gave a neutral shrug. His body language said that he didn't care *who* she was seeing, but Luca was not totally convinced. "Inspector, you don't think that Gina could be involved, do you?"

"As I said, the investigation is just beginning. I must assume nothing and suspect everything."

"Of course. And I suppose I should tell you where I was at the time of the murder. Isn't that what always happens in these investigations?"

"Well, Signor Sindaco, I really—"

"No, we must do it by the book." He tapped his finger to his forehead and closed his eyes in thought. Somewhat theatrically, in Luca's mind. "It's difficult to remember every minute of Saturday, or any other day for that matter. I like to move around the town."

"Keep your finger on the public pulse, so to speak."

Grandi glanced up and nodded vigorously. "Yes. Yes, indeed. I take my job as mayor very seriously. On Saturday I went by the tourism office, to get a reading of how business was doing. Then

I stopped at the ski lift consortium, where they sell ski passes, and found that the numbers were very good. Lots of people getting the weekly pass, meaning they are here for the entire week, staying in hotels and eating in restaurants. And I also—"

"Was that in the morning? Early?"

"No, that would be mid-morning. Earlier, I was here working." He gestured at the block of wood, its eventual shape still anyone's guess. "Early morning, before the shop opens, is the time I get some of my best carving done."

"What time do you open?"

"Ten. During the season we are open every day, and my salespeople arrive a few minutes before ten. Unless there's some reason to be here, that's when I make my rounds about the town. My staff is very dependable. So I was out most of the day."

"Lunch?"

Grandi pondered the question, as if he had been asked something more profound. "Let's see. Saturday I just had a *panino* and a glass of wine at the bar across the *piazza*. No time for a regular lunch. Then more calls around town." He had been looking at the wooden ceiling as he tried to recall his movements, but now gazed directly at the policeman. "You know, of course, that I am running for re-election."

"Which explains your busy schedule."

"Well, Inspector, during the ski season I'm always on the move, especially on weekends, but if you are thinking that I may be doing more of it because of the election, well, guilty as charged." He held up his hands defensively. Another try at humor.

"So you didn't come back here at all on Saturday?"

"I returned at about six and stayed until we closed at seven thirty. No, that's not true. I worked here by myself until a little after eight thirty. I had dinner by myself at home. I live a few blocks away."

"When you make your rounds, if that's the word, how to you get around town?"

"Mostly on foot, of course. But if there's someone I need to see who is more distant, or if I have to go up to the ski lifts north of town, I use the city vehicle."

"That's a nice perk."

"Yes it is. A Land Rover. My predecessor picked it out; I might have gone with something else. Something Italian. But I've never been stuck, even in the heaviest snow."

"I trust you ski?"

Grandi gave the policeman a puzzled look. "Of course, Inspector. Everyone here skis. I don't get out to enjoy the trails as much as I'd like, what with my responsibilities to the town."

"And you do get some good snowfalls in Campiglio."

"Yes, Inspector, for business, thank God that we do. Such as last night when that horrible attack took place."

"I was going to ask you about that, Signor Sindaco."

Grandi looked at the policeman's face and squinted his eyes. "Surely you don't think it is connected to the American's murder."

"Two violent crimes within days in a town this size. What would you think?"

Grandi clearly did not want to think anything of the sort. "Pure coincidence. Guido had a reputation with the ladies. My guess is that his attack had something to do with those activities."

"He works on your campaign."

"That's correct. But what…certainly you couldn't think that his attack could be politically motivated."

"Politics can become heated."

"Inspector, Campiglio is a civilized place."

Luca did not point out that crimes often happen in the most civilized of places. Even murder. "A zealous supporter in the opposing campaign?"

Grandi waved the suggestion away with a flick of his hand, but then used it to rub his head in thought. Luca waited, not wanting to interrupt what was going through the man's mind. "Last week Guido got into a shouting match with someone who works for the other candidate. It got ugly but certainly not violent."

"Who was that?"

"It was an isolated event," Grandi said, putting a weak smile on his face and holding up his hands. "I should not have even mentioned it. It makes me appear to be engaging in dirty politics."

"But Signor Grandi, I really must—"

"No, no. I've said enough. Perhaps you should talk to my opponent."

Chapter Eight

Gnocchi verdi alla gorgonzola was the pasta course at the hotel that evening, a dish firmly based in the north of Italy with touches from various regions. The spinach that made the potato dumplings green was a Tuscan staple, but the gorgonzola cheese was arguably as Milanese as the Duomo. There was even a stop on the Milan metro named Gorgonzola. And the slight bacon taste in the *gnocchi* could have come from the eastern Po Valley, where not all pork went into the production of *prosciutto*. But the origins of the various ingredients were not important to the three men savoring the *gnocchi*. The dish's various features had joined perfectly together in the kitchen before arriving at their table, and that was enough for them. Luca sat back in his chair and picked up his glass. The straw yellow liquid swirled softly inside it.

"Flavio, you outdid yourself in the selection of this bottle. Its match with the *gnocchi* was something magical."

"You are too kind, Luca. You likely passed the vines that produced this bottle's grapes when you drove to Campiglio. It is an Etschtaler pinot bianco. Unfortunately a small vineyard. I could sell twice as many bottles as they produce."

Since moving to Italy, Rick was increasingly finding himself drawn into discussions of food and wine. It was simply something Italians did, along with complaining about the government and worrying that the economy was finally going to collapse. He found it more than ironic that at the same time they complained and worried, Italians were enjoying a lifestyle that would have been the envy of most of his friends back in the States. Now, as the table was cleared of the first course dishes, the conversation, as he knew it would, left food and returned to crime. After the waitress cleared the plates in front of each of them, in anticipation of the *secondo*, Rick began the questioning.

"So, Luca, how did your meeting with Melograno go? I don't suppose he confessed to the murder."

"He did not, Riccardo. I asked him about his movements on the day of the murder, Saturday."

"And?"

"Not exactly exculpatory. He said he was working in his office, and I confirmed with someone on his staff that he was there most of the day."

"That sounds like a good alibi," Flavio said, "if someone vouched for him. You think that person can't be trusted since he works for Umberto?"

Luca drank the last drops of the wine in his glass. "No, it's not that. The problem is that if Melograno was in his office, his assistant wouldn't know if the man was actually inside the whole time."

"That's true," said Rick. "There's a door to the back stairs. We saw it."

"Exactly. So he could have been in and out several times and the kid sitting in the outer office wouldn't have known. Melograno told me he'd gone to a bar nearby when he left the office at about five o'clock. I talked to the barman who said Melograno goes in there most days at that time, and he's quite sure Saturday was one of them."

"Quite sure but not positive," Rick said. "That was about the time the body was being dumped from the gondola."

Flavio finished his wine. "But if he was at the bar, that lets Umberto off the hook."

"For the drop of the body, yes it does." Luca pondered his statement and then snapped out of his thoughts. "Wine steward, are we going to continue with this wine for the second course?"

"No, of course not." answered Flavio. "The *secondo* tonight is *involtini*, so a red is required. There's a winery just north of Sondrio I deal with that makes an excellent Valtellina. We will have one of their bottles." He signaled to the waitress who scurried over and took his order.

Rick watched her disappear into the kitchen. "Luca, Flavio and I ran into two of our suspects this afternoon, if I can call them that."

"Really? Tell me."

"First, Gina Cortese. We bumped into her when she was between classes, and of course the murder of Taylor came up. She broke down when talking about the guy, and it was real. Don't you think so, Flavio?"

"Hard to tell, but I think so."

"She's got the best alibi of anyone, being with classes Saturday," Luca said. "Well, let me clarify that; she was in classes from ten o'clock on, so I suppose there may be a gray area early in the morning. But what would be her motive? They could have had a fight Friday night, but it would have been quite a violent one for her to go home and find someone to murder the man."

Rick recalled Gina slapping her ski school colleague, but said nothing. Three new glasses and the wine had arrived at the table. The bottle was opened and quickly vetted by Flavio before it was poured for Rick and Luca. They tasted and approved.

"I can't think of any other motive she could have," said Rick as he studied the dark red color of the Valtellina. "More likely would be her ex-husband, if she was really fooling around with Taylor before the divorce was final. Taylor could have even been the reason for the divorce."

"I brought up his ex-wife when I talked to the mayor this afternoon. He gave the impression that he's not shedding tears every night because of the divorce, not that he couldn't also have had a grudge against the dead man. But now he's married to his job as mayor, which, ironically, he is trying to use for an alibi. Essentially, he doesn't have a real alibi, since he spends his days going around town glad-handing the electorate in anticipation of the election. So he was nowhere and everywhere on Saturday. But what intrigues me is his relationship with Melograno."

The second course arrived, thin cutlets of veal that had been spread with bread crumbs, cheese, and mushrooms, rolled into meaty tubes, and lightly sautéed in oil and butter. They were arranged on each plate at right angles to a bundle of green asparagus sprinkled with *parmegiano reggiano*. The three men silently admired the food before putting knife and fork to it. After a few bites Luca returned to his point.

"I remember what you said, Flavio, about Melograno being the mayor's largest contributor, and I know that the election campaign is heating up, but…" He tried to find the words. Rick and Flavio waited patiently, enjoying their veal and asparagus while they did. "Is there more to their relationship than the need to get Grandi re-elected?"

"It's no secret," said Flavio, "that Umberto has designs to increase his influence outside of Campiglio. The bribery case that was dropped involved a regional politician, not a local one. But he cultivates the local economy very carefully, winning friends, and weakening enemies whenever he can. Bruno Bauer, for example…Umberto lent him the money to renovate his store."

"Bauer's store looked brand new when we were there, didn't it, Luca?"

"Yes it did. New carpeting, lighting. It looked very elegant. To go along with the merchandise. The hats, for example." He pretended not to notice Rick's grimace. "And who was the other person you two saw on the mountain while I was working?"

"Daniele Lotti," Rick answered. "He was having a beer in a little place halfway down. He did not seem very happy, with a good friend dead and the sister ignoring him."

"Did you ask him to describe all his movements on Saturday?"

"Hardly, Luca. But he did tell Flavio and me that all he's done since he got here on Friday night is ski, so I assume that's what he did on Saturday. Or will say he did." Rick put the last piece of veal into his mouth. The asparagus spears were already gone. "If that's the case, he has no alibi whatsoever for Saturday."

"What's his motive?" Flavio asked.

"His motive, Flavio, is Signora Taylor's motive." Rick and Flavio looked at Luca, waiting for him to continue. "It is clear the young lady has a motive, which is what we must assume is a large inheritance, that now she does not have to share. It also appears clear that Lotti is attracted to her, even if she does not wish to reciprocate. But this gives her a power over the poor man. They did have dinner together the night before the murder."

"An interesting scenario," Rick said, "planning murder over dinner."

"And as possible, or unlikely, as any of the others we have come up with," Luca said. "There's really nothing else to make him a suspect, except for his lack of alibi."

"He told us something else that is a coincidence, but a weird one," Rick said. "Taylor told him the first sexual encounter between him and Gina Cortese took place the first summer he came here, in the very field where he was murdered. Taylor apparently liked to brag about his conquests."

That got the policeman's attention. "I am beginning to like our victim less and less. But I have to wonder: Who else knew about that tryst in the field?" The three of them pondered in silence until Rick spoke.

"Something else, Luca. Flavio thinks Lotti bought his apart-ments from Melograno."

Luca was about to take a drink of the wine, but now lowered the glass back to the table. "From Melograno? Is that significant?"

"I wondered the same thing, but Flavio thinks it's not," said Rick. "He's the most prominent real estate dealer in Campiglio, it would be logical for Lotti to have used him. So it would mean about as much as Melograno having bought a bear carved by Mayor Grandi."

"Ah, our delightful Mayor Grandi." Luca seemed about to comment on the mayor when he stopped in mid-thought. A grin split his face. "By the way, Flavio, I trust you know who is Grandi's opponent in this election?" Flavio nodded.

Rick looked from one face to the other. "Now what?"

"Well, Rick," said Flavio, "that other candidate would be Mitzi Muller, who is known to everyone in Campiglio as Zia Mitzi. Nobody gives her much of a chance to unseat Grandi."

"From the way he's campaigning," said Luca, "it appears that Grandi's not taking any chances. And, Flavio, what does Aunt Mitzi do around here that makes her known to everyone?" Rick knew from the ever-present grin that Luca knew the answer to his question.

"She runs the best pastry shop in town. That may be why she isn't given much of a chance of winning. Nobody wants her to be elected, for fear she'd spend less time baking."

From Luca's expression one might have thought he'd pulled a rabbit from a hat.

"Wait a minute, Flavio," said Rick. "Is her shop right on the main street, across from Bruno's ski shop?"

"Aha, so you've been there and didn't tell me. I would have asked you to bring back some of her almond cookies. Best cookies in the Dolomites."

"Her *mille foglie* was pretty good. You can still see traces of it on Luca's jacket lapel."

Luca instinctively glanced down at his jacket and laughed. "Well, I think such a prominent citizen of Campiglio should be questioned about the case. Riccardo, we will have to make a return visit to her establishment. And we won't forget the almond cookies." Luca held up a finger. "But, Zia Mitzi does not seem like the kind of person who would use violence to win the mayorship." His comment was greeted by blank looks from the other two men at the table. "I'm talking about the attack last night. Remember that the victim worked for Grandi's campaign."

Rick nodded. "One theory, Flavio, is that the attack on Pittini had something to do with his work for Grandi."

"When you told me about the attack, Rick, you failed to mention that."

"I suppose I was too concerned that I could have been the target."

"You're forgiven." Flavio turned to the policeman. "But an attack on the street over who should be mayor of Campiglio? That doesn't sound like my beloved hometown."

Luca nodded. "That was exactly the mayor's initial reaction today when I broached the possibility, Flavio. And if anyone suspected Mitzi of such activities, or suspected someone on her campaign, Grandi would be the one to know."

"By the way, Luca," Rick said, "what's the condition of Pittini?"

"He still hasn't regained consciousness. His wife remains at his side, and a policeman is on call, ready to get any kind of information out of him if he comes to. Even though the attack was from behind, he may well know who it was. Or suspect someone." The policeman watched the waitress take away his empty plate.

Rick watched his own plate disappear. "The mention of Mitzi reminds me of her cookies, which logically brings us to the issue of *dolci* to finish off this wonderful meal." He pushed the chair back slightly from the table. "I, for one, will skip the sweets and have some fruit. What about you, Flavio? Flavio?" Rick turned to follow his friends eyes, and saw that Lori Shafer, still dressed in her working pantsuit, had taken her place at a table in one corner of the room. "Aha. The lovely Ms. Shafer returns from her consular duties. She was working late."

Flavio turned back to his tablemates. "I can't let her dine alone, my friends, that would be rude."

"So that is the American diplomat," said Luca. "Of course, Flavio, do the needful. The waitress will find you for your dessert and coffee order." Flavio rose from their table and walked across the room, saying a quick hello to the Smiths on the way. The Americans were just finishing their *involtini con asparagi*. Rick and Luca watched as Flavio greeted Lori and took the chair across from her, flashing a quick grin back at their table as he sat. She looked up and waved at Rick.

"I think you are correct about needing something sweet, Riccardo. With our coffee. Just to clear the palate, of course."

"Of course, Luca. They have an excellent *panna cotta,* I had it a few nights ago."

"Small portion?"

"Tiny."

"Then that's what I'll have." Luca got the attention of the waitress and ordered the dessert. Rick asked for the *frutta fresca.* "Riccardo," the policeman continued, "there is someone else we should interview, besides the other mayoral candidate."

He's back to using "we" again, Rick thought. "And who would that be?"

"Bruno Bauer, of the hat emporium. You said that Signora Taylor spoke of him like they knew each other, and now we find that he got a loan from Melograno."

"I don't see any motive for Bauer to murder Taylor."

"Nor do I, Riccardo, nor do I. Unless, again, the murdered man's sister is actually behind the crime, and we substitute Bauer for Lotti in that scenario."

"The picture you're painting of Cat is one of a scheming woman who can wrap men around her little finger."

"Well, Riccardo, I assume you noticed that she is a beautiful woman, and—"

He was interrupted by the arrival of the custard in a small ramekin. A brownish liquid had been dripped over the white surface. The waitress also set a bowl of fruit on the table, which Rick began to study after gesturing for Luca to eat. The inspector took a small spoonful of the custard.

"An excellent *panna cotta.* Smooth with a dash of amaretto serving as the perfect foil for the cream. Your suggestion is much appreciated."

Rick pulled an orange from the bowl and placed it on his plate. Using the knife provided by the waitress, he sliced off one end and peeled the thick skin, happily finding that it was a Sicilian blood orange, his favorite. After separating the slices, he picked up a fork, sliced one of them, and put it in his mouth. Italians always used a knife and fork to eat fruit, even bananas. Luca watched the process as he enjoyed his sweet.

"Enough murder talk, Riccardo. Tell me, where do you live in Rome?"

"I have a small apartment near Piazza Navona."

"Ah, right in the *centro storico*. How were you able to come across such a place?"

"A distant relative owns it."

Luca had made quick work of his dessert and was scraping up the last bits with his small spoon. "Of course. That's what family is for. I lived with my parents until I got married, a typical Italian story, and then managed to find an apartment only a few blocks from where they live."

"Much to your mother's delight."

"And my wife's. Fortunately they get along well. When I was transferred up here I don't know what upset Mamma more, losing her son, or her daughter-in-law."

Try moving to a different continent, Rick thought, and see how your mother takes it. "Where was your apartment?"

"Outside the walls, the Porta San Giovanni area. Near Piazza Zama."

"I've been to Piazza Zama," Rick said, "There's a restaurant—"

"Severino. Best *saltimboca* in Rome, which is saying a lot." His empty custard bowl was whisked away, a coffee cup put in its place. "Riccardo, do you know what Piazza Zama is named for?"

"The Battle of Zama, if I remember my Italian history correctly."

"*Bravo*. The final and decisive battle of the second Punic War, Scipio defeating Hannibal outside Carthage. Here it is the twenty-first century, and we Romans think it important to name a square after an event that took place in 202 BC. Quite a long collective memory, don't you think?"

Rick drank the last of his coffee. "There's simply more history to remember here, Luca. The state I come from in America boasts the oldest capital in the country, yet it only dates back four hundred years."

"The one with the Roman street grid."

"Your short-term memory is pretty sharp too." Rick glanced at Flavio and Lori, who were in the middle of a deep conversation. He wondered what language they were using, but suspected it was English. Despite the jokes, Flavio's English was excellent, as was his accent—when he wanted it to be. Rick returned his attention to the inspector. "Do you really want me to go with you to talk with Mitzi and Bruno Bauer tomorrow?"

"Absolutely, having you present when I talk to people keeps them off guard, better than if I took one of the local police with me. And I value your opinions."

"That's good of you, but I—" Rick was interrupted by his cell phone, which he pulled from his pocket. Not a number he recognized. He glanced at Luca who gestured for him to take the call.

"Montoya."

"Rick, this is Cat. I need your help. Can you come over right now?"

◇◇◇

Rick looked at himself in the mirror of the elevator as it rose to Cat's floor. He wore the shearling coat from a small shop in Taos, bought when he was on a ski break from college. The leather on the sleeves was beginning to get shiny, and it had a small hole on the bottom of one side from when he'd caught it in his seat belt lock. It was too expensive to have the hole repaired, and over time the story of the bullet hole had proven to be worth gold at Albuquerque singles bars. He would never get rid of the jacket; not just for its warmth, but the memories it held of cold times past. And it went with his cowboy boots, as well as with the wide-brimmed hat he now held in one hand.

He didn't remember the elevator being so slow. Finally it lurched to a halt and released him into the hallway. After two rings of the bell, the door opened. Cat was dressed in jeans and a sweatshirt, her face scrubbed of makeup, hair pulled back. If he hadn't gotten her call he would have thought that she wasn't expecting visitors. Her appearance did not detract from her looks. She closed the door and put her arms around him, that same perfume hitting his senses.

"Thank you for coming so quickly, Rick."

"What's wrong? From your voice it sounded like there's some crisis."

"Did I give that impression? Come sit down, I'll tell you." Rick stamped the caked snow from his boots onto the door mat, shed his hat and jacket, and followed her into the living room. A book lay open next to the chair where she was sitting down. He took the place opposite her.

"It's that woman."

He frowned. "What woman?" Had Gina Cortese contacted Cat? Made some kind of threat?

"That woman from the consulate. She's driving me crazy."

Rick couldn't decide whether to laugh or get pissed off. He opted for the latter. "You had me rush over here because you can't get along with the person who drove up here to help you in your time of crisis?"

Cat's expression turned into a pout, and it was not becoming. "Rick, she's just…stifling. She hovers like the dorm supervisor we had in school. I can't stand her."

"Well, you can't always choose the people you have to deal with in life, Cat." He got to his feet.

"Don't go, Rick. I'm sorry. It's just that, well, this is not an easy time. I'm on edge."

He studied her face and slowly sat back down. She was right about finding herself in a tough situation, and it wasn't his place to be judgmental. He knew he had to give her the benefit of the doubt. What happened to her brother wasn't her fault—at least he didn't think it was.

"Okay, Cat, you got me here. How can I help?"

"First let me help you." She bounced to her feet and Rick noticed that the sweatshirt, though roomy, still fit well. "I am remiss in my duties as a hostess. What can I get you to drink?"

"Do you have any beer?"

"I think so. But it's Italian."

"Well, we are in Italy, Cat, last time I checked. That will be fine."

She disappeared into the kitchen. He got up and looked around the room, which hadn't changed since his last visit. The cover of the book she was reading was dominated by a woman barely dressed in futuristic armor, facing off with a tentacled creature not in the least intimidated by her ray gun. Rick always wondered what kind of people read such books, and now he knew. He heard the pop of a bottle cap being removed, then the beer pouring into a glass. Even at many of the best places in Albuquerque, patrons were always asked if they wanted a glass or just the bottle, but this wasn't New Mexico. Cat reappeared, a beer mug in one hand and a crystal glass with something on the rocks in the other. Rick took his beer, tapped it with her glass, and returned to his chair.

"Is there any news on the investigation?" Cat settled back into the cushions.

"I don't really know what Inspector Albani is up to," Rick said. It wasn't true, but he didn't want to get into any details with someone who was at least peripherally considered a suspect. "I know he's been interviewing a lot of people."

"I thought you were, you know, working with him."

Rick took a sip of his beer to give him time to respond. It didn't taste like one of the big national brands, like Peroni or Moretti; it was probably something local. With the number of German speakers in the Dolomites, there would have to be lots of local beers.

"I was here to help translate, Cat. But if you have something else he should know, something you've remembered, I can tell him. We're staying in the same hotel."

"No, nothing new. I just thought…"

Rick studied her face silently, considering various possibilities. The most obvious was that she truly was upset, outside her comfort level, and in need of some support. Of course Lori had been giving that support all afternoon, but perhaps in a manner that was more overbearing than comforting. Or perhaps Cat was somehow involved in the murder and was probing to find out how much he knew. If that was the case, their interaction now would become a game of cat and mouse, or rather Cat and Rick. The third possibility was that she was simply attracted to him, and that's why she'd called and asked him to come over. He had to admit he preferred that one to the first two. There was a fourth possibility: some combination of the first three.

"The inspector is tracking down various leads, I know that. He seems very efficient."

"It was someone local, wasn't it?"

"I doubt if someone came up from Milan, or from the States, if that's what you mean."

She took a strong pull of her drink. "I just wish there was something I could do."

"Cat, perhaps it's best for you to try and take your mind off things. Being with the vice consul all day, dealing with the details you had to talk about, has taken its toll."

"I had no idea there were so many decisions to make."

"I'm sure. And you've been cooped up here all afternoon. Why don't we go out for a walk around town? Getting some fresh air will do you good."

"Oh, I'd love that, Rick." She stood up, and to his surprise, drained her glass. "Take your time with your beer, I'll just freshen up."

Before he could get to his feet she disappeared down the hall. His hand reached for the mug on the table next to the chair. After another drink of the beer he held it up and studied the frowning face of the Irish leprechaun, his fists up, ready for a fight. Perhaps this had been Cameron Taylor's third-favorite possession, after his cap and expensive skis. Rick put down the mug and walked to the window where he could see people walking slowly along the sidewalk below. He couldn't tell if the flakes swirling on the street were falling from the sky or being picked up from the ground by a passing gust of wind. Whatever their source, they gave the couples he watched a good excuse to pull closer.

He walked back to the chairs, picked up his mug and Cat's glass, and walked into the kitchen. In the sink were some dishes and a frying pan, but he found room for the glass and mug, into which he ran some water. In the drain were a few strands of spaghetti, the remnants of what looked like a simple meal. Probably all that Cat would be capable of, Rick decided, without Maria in the kitchen. He walked back into the living room and sat down, stretching his legs out toward the coffee table, noticing his boots. They would need a good polishing when he got back to Rome, thanks to the slush of Campiglio's streets. They were ones from the Boot Barn in Albuquerque, not the fancy place in Santa Fe where he'd gotten his other, more dressy pair. These were more comfortable.

"I'm ready."

Rick looked up. Cat had changed into something which looked like a long sweater, but which he quickly realized was a dress of heavy wool that ended just above her knees. Loose-fitting snow boots rose to meet the hem, but ended just below the knees. The dress was not loose-fitting. Quite an outfit to stroll about the streets of Campiglio, he thought. She had brushed some color to her face, added a light coat of lipstick, and changed the ribbon holding back her hair. After taking it all in, he rose to his feet.

"That was quick. Where's your coat?"

"The closet there by the door."

Rick opened the closet door and found the coat she had worn that morning. Next to it were two that must have belonged to her brother. She turned her back to him and he slipped it up over her arms, noticing that she'd added a few new sprays of perfume. He pulled on his own coat, took his hat, and opened the door to the apartment.

When they emerged on the street a gust of snowy wind swirled around their two bodies. Cat pushed herself against Rick's chest.

"You should have worn a hat, Cat."

"I'll be okay. It feels good to be out of that apartment."

The violent images of the previous evening, pushed from his mind, reappeared. It was just ahead that he had been jolted by the cries of Pittini and rushed up to find him bleeding in the snow. He instinctively glanced around to find that now several people strolled the sidewalk. That would be expected since the snow was not as heavy and the hour not as late. He toyed with the idea of telling Cat about the incident but rejected it immediately. She had enough on her mind. He wasn't sure how much she wanted to talk, so he decided to wait to let her start the conversation. They came to a shoe store and stopped to gaze at the pairs lined up on the shelves inside the long glass window. The stock was dominated by boots, as would be expected in a mountain town in the winter.

"This is where I got these boots," Cat said, extending her toe. "They're very warm."

"These are warm too," he said, noticing that she was glancing at his footwear.

"Do you always wear cowboy boots, Rick?"

"When I'm in the States, I wear Italian shoes."

"Really?"

"Pretty much. Loafers, mostly, when the weather's not too cold."

"Clever. American women think the Italian shoes are cool, and Italian women are fascinated by the cowboy boots."

"That never occurred to me."

"I'll bet it didn't."

They continued walking slowly along the sidewalk and reached the pedestrian-only area around the main square. Despite the hour, people still milled around in small groups, but they were younger couples instead of the pensioners of the mornings. On leaving the protection of the storefronts Cat clutched Rick's arm more tightly and pushed herself into his shoulder.

"Shall we go in there for something warm?" he asked. "I went there with Flavio the night we got here." His eyes pointed to the large bar on one corner of the *piazza*. Its porch area was covered with snow, but through the frosted windows they could see the heads of people sitting inside.

"Yes, let's. You haven't told me about Flavio."

"College buddy. We've been trying to get together since I moved to Rome and finally managed to work it into both our schedules. He lives down in Trento but grew up here."

They climbed the few steps, crossed the porch and pushed through the heavy wooden door.

The inside was one large room on two levels, perfect to see and be seen, which Rick decided was the idea. On the upper level a bar ran along the entire back wall. Behind it various espresso machines gleamed between rows of bottles and glasses. Chrome stools lined the bar, but most of the customers on the upper level were at the tables along the railing in front of it, or sitting at the area below. A harried waiter rushed past Rick and Cat, giving them his best "sit wherever you'd like" look. They found a table for two at the far end of the upper row with a good view of the entire room. In contrast with the square outside, it was bright, warm, and noisy. They slipped off their coats and draped them over the empty chairs.

"What would you like, Cat?"

"I'd love a cappuccino."

Rick got the waiter's eye and he hurried to their table, dropping napkins in front of each of them with a quick movement of the hand. "*Un cappuccio e una spina*," said Rick, and the man disappeared.

"Did you say *cappuccio*?"

"You have a good ear. Yes, it's more informal, but the same meaning."

"And what's a *spina*?"

"A draft beer. Watch the bartender." She looked up and saw the man holding down a tall plastic handle, filling a glass with beer.

"I think I get it. He's pulling on a thing that looks like a spine. So, *spina*."

"*Brava*, Cat, you'll be fluent in Italian before you know it."

"I doubt that." Their drinks arrived at the table. She stirred sugar into her coffee, blew on it, and took a sip. "Perfect. I didn't think I was cold, but this hits the spot." She held the cup in two hands and looked over its rim into Rick's face. "It was awfully nice of you to come to my aid, Rick.

"Glad to help out, Cat."

"So, there really are no leads on the murder? Must be something."

He took a sip of his beer, giving him time to think of an answer. It was smoother than the bottled stuff he'd had at her apartment, but that could have been in the refrigerator for weeks. "There are some local leads, I think, but I don't know the details."

"I got the impression you were in tight with the inspector." She took another drink of her cappuccino and placed the cup back in the saucer.

"I don't think I can be described as 'in tight' with the man." The way she was pushing him made it easy for Rick to lie. He shrugged. "As I said, he's staying in the same hotel."

"Well maybe you could ask him for me the next time you see him. It's my brother, after all, I have a right to know. If it makes you feel any better, you don't have to say I asked."

"I'll see what I can do."

Her hand moved to cover his. "Thank you, Rick." Her eyes moved from his to over Rick's shoulder. "Well now," she said, her voice lowered slightly, "you know this is a small town when even I start to see people I know."

Rick turned to see Bruno Bauer walking through the door. He shook snow off his thick black hair with his gloved hand and surveyed the room. After a few sweeps he spotted someone and walked toward a table near the front where a blond woman sat with her back to Rick and Cat. Bauer bent over the woman who turned her face so he could kiss her on both cheeks before sitting in the opposite chair. Well, well, thought Rick. Bauer and Gina Cortese seem to be friends.

Bauer pulled off his gloves and coat and found the waiter. After giving his order he looked up and spotted Cat. He leaned forward and said something to Gina, who turned around. She was a different woman from the one he'd seen drinking with her colleagues, starting with a tight sweater and slacks. The hair was now puffed up to double the previous size, hoop earrings dangled from her ears, and she had enough makeup on to cover several faces. Her expression showed puzzlement with a dash of annoyance. Bauer got to his feet and walked toward them.

Rick was standing when Bauer reached the table and took Cat's hand in both of his. "Caterina, I am so sorry. My condolences." His English was thickly accented but passable. It came from dealing with the few American and English tourists who come through Campiglio, Rick thought.

"Thank you, Bruno. This is Rick Montoya, an American friend."

Rick shook Bruno's hand and stayed in English. "Bruno and I have met, Cat. I rented my skis at his shop on this trip."

The man was uncomfortable, but Rick couldn't know if it was because of Cat's loss or finding she was with the person who'd come into his shop with the policeman. Or his limited English. Whatever the reason, Rick expected Bruno to beat a quick retreat, and he did. After mumbling some more words to Cat he went down the steps to the lower part of the room and returned to his seat facing Gina Cortese. Cat had not recognized Gina, and Rick thought it better not to point her out.

"Do you know Bruno well?" Cat asked before sipping her coffee.

"Not really. Flavio introduced me when I was renting the skis." No use mentioning the encounter with Luca, Rick thought. "And how well do you know him?"

"The same."

Rick would not have expected Bruno's tender condolences, even from an Italian, if his relationship with Cat was based purely on determining her boot size. Watch it, Montoya, he thought. Your Italian side is taking over, the one that's always looking for something hiding behind even the most innocuous statements. He drank another sip of beer, noticing a slightly bitter aftertaste.

"What are your plans, Cat? I mean in the next week or so."

She stirred the cappuccino and pondered the question. "Cam's body won't be released for a few days, and I'm not in any rush to get back to the States. The apartment here is paid for through the end of the month, not that Daniele would throw me out. I really don't have anything to get back to." She had been staring at her cup and now she looked at Rick. "That's why I came here in the first place, to get away from what was going on back there."

"Your divorce is final, isn't it?"

"Yes, but that's not the problem. I'm just not sure what I'm going to do next."

"Like work? Or where you want to live?"

"Both those things. I have a lot of questions to answer."

"I get the sense you don't even know yet what all the questions are."

"Perhaps you're right, Rick. Perhaps you're right."

The woman is aging before my eyes, Rick thought. For him, life had moved easily from one stage to another without many agonizing decisions. From as far back as he remembered he'd wanted to go to college where his father had graduated, and once at UNM getting into language study was another logical choice. After all, he was already fluent in English and Italian, and almost the same level in Spanish. The translation work had started in college, helping pay his tuition, so it was easy to hang out a shingle after he got his graduate degree. Even moving the business to Rome was an easy decision. And it all had turned out well so far. Unlike this poor woman who had already messed up her life by getting into a bad marriage. And now she didn't know what to do with herself, or even where to do it. At least money wasn't a problem for Catherine Taylor. He watched her as she stared blankly around the rest of the large room.

"Let's get you home, Cat. You look exhausted."

"It has been a long day. The cold outside and this cappuccino woke me up, but now it's starting to get to me."

Rick rose from his chair and walked to the bar, behind which their waiter was pouring drinks into glasses on a tray. From a wad of tickets in his pocket he found the right one and passed it to Rick, who checked it, counted out some euros, and thanked the man. As he walked back to the table he saw a familiar figure standing at a table near the door. He was chuckling as he slipped Cat's coat over her shoulders.

"What's funny Rick?"

"That man over there is the mayor of this wonderful town. As you may be able to tell, he is up for re-election." He watched Grandi work the room like a pro, shaking hands with the tourists but giving more familial hugs to the locals. It reminded him of his father showing the flag at a diplomatic reception. "Wait a second, Cat, I am curious about something." She pulled out a small mirror from somewhere and checked her makeup while Rick watched Grandi shake hands with Bruno after giving his ex-wife a peck on each cheek.

Cat took Rick's arm as they walked toward the door. "You know the mayor, Rick?"

"You're the one who said it's a small town, Cat." He pushed open the door to let her pass. Leaving the heat and stuffiness of the bar, the crisp outside air felt good. Rick pulled down his hat and looked up to see Flavio, with Lori Shafer in tow, coming across the snow-covered porch, heads bent against the wind.

"Out for a night on the town, Flavio?"

His friend's head popped up. "Rick, what a nice surprise."

"Ciao, Rick," said Lori. "Hi, Cat. I don't think you've met Flavio Caldaro. Flavio, this is Cat Taylor."

Flavio pulled off his glove and took Cat's hand. "It is my pleasure, Caterina. I only wish we were meeting under better circumstances. I am so sorry for your loss."

"That's kind of you. And I am so glad to meet Rick's friend. He has told me about you."

"Only things that put me in a good light, I hope."

Rick watched his friend work his magic. He had always been good at making a first impression, especially when it involved beautiful women. Lori held Flavio's arm tightly.

"You are just leaving?" Flavio asked. "Can we talk you into going back in and joining us for something?"

Rick was about to beg off, but Cat spoke first. "Thank you, Flavio, but I really need some sleep. I've had a difficult day."

"Of course, Caterina. We will do it another time. Right, Lori?"

"Yes, another time," said Lori. "Cat, I'll see you tomorrow morning."

Cat shivered, and Rick wondered if it was the cold. "You know, Lori, I think I need to rest in the morning. Make some calls back to the States."

"Certainly. I'll be over after lunch."

Cat glanced at Rick, who was watching the exchange. He wondered who she would be getting out of bed by calling the States in the morning.

"Actually, Lori," Cat continued, "Rick has been nice enough to invite me to go skiing in the afternoon. He thought it would be good to get my mind off things. So maybe I'll see you around, say, four?"

"Sure, four o'clock is fine."

Rick thought he noticed Lori squeezing Flavio's arm, but it could have been his imagination. Air kisses were exchanged and Rick and Cat descended into the square, now virtually deserted. When he heard the door of the bar close he stopped and put his hands on Cat's shoulders.

"The two beers may have clouded my memory, Cat, but I don't recall asking you to join me on the slopes tomorrow."

She took one of his arms and folded it over her shoulder while she pushed against him. "I said it without thinking, but you don't mind, do you? I couldn't face another whole day with that woman."

Rick had to admit that he wouldn't mind, as long as it didn't interfere with assisting Luca in the morning. He kept the arm around Cat's shoulder as they crossed the plaza, their footprints beginning to fill with snow as soon as they stepped out of them. It was going to be another good night for skiers.

Chapter Nine

After a night of heavy snowfall the morning had arrived with clear skies. The first rays of sun cut between the eastern peaks and exploded into bright prisms on every white surface they hit. A snowy night followed by a sunny morning; nothing could have made the skiers—or the tourist office—more pleased. Skiers in small streams clomped along the town's sidewalks toward various *impianti*, eventually converging into rivers of jostling bodies as they neared the lift lines. Everyone knew this would be a perfect day, and they wanted to get the most of it.

Rick, with no skis over his shoulder, walked against the current. The pointed footprints of his boots contrasted with the snub-toed marks of the skiers he passed heading in the opposite direction. If he hadn't known it already, their faces told him he would be missing an ideal morning on the mountain. But the excitement of the investigation easily made up for it, and the snow would still be there in the afternoon when he took to the mountain with Cat.

He was becoming an accepted member of the station team, despite his quasi-official status with the *Polizia dello Stato*. The uniformed policeman at the front desk barely looked up when Rick pushed through the front door and made his way to Luca's office. The door was ajar, and he tapped lightly.

"*Avanti*."

"We missed you at breakfast, Luca." Rick took his usual seat opposite the inspector.

"That's because you came down at a much later hour. I had to eat early since…" He spread his arms over the papers. "Since I had all this waiting for me. It's been so long since I had my coffee I am ready for another, but let me first bring you up to speed on what is happening in the investigation."

"Some developments?"

"You could say that. One of the men who helped search the field yesterday was talking with his wife about it, and she told her cousin, who happens to work in a real estate office."

"Melograno's?"

"No, a competing one. Anyway, the cousin is sure that the field where the cap and blood were found is the one that Melograno is trying to purchase with the loan from Taylor's bank."

Rick's eyes widened. "An interesting coincidence."

"I'm sure your uncle has talked to you about such coincidences, Riccardo."

"He has, he has. So what could—"

"Wait, it gets better. This person also said that it's well known in local real estate circles that there is another bidder on that plot of land." He leaned back in his chair.

"Don't keep me hanging, Luca."

"It is a certain Lauro Muller, the owner of a local hotel."

"Lauro Muller. Hmm. Am I supposed to recognize—wait a minute. Zia Mitzi is named Muller. Has to be a relative."

"Her husband, to be exact. He's what could be described as a prominent businessman, and the manager of her mayoral campaign. Apparently he wants to buy the property to build another hotel. It would be a perfect place for one, I must say. People staying there could ski out the back door."

"The same reason Melograno wants to build an apartment complex there."

"Exactly. And it is one of the last choice pieces of undeveloped land in Campiglio close to the ski trails. I asked the sergeant to track down exactly who owns it. And something else about the Muller family: There is a son. He came back to Campiglio a few months ago after spending several years in Milano, where he was involved in some petty crime. Since returning home, however, he's been working in his mother's bakery and hasn't gotten into any trouble."

"His mother has whipped him into shape."

"Mammas often do that."

The two men silently pondered mothers. It was something Italian men did often.

"Has Pittini's condition improved?"

"No, still in a coma. The stab wound is healing nicely, however. I did confirm that he was working the gondola on the night of the drop, so the possibility that he was involved in the Taylor case becomes stronger."

"That's good, since it weakens the possibility that the attacker was after me."

"I suppose it does." Luca pushed his papers to one side and got to his feet. "Let's get a coffee on the way to see Mitzi Muller. I'd rather not get one from her if we are going to be asking her questions about the case. Wouldn't be professional."

"And that means we shouldn't buy any almond cookies either. Flavio will be disappointed."

While Luca pulled on his jacket, Rick walked to the wall and pulled out the thumbtack from where it was stuck near one corner of the poster. He smoothed down the curled corner with his left hand and carefully pressed the thumbtack back in place. The poster now showed the tips of the woman's skis. It had been driving him crazy.

◇◇◇

The same rich *profumo* of baked goods washed over them as they came through the door of the shop, even richer than their previous visit. Rick surmised that today they were closer to the morning baking hour, and the strong flavors of the ovens still hung in the air. He immediately regretted that Luca had vetoed any purchases. Besides the almond cookies, which he immediately spotted behind the glass, there were rows of other goodies to tempt him. Any one of them would have gone perfectly with an espresso.

There was no one behind the counter when they entered, but soon a figure appeared through the door. He was in his early twenties, unshaven, and stared at them through tired eyes. The long, white apron was stained with flour or sugar, and dark hair pushed out from under a blue baseball cap with a yellow M on the front. The way he stared at Rick and Luca, one would have thought he had just emerged from a cave after a long hibernation. After several seconds he spoke, but it was not to the two visitors.

"*Mamma! Clienti!*" He kept his eyes on them as he called out, then turned and disappeared into the back. Rick and Luca were left looking at each other for several seconds before Zia Mitzi hurried through the door. She had the same work outfit as their previous visit, but this time her hair was covered with a white scarf tied in the back. Perhaps she had been frosting a cake when they arrived.

"Yes, gentlemen, what can I—oh, it's you, Inspector." She tried to put on a more serious face, but it seemed to go against her nature. While other women her age had wrinkles caused by worry, Rick surmised that those around her eyes and mouth had formed from too much smiling. This was a resolutely cheerful woman. "Such a terrible thing, with that American man. I feel so bad for his sister. She lives upstairs, you know." She cleaned her hands on her apron. "But you're not here to talk about that, I'm sure. Can I get you another coffee? And some pastry?"

"Thank you, Signora Muller, but we are here regarding the investigations, and hoped you could be of help." A perplexed look crossed her face as she waited for the policeman to continue. "I don't believe you've met Signor Montoya." Rick nodded.

"I had heard that an American was helping in the investigation, so I assumed he was the one who came in here with you the other morning. Welcome to Campiglio, Signor Montoya." Her natural smile returned.

"Thank you, Signora."

"Please, both of you, call me Mitzi. Everyone else does. Would you like to sit down?" She motioned to three small tables at one side of the room, near the window.

"Thank you," answered Luca, "but we just have a few questions to ask. Let me start with the attack of two nights ago. Since it happened only a few steps from here, do you have any idea who could have done it?"

"The sergeant who came by yesterday asked me if I had heard or seen anything, but I told him we were closed at that hour. Since I get up so early every morning to bake, I was fast asleep when it happened, and since I sleep so soundly…"

"You live close by?" asked Rick.

"We live just down the street, Signor Montoya, on the first floor, but facing the mountain, not the street." She pointed in the direction of the attack. "Lauro, my husband, was still up, he works a different schedule than I do. But he didn't hear anything either."

"Your husband owns a hotel, I understand."

"That's right Inspector, the Hotel Trentino." She turned in the other direction. "Two blocks down and one block back to the east."

"The victim worked for your opponent, Mayor Grandi."

For the first time she showed some annoyance. "It is impossible that Guido's attacker could have had any political motive. I'm sure you know that there are many men around Campiglio who have reason to be angry with him, and it has nothing to do with local politics." Her face changed to a slightly darker hue of pink.

"Did your son hear anything, Signora?" asked Rick. He couldn't bring himself to call her Mitzi. "I assume he lives with you."

"Vittorio has to be up even earlier than I do, Signor Montoya, since he lights the ovens and prepares the bread dough. He was asleep before I was." The bell rang over the door and two women came into the store. Mitzi looked at them and back at the two men. The smile returned, but Rick thought it was more for the new arrivals. "Is there anything else I can help you with?"

Luca looked down at the cookies and Rick wondered if he was going to change his mind about purchasing some. "One more thing, Signora. I understand that your husband is trying to purchase a plot of land just outside of the town."

Mitzi held up her hands, and Rick could see specks of what looked like white cake icing on some of the fingers. It matched most of the cakes under the glass case. "I don't get involved in my husband's business, Inspector, and he doesn't tell me how to bake cookies. It works out well for both of us."

Rick watched Luca slowly retie the ear flap strings before carefully placing his hat on his head. It was starting to be a ritual with the man when he emerged into the cold. Just wearing the thing was bad enough, but treating it like some kind of heirloom was a bit much. The policeman glanced at Rick and grinned.

"Next stop, Riccardo, the Hotel Trentino. We have some questions for Signor Muller." Rick heard the muffled sound of Luca's phone, which was quickly fished out and answered. The inspector nodded, wedged the *telefonino* between shoulder and ear, and scribbled notes as he listened. "Thank you, Sergeant. We're going to see Signor Muller now, and then we'll be back at the station to get the car." He stowed phone, pen, and pad, and turned to Rick. "We have the name and address of the owner of the empty lot. He lives in Folgarida, the next town to the north. We'll drive there after our visit to the hotel."

"We passed Folgarida when Flavio and I drove into town last week. It has its own ski lifts and trails, but is connected with Campiglio's. You can get a special lift ticket and ski both places."

"Were you tempted?"

"Not really. There are more than enough trails here in Campiglio to satisfy a skier like me, I don't need another valley. The way Flavio talked, the special pass is more for people staying in Folgarida who want access to Campiglio, not the other way around."

They crossed the street, which had little traffic at this time of the morning, and started up a side street. On the corner they had passed two signs for the Hotel Trentino. A rectangular brown sign on a light pole was courtesy of the traffic authorities, with the same size and lettering used all over Italy to help tourists find lodging. The other was a carved wooden sign, complete with a little chalet roof and a small spotlight. Attached as it was to the corner building, it reminded Rick of the *madonnelle*, the small but elaborate religious shrines found on so many corners in Rome, put there in commemoration, or as thanks for some answered prayer.

"The sergeant gave me another new piece of information, Riccardo, and just in time for our meeting with Signor Muller. Signora Pittini told the policeman on duty at the hospital that her husband had an argument a few days ago with one of Zia Mitzi's supporters."

"Violent?"

"They didn't come to blows, but from what she heard from her husband, it was very heated."

"She's just remembering that now? Maybe she wants to make the attack seem political, since everyone in town is assuming that it had to do with women, which reflects badly on her."

"Your cynicism shocks me, Riccardo. The poor woman was under such stress after the attack, and so consumed with nursing her beloved husband back to health, it just slipped her mind." He pulled the notepad from his pocket. "Fortunately we have a way to confirm the story or not. Gaetano Spadacini, the man her husband argued with, happens to work at the Hotel Trentino."

The hotel stood at the end of the short street. Its brown wood contrasted with the green of the mountain rising behind it. The inverted V of its sharply pitched roof covered a row of balconies, which in turn covered more balconies, four floors in all. Rick wondered if the rooms in the back, with the view of the mountain, fetched more than those overlooking the roofs of Campiglio. Perhaps they were equally pricey. The hotel where he was staying was very comfortable, but clearly the Hotel Trentino was in a higher category. In fact, as the signs at the corner had indicated, it boasted four stars, based on the amenities checklist set up by the national tourist authority. Or was that another regulatory function taken over by EU bean counters in Brussels?

They passed the entrance to an underground garage and mounted steps to a covered porch running the width of the building. Rustic chairs, all empty, enjoyed a view of the street and across to the other side of Campiglio's narrow valley where skiers floated down the one white strip of trail visible amid the mountain's heavy green cover. The lobby of the hotel was open and inviting. On the left a lounge area was furnished with leather chairs, each as large as Rick's dining table in his small apartment in Rome. To the right, a bar covered most of the wall. Small tables allowed guests to sit and enjoy a libation indoors if they didn't want to brave the chill of the porch. Directly across from the door was the reception desk, behind which stood a smiling young woman wearing the plain uniform of the Italian hotel clerk, another item on the checklist for earning the fourth star.

"May I help you?"

Luca pulled out his document. "Inspector Albani, Signor Montoya. We'd like to talk to Signor Muller. Is he here?"

Rick expected her expression to become more serious, but she kept up the smile. "Yes, of course, I'll tell him you're here. If you'll excuse me?" She hurried through a door behind the desk.

Luca cast his eyes around the room. "Nice place. Too dear for my expense account, and I love where we're staying. Can't beat our food."

A man appeared from another part of the room, his features trying hard to mask his concern.

"I'm guessing Zia Mitzi called ahead," Rick whispered.

Lauro Muller wore a suit, the first Rick had seen in Campiglio other than Luca's. Unlike the policeman's, Muller's was measured to fit perfectly and looked like it just came from the dry cleaner. The tailoring had been done with such skill that the man's girth was not immediately noticeable, but his height could not be disguised. Rick, who was more than six feet himself, found himself looking down at the man. What he looked at was a face whose shape matched Muller's body, with a neatly trimmed goatee that blended into his neatly trimmed hair, both flecked with salt and pepper to add seriousness to his demeanor. Anyone meeting this hotel owner would immediately think—even without seeing the hotel itself—that his was a serious establishment. He introduced himself to the two visitors with firm handshakes and gestured toward the back of the room.

"Gentlemen, please come back to my office so we can talk without interruption. Allow me to lead the way."

A door led into a cramped rectangular room with two metal desks, each with a computer. A young man, jacket-less but with a dress shirt and tie, sat at one, an earpiece and filament microphone clipped to his head. He was discussing reservations with someone at the other end of the line. Despite the computers, shelves lining the wall were filled with the thick notebooks that Italian businesses and bureaucrats had been using for decades. Rick wondered if Muller had a plan to put everything on discs during the off-season. They followed the man through another door into his office.

"Please sit down. Can I get you something, perhaps? Coffee?"

Luca held up a hand. "No thank you, Signor Muller, we don't want to be any trouble."

They took their places on a leather sofa at least six inches lower than Muller's high-backed desk chair. Now they were looking up at him.

The office was small but well furnished. One wall was covered with photographs which Rick at first assumed were of Muller with important personages, perhaps famous people who had been guests at the hotel. A closer look revealed that while other people were found in the photos, most of the images included cars of various vintages and styles. So Muller was a car aficionado, and perhaps a collector. It was a hobby Rick had toyed with when he'd started working in New Mexico after college, but he'd never had enough money to become serious about it. One photo, a large one centered on the wall, caught his interest. It showed Muller wearing mechanic's overalls, standing next to a small greenish vehicle, a wide grin splitting his round face.

Rick pointed at the photo. "Is that Willys MB yours, Signor Muller?"

The man's mouth dropped open, forming an oval that matched the shape of his head. "Why, yes, yes it is. You…do you know about Jeeps, Signor Montoya?"

"I had a friend back in America who had one like yours. It looks like about a 1943."

"1942, actually, it probably landed in Sicily, or Anzio."

Rick turned to Luca who had been silently following the exchange. "The United States made a decision not to ship back most of their Jeeps after the war, which ironically has meant that parts for collectors are now easier to find here in Europe than in America."

"So you won the war but lost your Jeeps."

"You could say that, Inspector," Muller piped in. "But Signor Montoya, your friend in America, his is the Willys, not the Ford model?

"Willys, for sure. He let me drive it a few times, an amazing engine."

"The go devil engine," Muller said in English.

"Bravo, Signor Muller." Rick glanced at Luca's frown. "But perhaps we should get to the business at hand."

Muller's face became serious and he turned to Luca. "Of course. Inspector, how can I be of assistance? You are looking into this business of the American?" He rocked back in his chair. The desk hid the lower part of his body, but Rick guessed that his feet were suspended above the floor.

"That's correct," answered Luca. "As well as the attack on Guido Pittini."

"You don't think the two crimes are related, do you, Inspector?"

Luca shrugged and pulled out pen and pad. "We understand you have been trying to purchase a piece of property on the north edge of town."

"Yes, I'd heard that the police had been up there looking around. Is that where the murder took place, Inspector?" The reply was a silent glare. "Of course, of course, Inspector. You are the one asking the questions." He adjusted his tie, blue with small white polka dots. "Yes, I have been bidding on the property, and as I'm sure you know, Umberto Melograno has too. There may be others, but I suspect we are the only two serious potential buyers. It will be a perfect location for a new hotel. Access to the lifts, beautiful views—it has everything. It would be a shame to build anything else there." The voice of the businessman had returned.

"But you had not been in contact with the murdered man regarding financing?"

"*O dio*, no, Inspector. I have my own funding sources."

Rick thought for a moment that the man would explain further, but he did not. "Signor Muller, when was the last time you visited the property?"

He rubbed his beard in thought for several seconds. "It's been a while. Last year in the fall. It hadn't snowed yet, so it must have been around October. I went there with an architect."

Luca looked up from his pad. "An architect? Isn't that somewhat premature?"

"I am confident the sale will go through, Inspector. We have to be ready to start construction immediately when the spring thaw arrives."

"Had you met the American, Signor Taylor?"

Muller tugged at his goatee, which didn't have much to tug. "Last summer, or perhaps it was the summer before, he stayed in the hotel. I met him briefly. I try to greet all our guests at some point during their stay. He told me he was looking to rent something, which I understand he did."

"Was he alone?" It was Rick who asked the question.

"I'm quite sure he was, but I can't remember every one of our guests."

"One more thing. I trust you were in Campiglio on Saturday?"

"Certainly, I'm almost always here during the season, except when I'm at another hotel I own in Pinzolo, a few kilometers down the valley. I check in with the manager there frequently."

"You were here on Saturday?"

Muller's questioning look turned to a weak smile. "Ah. I see what you're getting at. I was here all that day, yes. I don't remember my exact movements hour to hour, of course. I move around the hotel seeing to things. It's the way a manager must be, always on the move. I doubt if my staff can be more exact than I on where I was at any given moment."

Luca flipped a few pages back in his notebook. "You have a Gaetano Spadacini working here at the hotel?"

Muller did not seem surprised by the question. "Yes, he's my electrician, and he does other maintenance work. In a hotel this size there is always something going wrong and it usually needs to be fixed immediately."

"He also works on your wife's election campaign."

"That's correct, Inspector. He is her liaison with the unions, since he's active in the electricians' confederation. The labor vote is important in this town."

"We'd like to speak with him. Is he here today?"

"I believe so." Muller picked up the phone on his desk and punched some buttons. "Gaetano, where are you?…I'm sending someone up to see you." He hung up and leaned forward in the chair. "He's working in room 304."

Luca got to his feet. "You didn't ask me why we want to speak to the man."

"I think I know," answered Muller as he slid off his chair. "And I'm sure Gaetano is not the man you are looking for."

"Your wife told us that you didn't hear anything the night of the attack on Pittini. You were home? It happened at 11:35."

"Mitzi was asleep when I got home at a little after ten. I watched the news. I must have been asleep, too, by that time. To answer your question, no, I heard nothing."

Rick noticed an especially strong grip as he shook Muller's hand. He was short, but strong. As their host walked his two visitors to the door of the office, Rick asked, "Signor Muller, do you drive your MB around Campiglio? I imagine it's good in the snow."

Muller chuckled. "Certainly not. It stays inside under a cover in the winter. I only take it out once the weather is warm, and not too often then."

"So how do you get around?"

"I remain loyal to the Jeep brand, Signor Montoya. I drive a Grand Cherokee."

Luca pressed the third-floor button and the elevator lurched slowly upward. "I trust, Riccardo, that extracting information about Signor Muller's vehicles was done on purpose?"

"Taylor's body didn't walk from the field to the gondola by itself."

"And the motive is that if Melograno's financing source is eliminated, Muller could waltz in to make the purchase, without having a bidding war."

"It makes sense."

They left the elevator and walked down the narrow hallway to room 304. The door was open.

Gaetano Spadacini sat between the two beds, studying a snarl of wires poking from a hole in the wall. The small table which held two reading lamps had been pushed to the opposite side of the room to make space for his chair. He pulled a pair of pliers from a leather satchel, elegant enough to hold a physician's tools, and glanced at Rick and Luca.

"They shouldn't have put these *tapparelle* on a switch. The manual kind would have been just as easy for people to use, and they wouldn't break as often." He touched two wires together and the shutters over the window began to grind down, stopping only when the wires were separated. "I don't know how many of these I've had to fix." He swiveled in the chair, which had come from the small desk near the window, and faced his visitors.

Spadacini's starched shirt was embroidered with the logo of the hotel and matched his blue pants. He looked to be in good shape, but his most striking feature was his hair. Almost Tarzan-like in length, it was cut in a style which was virtually a caricature of the Italian romeo. He had looks to go with it, and a tan that sharpened his features even more. He either spent his days off on the slopes, Rick decided, or used a sunlamp. He was also, clearly, well aware of his good looks.

Spadacini tapped the phone on his belt. "Signor Muller said you wanted to ask me some questions. I hope it won't take long, there may be a client arriving soon to check into this room."

Luca leaned against the side board. "It shouldn't take long. Where were you Monday night, at about eleven thirty?"

"Monday? Let's see… at my apartment. I try to stay in a few nights a week, to get my sleep and regain my strength. Monday was one of them."

"Can anyone confirm that? Your wife?"

"I'm divorced, Inspector." He glanced at Rick and back at Luca. "I assume you're the inspector. Italian police I've met don't wear boots like his."

Rick chuckled. "You're correct, Signor Spadacini. And you know why we're asking?"

"Of course. Pittini. He went too far and got someone very annoyed. I can understand that. But it wasn't me."

"The argument you had with him?" said Luca. "It was apparently quite heated."

Spadacini shrugged and pushed his hair back from his forehead. "Ask anyone who was there and they'll tell you that he was getting in my face first, and I reacted. But just with words. It happens. Guido can be a *stronzo* at times. Ask anyone that too."

"What was the argument about?"

"I don't remember exactly, Inspector. Something he said about Zia Mitzi, I think."

"What's your usual work schedule, Signor Spadacini?"

"During the season I'm here six days a week, but I'm always on call. Like today. It's my day off, but this damn shutter motor brought me in. I won't get out of here until lunch time."

"You must do well on overtime pay," said Rick.

"But when can I spend it?"

"On those nights when you're not regaining your strength."

Spadacini's mouth formed something between a grin and a leer, showing that in addition to everything else, he had perfect teeth.

Chapter Ten

Rick looked up as they walked back to the station from the hotel. The sky had clouded over, bringing lower temperatures and a chill wind. It could mean less than ideal skiing conditions in the afternoon when he was meeting Cat, but Flavio had told him that the weather could change quickly—for better or worse.

"So, Inspector, what did you think of Spadacini?"

"Gaetano the heart-stealer? He appears to be an ideal employee for Muller, Riccardo. Clearly a competent electrician, and a loyal soldier in his wife's electoral campaign. I expect he's good at winning over female voters as well as members of the electricians' union."

"In that regard, he may service more than just the electrical system in the hotel."

Luca shook his head and frowned, but it was a weak frown.

They turned the corner onto the main street, and Rick had taken a few steps along the sidewalk before realizing that Luca was not next to him. He turned to see him peering into the window of a store.

"Look at this, Riccardo." Luca motioned to Rick with a hand gesture that in the States would indicate "good-bye," but in Italy meant "come here."

Elegantly arrayed on satin inside the glass were handmade knives, fine cutlery, and other kitchen instruments not found in the average kitchen. The ornate bone handles on the knives, many carved in the form of wild animals, almost discouraged being covered by someone's hand. These items would be purchased for ostentation, Rick decided, even a shiny gadget like the truffle slicer. Come to think of it, *especially* the truffle slicer. Cheese knives, including the ubiquitous *parmigiano reggiano* blades, lay against dark wood cutting boards in all shapes and sizes.

Luca tapped on the glass. "Who would come to this town and buy that?" He was pointing at a chain mail glove, next to which lay a knife with a short blade and ebony handle. Between them on a laminated wood board was an oyster shell. "If they didn't have the shell there, I wouldn't have known what that was for. So you live in Milan, come up to Campiglio to ski, and decide to pick up equipment to open oysters?"

"You never know when you'll need to shuck an oyster, Luca. It pays to be prepared."

"I suppose so."

A few minutes later they reached the station, where the car was waiting for them in front. Rick got in the passenger side and put his Borsalino in the backseat. Luca didn't take the hint, keeping the deer stalker on his head. They drove out of town to the north, the road climbing steeply before flattening out and passing a large parking lot where trails came down from the two sides of the valley. A covered foot bridge connected the trails for those skiers who wanted to change mountains. Through the glass Rick could see people moving in both directions, their skis over their shoulders, clomping toward the lifts. They drove under the bridge and climbed past the full parking lot, beyond which the valley opened into a treeless expanse that in the summer, Flavio had told him, was a nine-hole golf course. Cross-country skiers followed thin trails through the valley, moving like stiff puppets on connected strings. It was a form of skiing that had never interested Rick. Too much like work.

The road reached the top of the hill and entered the forest, broken initially by some apartment buildings on the left and an occasional glimpse of the open valley through the trees on the right. As they passed one break in the trees, Luca took his right hand off the steering wheel and pointed. "That's where the hat and the blood were found. Back in there."

Rick turned his neck to look before they passed the opening. "I can see why Melograno and Muller want that property. Perfect location for either a hotel or an apartment." A location to die for, he could not help thinking.

The forest had begrudgingly given way to the road. Large trees stood menacingly on both sides, their branches touching in solidarity as if ready to reclaim the thin strip that civilization had sliced through them. Despite the heavy cover, the forest floor was deep with snow, blown there by the wind. Rick guessed that even in summer this would not be inviting terrain for *alpinisti*—it would be much more practical, and pleasant, to hike the high, snow-less ski trails.

The road bent sharply for a bridge over a small stream, its icy water flowing back toward Campiglio. Gradually the forest began to thin out, a house or two appeared, then a ski trail flowed down from the hills on the left side of the road. After a few bends they descended into Folgarida, a tiny town on the north side of the mountain. Luca spotted a policeman, rolled down his window, and after identifying himself, asked directions.

The man saluted, but not too formally. "The building is that one, Inspector. And if you leave your car over there, I won't give you a parking ticket."

"That's very kind of you, Corporal. We won't be long."

The space the policeman had indicated was behind a set of covered benches in the middle of what Rick guessed to be the main square of the town. A very tiny main square. Two people sat on one set of benches holding skis and poles, waiting for a ride or perhaps a bus. Rick looked up the street lined with hotels and could see that it ended about a hundred meters from where they stood. Space here was clearly at a premium; the town clung tightly to the side of the mountain, like it wasn't supposed to be there. The narrow ribbon of pavement and its thin sidewalks were relatively flat, but everything else was on an incline. On both sides of the street, buildings had been squeezed into the mountain. Like some of the neighborhoods Rick had been to in Rio when he'd visited his parents, the buildings on the lower side of the street were entered on the upper floors. But instead of offering a view of Guanabara Bay, their windows looked out over snow-covered trees.

Not many people were out walking, but the town was much smaller than Campiglio, so that would be expected. People came here to ski, and at this time of day they were on Folgarida's trails or over the mountain on Campiglio's. Judging by the number of cars squeezed along the length of the street, there were quite a few skiers, and that didn't count cars parked in the underground garages of the hotels. On one side of the *piazza,* a tourist office shared its space with a real estate company, and on the other a row of low apartment buildings wedged themselves into the mountain. It was at one of these buildings that the policeman had pointed.

They walked across the street and up some stairs to the entrance. It was chalet style, like everything else in the region, but older and shabbier than the buildings next to it. Luca scanned the eight names and pressed the button under one of them. Almost instantly the door buzzed open. He looked at Rick and lifted his eyebrows before pushing open the door.

The apartment they were seeking was on the second floor—or first by Italian designation—so they had one flight of stairs to climb. The stairwell was lit, but dimly, as was the hallway, but Luca found the door number without trouble. He rapped lightly.

"It's open!" called a voice inside. This time it was Rick's turn to raise his eyebrows before turning the knob and pushing open the door. They saw the back of a man who adjusted a scarf around his neck before pulling on a black leather coat. "I'm glad you're here early," he said before turning around to face Rick and Luca. His movements stopped. "Who the hell are you?"

"Signor Peruzzi?"

Rick got a strong whiff of aftershave lotion, which went with the man's clean-shaven face and perfectly coiffed hair. After regaining some composure, he looked from one face to the other and settled back on Luca's. "Uh, no. That's my uncle. But who are you?"

"Inspector Albani," Luca said, showing his identification. "And Signor Montoya. Does Signor Peruzzi live here?"

"Yes, he's here. I thought you were the cleaning lady. I have an appointment so I was glad she came early, but—"

"But we're not the cleaning lady. *Per favore*, can you tell your uncle we're here?"

"Of course, of course. Is this about the murder in Campiglio? I heard that the police, I mean that you, found the body on Uncle Lamberto's property, and—"

"If you can just tell your uncle we're here, you can get to your appointment."

"Yes. Yes, certainly. Thank you. I'll do that." He hurried down the hall and disappeared.

Rick watched him dart into a room. "I wonder where he heard that?"

"Stories can change while traveling between one person's mouth and another person's ear, Riccardo. It's not surprising that this one didn't make it over the mountain road intact."

"Inspector." They looked down the hall to where the man stood. "Please come down here, my uncle will see you in his room. He doesn't get around very well." Rick and Luca walked down a hall that was bare except for some closed doors to reach the waiting man. "Zio, this is Inspector Albani and…I'm sorry I didn't—"

"Montoya." Rick looked into the room, which was on the back of the building. Despite open curtains and shutters, thick branches just outside the window allowed little light to enter. Much of the space in the room was taken by a large bed covered by a heavy quilt. Next to the bed a white-haired Lamberto Peruzzi sat in a high-backed reclining chair set about a third of the way to horizontal. A book, open pages down, sat within reach on a table next to him, and next to it a glass of mineral water. Light came from a gooseneck floor lamp.

"Please sit down, gentlemen. I regret I cannot greet you properly, on my feet. Please also excuse the lack of comfortable seating." He waved a thin hand at two simple wooden chairs and looked at his nephew. "You can be on your way, Massimo. Be careful driving over the mountain."

"But Zio, if you—" The old man silently raised his hand, which apparently was enough. "Very well, Zio, I'll see you this evening." He nodded at Rick and Luca and left the room.

"We won't take much of your time, Signor Peruzzi."

The man settled back into the chair, legs propped on a leather ottoman and covered with a thick wool blanket. His gaunt neck stuck out from a gray turtleneck sweater which may have fit him once but now looked at least a size too large. He had not shaved, or been shaved, in a few days, and perhaps realizing this, he rubbed the stubble with his hand.

"My time is yours, Inspector. As you might surmise, I don't get many visitors, so I may be that rare person who actually enjoys being interrogated by the police."

"We're not here for an interrogation, Signor Peruzzi, we just have a few questions."

"Call it whatever you'd like, but don't feel rushed. I am at your disposal."

"You live here alone?"

"No, Massimo is here with me. My sister, his mother, used to come in to see to my needs every day, but when she died three years ago, he moved in."

"A very devoted nephew."

The old man stared at Rick, a sad smile on his face. "Yes, perhaps you could say that. The fact is, Signor Montoya, my nephew is waiting for me to die. Massimo is already very comfortably set, since he owns a very successful grocery store here in Folgarida, made successful by his late father and my sister. They worked tirelessly to make it what it is, but Massimo has found it easier to hire a manager. Fortunately he hired a very good one. When I die he will inherit an even larger sum." His eyes moved from Luca to Rick and back. "You will excuse my frankness, gentlemen. I have no reason, at my age, to speak otherwise."

"Your estate can go to someone else."

"I have no other family, Inspector. And I owe it to my sister to pass it to her son. She was a lovely woman. She and my brother-in-law would be disappointed that their only child has little interest in anything except…" The voice trailed off. "But he's still young, perhaps someday he'll settle down. I doubt if I will live long enough to witness it, but it could happen."

"He will inherit the property in Campiglio."

"Yes, Inspector, or the money from its sale. Which is why you are here, I am sure, to ask about that land. You must forgive me for boring you with my family problems. Please don't think ill of Massimo. He is not a bad person."

"Is the sale imminent?" asked Rick.

Peruzzi thought before answering. "The two bidders—I assume you know who they are—would certainly like the sale to happen soon, no question about that. And so would my nephew." He rubbed the back of one hand, like it had a rash. "I must confess that I am in no hurry. What money I have made over the years has been in these transactions, buying and selling land. Much of the buying was done many years ago, before the town changed, before the skiers mounted their invasion of the Dolomites. Some people say I was smart, others that I was lucky. The truth is somewhere in between, but one thing is certain, I loved all of it. I don't mean the money, though I can't complain about that part, I'm talking about taking a risk and seeing it bear fruit. There is nothing like it. Nothing. Yes, there were some bad bets, some losses. They only made the successes that much sweeter." He had been hunched forward as he talked, and now he settled back into the chair and took a long breath. "You see, gentlemen, this is the last transaction, the final sale. I know it has to end, like my life will have to end. But I want to savor it a little longer."

The three men sat in silence until Luca spoke. "When did you last have contact with the two potential buyers?"

"Let me see. With Muller, it's been at least a week. He called to ask when I was going to make a decision. He was pleasant about it, as he always is. Soon, I told him." He made a sound which was somewhere between a cough and a laugh, and followed it with a sip from the glass. "Melograno came here five days ago."

Luca's head jerked up from his notebook. "Friday? Are you sure?"

"Absolutely, Inspector. As I told you, I don't get many visitors."

"What time was it?"

"In the morning, I don't remember exactly. Ten, eleven."

"How did the meeting go?"

A twisted smile came over Peruzzi's face. "Well, I've dealt with Umberto many times, from when he first got into real estate until now. His style of doing business is not one I share, but he would probably tell you that times have changed. Perhaps he's right. But you asked how our little meeting went. He was more insistent than ever, and the fact that he came here to my home, rather than calling, surprised me somewhat. But he got the same answer as Muller."

"We think that the murder took place on your plot of land."

The old man stared at Luca and nodded his head slowly. "That saddens me. I hope it is just coincidence, given its secluded location, off the main road. I know it's been used for unsavory activities over the years, but never murder. Very sad."

Rick shifted in the wooden chair. "Does your nephew have any preference as to who should buy the land?"

Peruzzi's eyes bore into Rick, and then softened. "The decision is mine, Signor Montoya, not my nephew's."

"Have you made that decision?"

The man did not reply, but the silence, combined with the tired look on his face, were answer enough.

Rick felt a nudge. "Riccardo, we should be on our way back to Campiglio, and let our host get back to his reading."

"I am in no rush to see you leave, Inspector, but I'm sure the investigation calls."

"What are you reading?" Rick said. "If you don't mind me asking."

The man glanced down at the book. "Not at all. I often read the classics, but I must confess that I have a taste for novels of the American West." He held up the book, a paperback. The cover showed a sheriff's star, a smoking bullet hole cut through one of its points. "I thought you might be familiar with it, Signor Montoya." He inclined his head and looked at Rick's cowboy boots.

Rick laughed. "It's not an author I know, Signor Peruzzi. Though as you have noticed, I did spend many years in the American Southwest."

"You did? What part?" It was the most energy the man had shown since they'd entered his room.

"New Mexico."

"Where Pat Garrett shot Billy the Kid?"

"That was to the east of where I lived, but yes, sir, the same state."

Peruzzi settled back in the chair and slowly closed his eyes. "I can just picture the tumbleweed and sagebrush."

They separated outside the Campiglio police station. Luca went in to see if anything had come from the lab, and to make contact with his office. Rick started the walk to the hotel to check his email. They would meet at lunch after separately mulling over the case, but from the mostly silent drive back over the mountain Rick sensed that Luca was as stumped as he was. There were some suspects, a few motives, and a lot of alibis, but no obvious trail that could lead them to the murderer. He knew from conversations with Uncle Piero that this was the critical point in an investigation. They needed to catch a break now, or the trail could go cold, perhaps permanently. He took a deep breath and started up the hill. The trail may be going cold, but the temperature today was not. He looked at the sky, watched a few wispy clouds floating between one mountain and the next, and knew it would be a good afternoon to be skiing after all. There were worse ways to spend a few hours than out in the snow with a beautiful woman. If only he had some progress to report to Cat.

The main street he was on continued to the gondola station, but Rick stepped onto the smaller one, without sidewalks, which took him up to the hotel. His boots sloshed through snow that was beginning to melt despite the shade from tall fir trees on either side of the pavement. The road bent to the right, but opening on the left was a narrow pathway, barely wide enough for a car. A few fresh footprints ran up its center, as well as others that had been filled with the snow of the past few days. At the end of the road, about thirty meters distant, he could see a metal gate in a stone wall. While he could not read the writing that was written on the arch over the gate, there was no question in his mind what was beyond it. This was the town cemetery.

Rick had been fascinated by cemeteries since childhood when he'd been taken to visit family graves, a tradition shared by both the Montoya and the Fontana sides of his family. Many of his favorite family stories he'd heard for the first time while standing quietly in front of a grave marker. They were often stories that had made him laugh, like learning about an uncle in New Mexico who had been treed by a bear for three days, or his Italian great-grandmother who never, even on her deathbed, revealed her recipe for mushroom soup. Each story was like shining a flashlight into a corner of the family attic. Now he found it hard to pass a cemetery without going in to see if it might reveal something, even if he had to imagine it for himself.

The metal gate creaked as it opened as Rick stepped carefully inside the walls. Gravestones of different sizes poked out of the snow, closer together than they would be in the States, but then space was at a premium here. Standing guard behind the graveyard loomed the town church. The regular lines of its rectangular side wall were broken by a pointed bell tower at one end and the curved stones of the apse at the other. Rick walked the narrow paths that separated the graves, their snow tamped down by recent visitors. Flowers, some more withered than others, adorned a few of the graves, placed in metal vases set into the stones, often next to an oval black-and-white photograph of the departed. Rick walked slowly, reading the names and studying the photographs, wondering if the people buried under the frozen ground had been consulted on choosing which image would be used. The faces in the photos were stiff and frowning, as if saying they would rather be somewhere else. All but one—a smiling young woman whose color photo matched the bright plastic flowers set in the vase next to it. A few flakes from the recent snows had stuck to the photo and to the petals of the flowers. Rick brushed the gravestone with his hand to better read the name and date. After a few moments of thought he stepped back and noticed the gravestones on either side. The parents had died only a few years after their daughter. A slow death caused by grief? Perhaps this was one story he did not want to know more about.

He was turning to leave when he looked back at the side of the church. Its flat surface was broken by a door and two windows, but his eye went to a series of colorful frescoes. He walked closer to get a better view. Most of the wall's paintings were of saints and biblical stories, what would be expected, but at the top, just under the eaves, a striking procession marched the entire length. Thanks to the protection of the roof over the centuries, its figures had more vibrancy than in the lower scenes, but it was the theme that got Rick's attention. On the far left, on a crude throne, a crowned skeleton sat playing a bagpipe. The macabre king was accompanied by two other skeletons playing long, thin horns. Rick could almost hear the shrill music the three instruments produced. Moving toward the king of death, if that's what he represented, ran a long line of ornately robed figures: the lord, his lady, the cardinal, the merchant, the knight, the soldier—continuing to the end of the wall. Each of the living was being pulled along by a grinning skeleton, their partners in the dance of death, moving steadily toward an inevitable meeting with the skeleton king. The *dansa macabra*. Rick thought of Cam Taylor and shuddered.

He turned and walked back between the stones, avoiding the path that held the grave of the girl. He crossed himself, as he always did when leaving a cemetery, and closed the gate carefully behind him.

◇◇◇

Lunch began with a local specialty that Rick was looking forward to tasting, a dish not found on menus in other regions of Italy. *Canederli* were bread dumplings, the local equivalent of the *knödel* popular on the other side of the Alps. They were held together by egg and cheese, with more flavor added through herbs and bits of *speck*—smoked and cured ham. The dumplings arrived at the table bobbing in bowls of steaming meat broth, which Rick and Luca sprinkled with cheese. As tasty as they might be, there were not many first courses in Italian cuisine that could not be improved with *parmigiano reggiano*.

"Flavio doesn't know what he's missing," Rick said to Luca as he cut into one of the dumplings with his soup spoon. "But he told us not to wait."

"I doubt if he's going to skip this meal. He'll probably dine with the comely diplomat. Look at her table."

Rick turned his head and noticed that an extra place had been set at Lori's table. "I see what you mean." He poured more wine into their glasses. "I'm not sure if he would approve of our choice of wine, so it's just as well."

"The wine is more than adequate, Riccardo. And now that this wonderful *primo* is taking the edge off our appetite, we can return to the business at hand. Let me begin with what I learned at the station. The blood in the field is confirmed as that of our victim, so it is virtually certain that he was killed there. This brings in the question of how the body was transported from the murder scene to the gondola base. Concerning the autopsy, the only new information from it regards the murder weapon."

Rick glanced up from his broth, spoon in hand. "You know what the weapon was?"

"Not precisely, but the forensics people are almost sure it was a bottle. The wound was smooth, and there were specks of paint." He noticed Rick's frown. "I know, paint on a bottle doesn't sound right, but they seemed to be convinced. And there was something else. Grooves, or at least some kind of wavy pattern in the glass of the bottle, made a distinct impression on the skull."

"A bottle with grooves?"

"I have some men going over what was picked up in the field and along the road, when we first searched the area. The bottle could have been tossed away by the murderer as he drove from the field."

"It could have been something Flavio sells. Here he comes, we'll ask him."

Flavio walked toward them, dressed in jeans and a sweater, waving off the waitress. "Lori went up to change. I'll, uh, be having lunch with her." He sat down in his chair and squinted at the bottle.

"Don't say anything about our choice of wine," said Rick. "Luca has some serious questions for you regarding the investigation."

Flavio turned the wine bottle so that the label was facing away from him before giving Luca his full attention. "How can I help?" He listened to the explanation of the autopsy report and snapped his fingers. "That's easy. It's a prosecco bottled and marketed for the holidays. People pay extra for the same wine when it comes in a fancy bottle with grooves and painted decoration."

"Isn't there a parable in the Bible about new wine in old bottles?"

"There is, Luca, but it doesn't apply here. I can give you a list of wineries that produce holiday prosecco, but I'm not sure it will help much. It's sold everywhere, and wine shops don't keep track of who buys which bottles. A whole case, maybe, but a single bottle, there's no way to trace it."

"What kind of person would buy one of these bottles?" asked Rick.

"Could be anyone. Come the holidays, even people on a tight budget tend to buy a nice bottle or two of wine. It's the best season of the year for my business."

Luca finished the last of his dumplings. "Well, I can at least have the sergeant check the wine stores in town to find out if anyone bought any in large quantities."

"This hotel bought a case from me, if I remember right. In fact…" He got up from his chair and walked out of the dining room, allowing Luca and Rick to finish their broth. He returned with a bottle and placed it on the table with a flourish. "Exhibit A, the only one left after *capo d'anno*. There are other wineries that do the holiday bottles, but this is the one we sell."

More pear-shaped than straight, the bottle was made of dark green glass with surface grooves wound around the widest part to the base. The glass was thicker than in normal bottles, adding to the weight. The decoration, holly and Christmas balls, looked like they had been painted by hand.

"Very fancy," Rick said, running his fingers over the bottle. "I can see why these would sell well at holiday time."

"And it's a very good prosecco."

"We would expect nothing less, if you are distributing it, Flavio."

Luca tapped on the table next to the bottle, thinking. "A bottle is not the kind of weapon someone would normally bring to a crime scene if he intends to commit murder. Unless there is some strange statement that our criminal wants to make, it is more likely that the bottle was a weapon of opportunity."

"But," said Rick, "there had to have been a reason to bring the bottle there in the first place. And it had to have been the murderer, since Taylor was heading out to ski and not likely to be carrying a bottle of prosecco. So it was to celebrate something, or at least to give Taylor the impression they were driving up there to celebrate. So two possibilities: They were there because of the land or it was just a coincidence that the murderer and victim were on that plot of land." He looked at the faces of the other two men. "I can see that you agree with me that it's not a coincidence." He paused while the waitress cleared their soup bowls and replaced them with clean plates. "That would point to Melograno, since Taylor was dealing with him on the loan."

Luca repositioned the plate in front of him. "There were other people who knew about the loan. They could have gotten Taylor up there on some other pretense, to make it look like

Melograno did it. How about Lotti from across the hall? The sister could have told him."

"The sister could have told anybody," said Flavio.

"Exactly," answered Luca. "And then there's Muller. He met Taylor once at his hotel, he admitted that. He may have had more contact with the man than he claims."

Rick shook his head. "But why would Muller be in that field with Taylor and a bottle of prosecco?"

"My American friend, Taylor was the key to Melograno getting the land. But the other side of the same coin is that Taylor was the key to Melograno *not* getting the land."

"I need to think about that one a bit, Luca."

"And the arrival of our *secondo* gives you that opportunity." The waitress was approaching the table with a serving platter in one hand, spoon and fork in the other. "Flavio, your lady friend has appeared."

Flavio's head turned to see Lori wave before sitting down at her table. He waved back. "Got to go. But you'll find this interesting, Riccardo. Lori called the consulate as we were going out and told them to put down the morning as vacation on her time card since she wasn't helping Cat. Can you believe that?"

"Yes I can. What is surprising is that you find such honesty remarkable. But I suppose you are still smarting from the employee who embezzled your money. By the way, you didn't tell us how you spent the morning." He glanced at Luca who, as expected, was enjoying another exchange between the two friends.

Flavio got to his feet. "Skating."

"Did you say skating? Ice skating?"

"Yes, Riccardo. Lori wanted to skate."

"Did she wear one of those little skirts?"

"I'll see you two tonight." He turned and walked across the room to Lori's table.

The main course was *stracotto di manzo*, pot roast, with mashed potatoes. The waitress deftly transferred the meat slices to their plates, using the fork and spoon as if they were attached to each other like tongs. It was the perfect *secondo* to follow what had been a tasty but rather light *primo*, with enough thick, dark, *sugo* from the meat to drizzle over the mashed potatoes. As with any good *stracotto*, only a fork was needed to cut it.

"What you were saying, Luca, if I understand correctly, is that by eliminating Taylor, Muller eliminates Melograno's way to finance the sale." Rick put a piece of beef in his mouth. "But why would Taylor have gone up there with Muller?"

"To seal the deal with a bottle of bubbly. There would have been something in it for Taylor."

"Taylor was being bribed by Muller? But he was such a straight arrow in his business ethics."

The policeman sipped his wine and flashed a wry smile. "That's according to his sister. There may have been a darker side to our Signor Taylor that his sister was unaware of, or didn't want to admit. If you were completely Italian, instead of half, that would have occurred to you."

Rick put some mashed potatoes on his fork and ignored the jab. "Am I mistaken, Luca, or have we narrowed the field of suspects in this murder down to two?" Rick noticed that, without realizing it, he had said "we" instead of "you." Luca did not appear concerned by it.

"Well, two primary suspects because of possible motives and their connection to the crime scene. There could be others, such as Lotti or Grandi, and the main suspects could have been helped by someone else, like the electrician, or the mayor. In fact, since there were two key parts of this crime, the murder itself and later dropping the body from the gondola, and everyone has an alibi for one or the other, or neither, it appears very possible that there was an accomplice. The body could well have been handed off to someone." He took a piece of bread to get some stray meat sauce. "Which returns us to the issue of transporting the body. Everyone has a vehicle that could have done it: Muller has his Grand Cherokee, the mayor his city-provided Land Rover, even Gina Cortese, the ski instructor, has a small SUV, the sergeant told me."

"And Lotti has his car with snow chains and almost certainly a trunk large enough to hold a body. All but Melograno, whose Mercedes is in the shop."

"Which is something I have to check on tomorrow."

"What's on your schedule for the afternoon?"

Luca had left a small clump of mashed potatoes on his plate, perhaps so he could tell his wife that he was not overeating. "I have to talk with the public prosecutor, and another reporter has appeared to dig into the story. And I'm going to interview some of Pittini's co-workers to see if they can tell me anything about who could have attacked him."

"That's right, Pittini. I'd almost forgotten about him."

"He shouldn't forget you, Riccardo. I spoke with the doctor who said your first aid on the scene likely kept him from losing a dangerous amount of blood."

"What did the doctor say about his condition?"

"No change on the concussion. But the knife wound is healing well."

Rick felt himself shiver. Not since the attack had they discussed the possibility that he was the intended target of the attacker. And he didn't want to bring it up now.

"And you are heading for the mountain after lunch?"

"I am. Cat wanted to ski, to get her mind off things."

"That's very noble of you, Riccardo." He looked out over the porch that ran outside the window of the dining room. The sun glistened off the snow. "It appears to be a fine afternoon to take to the ski trails."

Chapter Eleven

Gazing down, Rick came to the conclusion that afternoon skiers were more languid and reflective than those who took to the trails in the morning. Fatigue played a part, as did the effects of food and wine at midday, but there was something about the afternoon which invited the skier to take in the experience as a whole and not think only of the joy of speed. Perhaps the angle of the sun caused it, or a shift in the wind direction. Whatever it was, skiers paused more frequently to enjoy the scenery, stopped more frequently to talk. Reaching the bottom was something faced with reluctance, even when there was time to return to the top.

He and Cat were floating inside one of the egg-shaped *cabine* that ran high above the clumps of skiers. It had passed through a wooded area as it steadily climbed, eventually bursting into the open spaces of the glacier where the cable slowed for an intermediate stop. This would be their last run, and they stayed on, as did the skiers who occupied two of the other four places in the cabina: teenage girls who stared silently through the windows while listening to music through ear buds.

"Can you make out what they're listening to?"

Rick shook his head. "Could be rap, could be Rossini. All I hear is a faint crackle."

"Do they have Italian rap groups?"

"I'm afraid so."

They faced each other, knees and boot tips touching, ski poles leaning against the empty middle seats. Cat wore the same outfit Rick had seen in the picture with her brother: a one-piece blue suit with white boots and a matching knit hat. Her blond hair poked from the sides and back of the hat. She had turned out to be a competent skier, as Rick had expected after her mention of family vacations in Vail. Fortunately for Rick's ego he was more competent, thanks to college outings to the less elegant slopes of the southern Rockies. His ski apparel was more appropriate to Sandia Peak, New Mexico, than Vail, Colorado—a pair of heavy rain pants pulled over blue jeans, and a red parka which he still clung to from his college days. The outfit had served to keep him warm thus far on Campiglio's trails, especially on this afternoon when the sun was unencumbered by clouds. Just before they began their first run, Cat had pulled a small tube from her pocket and spread sun cream on his nose and cheeks.

"You've been sweet to take care of me, Rick."

He lowered his eyes and touched his hand to his forehead. "It is my duty to help damsels in distress, Ma'am."

She giggled. "Stop that. I mean it. I don't know what I would have done without you."

"I enjoy being with you, Cat. Let's leave it at that. And I'm glad you picked me instead of your neighbor to unburden yourself." He wasn't sure how that comment would be taken.

"Daniele? Oh, please. He's a nice enough person, I suppose. But…"

Something better came along. He knew girls who did that kind of thing in high school, but ran into fewer of them now that he was in his thirties. He should give her the benefit of the doubt, in a stressful time she needed someone from her country, not just a guy who spoke her language. It's how his mother would have explained Cat's behavior, and Mamma knew a thing or two about finding herself in a strange country.

"Have you talked to him lately?"

She took off a glove and retrieved a strand of hair that had escaped from her cap. "He came to my door this morning and we talked. Wanted to know if he could help, and I told him that Lori was taking care of my needs. And I have to admit that Lori's been very helpful. There are things about the Italian authorities that I would never have known about, let alone been able to deal with. Daniele didn't know that the consulate had sent someone. He was impressed."

The *cabina* was starting to slow as it neared the end of the line. They went from light to shadow as it slid through the opening in the cement building that housed the gears and pulleys as well as a small snack bar. When they were shunted off to a slower cable the doors slid open automatically. As they had practiced on earlier runs, Cat grabbed their poles and stepped out first, followed by Rick who then pulled their skis from tubes on the outside of the door. When they reached the snow and sunshine, Rick dropped the skis in four parallel lines and Cat stuck the poles next to them. She smiled at him before adjusting her goggles.

"We make a good team, Rick."

"Easy for you to say, Cat. I had to carry two pairs of heavy skis."

She laughed and stepped into her bindings. "This will be the final run, let's make it last."

"I agree." He snapped into his skis and they both adjusted their wrist straps. Neither appeared ready to push off, they stood leaning on their poles watching skiers on either side of them start the descent. They also took in the view. They were at the highest point of Campiglio's system of interconnected trails, the saddle between two jagged peaks. Ahead in the distance was La Presanella, an isolated set of mountains under a snowcap year round. Behind them was Monte Corona and other smaller crests in the Gruppo Brenta. To the east, far out of sight, the terrain opened for the Adige River that had started near the Austrian border. It flowed past Trento and through Verona before veering left to make its own way to the Adriatic rather than losing its water and name to the mighty Po.

Cat finally pushed off, slowly sliding from the shelf where they had stood. Rick watched her make a first turn before following in her tracks while keeping his eyes on her back. Even in the bulky ski suit, the shape of her body was evident. He stayed behind her for a few more turns before moving next to her, and together they crisscrossed the slope until reaching the bottom of the run where other skiers were getting on a chairlift for the return to the top. It was the spot where he and Flavio had met Gina Cortese two days earlier, but he didn't mention this to Cat.

After a few days of skiing with Flavio, Rick was familiar with the trails, so he led the way as they continued down. They glided between the trees, though the trail was still broad enough for easy, wide turns. Most of the skiers had stayed on the higher runs which still caught the afternoon sun, so they had the trail almost to themselves.

They came over a hill and descended into a small valley where a four-seat chairlift raised them to the side of the mountain that descended into Campiglio. As Rick remembered, there were a few steep drops before the trails between the trees widened and smoothed out, and he pointed the way for Cat. It was on the second drop that Cat's ski stubbed on a mogul and she tumbled for about twenty meters before coming to a stop. Fortunately, Rick was behind her, and he was able to stop to pick up the loose ski before pulling up next to her. She was brushing snow from her goggles when he came to a stop.

"You okay?"

"Fine, nothing broken." She massaged the thigh on one of her legs. "Everyone has to fall once in an afternoon, don't they?"

He pulled her to her feet and dropped the ski next to her. "At least once. You're not testing yourself unless you take a few tumbles. You have to push the envelope."

She stamped open the binding of the rogue ski and then stepped into it. "I wasn't pushing anything, Rick, I just fell."

"Mogul mugging. It happens all the time, Cat. But take it easy the rest of the way, you may have twisted something."

She took his words to heart, bending less and making wider and slower turns. Rick hung protectively behind her in case she fell again, but she stayed on her feet and he decided she'd been unaffected by the tumble. Even so, when they reached a fork in the trail, and stopped for a rest, he recommended they go for the easier final descent.

"That way is less steep, Cat, and it has some beautiful views once we get through the opening in the trees. Let's take it."

"Sure, Rick, lead the way."

He turned his skis toward a trail that dipped down and to the right, Cat behind him. They were the only skiers choosing the easier route; everyone else continued down the more challenging main trail which was also a faster way to reach the chairlift to the top. The incline on this trail was about perfect for easy skiing. Rick dropped his arms and let his poles drag in the snow, allowing gravity to push him forward. Beyond the trees, they burst into an open field, the trail cutting through its center. The left side was open and flat enough to land a small plane in summer. To their right, the ground rose steeply and steadily until it reached a few clumps of trees after a hundred and fifty meters. Jagged peaks rose dramatically in the distance behind.

Something wasn't right.

Rick turned his skis, coming slowly to a stop so that he was facing back toward where they had just come. Cat slid down next to him, her skis pointing in the opposite direction from his.

"It's beautiful, Rick, this was a good—"

"Just a second, Cat." He held up his hand and turned his head toward the mountain. "It sounds like…but I thought they weren't allowed up here."

What had started as a soft purr somewhere up on the mountain changed to a louder hum before bursting into a rattling roar. Then a dark snowmobile shot out from one from the clumps of trees high above them and started weaving its way downward. It bounced along like a child's toy, but with each second became larger. Behind the handlebars crouched a black-suited figure who scanned the valley below him while he gunned the engine. Rick looked back at where they had come from and then down the trail.

"Let's go, Cat. I don't like the looks of this."

"But, Rick—"

"Move, Cat. Fast."

She moved, pushing hard on her poles. Rick turned himself around and followed her, looking up every few seconds at the snowmobile. Fortunately the snow was deep, and it was having trouble getting through. The driver revved the motor as he cut his sharp turns, the afternoon sunlight glinting off his windshield. He was now about a hundred meters above, and even though a helmet covered the driver's face, Rick knew he was looking straight at them. Cat apparently knew it, too, since she was struggling to gain speed. The soft incline, which had made the trail inviting, now worked against them. To make things worse, the warmth of the afternoon had turned powder into slush in some spots, slowing them even more.

"Who is it, Rick?" Cat yelled as she worked her poles and skis.

"I don't know," he called, "but somehow I doubt he just wants to ask directions."

Rick knew that once they passed through the field the trail went into more woods before rejoining the main trail. And in the woods the snow would be in the shade, so slicker and faster. There would be other skiers on the main trail, and, if they were lucky, also a stray pair from the ski patrol. Strength in numbers. Could they get there? He looked up and saw that the snowmobile had bogged down in the deep snow. The driver had gotten off his seat and pushed the handlebars from the side, while gunning the motor, making the tread spin and kicking up a wide, white plume. With him stuck, we might just make it, Rick thought. They were now only about seventy-five meters from where the trail cut back into the trees.

He was watching Cat struggle to make more speed when a different sound came from above. It was a low groan that slowly drowned out the raspy noise of the snowmobile's motor. Rick's eyes jerked up and saw that their pursuer had disappeared behind a curtain of powder now moving in their direction. A thought flashed through Rick's head that the snowmobile's intent all along had been to cause an avalanche. Just as quickly, he forced himself to forget intent—what mattered now was saving their skins.

At least they were pointed in the best direction. He'd heard many times that outrunning an avalanche was futile, and they were on just the right diagonal line toward the trees. Would they make it? Only about fifty meters left. Fortunately the effect of the danger on Cat was to push her to go faster; he couldn't see her face but her taut body showed intensity. Twenty-five yards. She was forcing herself to look straight ahead, but Rick kept one eye on the descending wave of white. Ten. If Cat's bad leg didn't give out, they would reach the trees in time.

Cat shot into the clump of trees just as the avalanche reached the trail, but the edge of it caught Rick and tried to turn him around. He fought the force of the snow and was barely able to escape it, managing to tumble into the protection of the trees. His body rolled twice before ending up against the base of a tree. He looked back and saw that the trail behind them was obliterated.

"Rick, are you hurt?" Cat's voice came in gasps. She lay on her side, skis still attached, her chest heaving.

"I'm okay." He struggled to his feet, shuffled to her side, and flopped on his back. "That wasn't exactly the way I had pictured our last run of the day."

"It was a run, all right. But what…?"

Rick had raised his hand and lifted his head from the packed snow of the trail. The sound of the avalanche had stopped when it reached the level field below the trail. There had been silence, but now they could hear a very faint rumble of a motor. They exchanged looks and quickly got to their feet. The sound did not seem to be coming closer, but they couldn't be sure.

"Let's hope he's buried under a few feet of snow, Cat, but we'd better not wait around to find out."

◇◇◇

Luca snapped shut his cell phone, dropped it into his jacket pocket, and took a long drink of beer. "The ski patrol has not found the snowmobile, and probably won't. He was lucky not to have been caught up in the avalanche. Had it started above him, they might still be trying to dig him out. There was a large indentation where you saw him get stuck, and tracks that showed he'd managed to get back into the trees above the hill. They followed the tracks, but when they merged onto a service trail, there was no way to differentiate them from those of other vehicles. They're checking registrations, but with so many of them, it's almost impossible to know whose snowmobile it is. And it could have been borrowed or stolen."

"I should have gotten the license plate number." Rick nursed a snifter of cognac, not his usual late afternoon drink, but the situation called for it.

"Don't tell your uncle," Flavio said. Like Luca, he was drinking beer, but an imported brand. "The lovely Caterina has come through this brush with danger as well as could be expected?"

"She was relatively calm when I dropped her off at her apartment." He watched the cognac as it swirled in the glass. "It's strange, I felt a certain exhilaration when we beat the avalanche, perhaps she was feeling it too. Now it's worn off."

"That's a typical reaction," said Luca. He took another drink of beer and stared at the wall of bottles behind the bar. "Riccardo, there is the possibility that this was just some snowmobiler out where he shouldn't have been. Got lost, didn't know he was in a restricted area."

Rick was sitting between the other two. He shot a look at Luca and shook his head. "The guy was looking right at me, Luca. Even through the tinted mask of his helmet I could feel his eyes on me."

Flavio coughed softly. "You realize that doesn't make sense."

Rick slapped his hand on the bar. "Look, Flavio, I—"

"*Calma*, Riccardo," Luca said. "We don't doubt you. We're just trying to understand what happened and figure out why. There is no doubt in my mind that whoever it was, they were attempting to intimidate you, Signora Taylor, or both of you."

"Yankees go home," Flavio said in English, bringing a chuckle from the other two and breaking the tension.

Luca brought the conversation back to the matter at hand. "Who would have known that you two were skiing this afternoon?"

Rick swirled the brown liquid in the snifter, thinking that cognac drinkers must spend as much time swirling as drinking. "Anybody, if they were following us. I picked her up at her apartment and we walked over to the lifts on the east side of town."

"You walked right in front of Bruno's shop," Flavio observed.

"I suppose we did. And past the window of Zia Mitzi's bakery."

Luca frowned. "Too bad you didn't clomp through Melograno's real estate office, past the mayor's shop, and across the porch of the Hotel Trentino. That would have covered all the bases. All right, we must conclude that anyone could have seen that you were going skiing, and on which trails." He let out a deep sigh. "Let's put aside today's incident for the moment and return to the murder. Forensics has confirmed that Taylor was struck with a bottle, the pieces of which were found along the road back to town from the murder site. And it is the brand of prosecco that Flavio had thought." Flavio raised an arm in triumph. "We've checked with the distributor," Luca continued, "and two wine shops purchased one case each in December, as did three hotels in town. One of them is the Hotel Trentino. However, before you ask me to arrest Signor Muller, I should tell you that the mayor bought a complete case himself. Apparently he does that every year and gives them to clients and friends."

"And political cronies," Rick added.

"I would also note, before you shift the guilt back to Muller, that cases also went to hotels in Pinzolo, just down the mountain, as well as Folgarida. And various shops and hotels in Trento. It is a popular wine." He noticed Flavio shaking his head. "You are skeptical, Flavio?"

"No, no, Luca. It's just that they're selling more wine than I thought."

Rick grinned. "It seems that one of the upsides of helping the police, Flavio, is you've gained some proprietary information about the competition."

"If we may return to homicide," Luca said, "the bottle was likely full or partially full when it struck Taylor's head. The contents would have given it the weight needed to do the job.

We didn't find the cork in the snow, but if it was opened there, he could have picked it up and discarded it later, as he did with the bottle. Same with cups or glasses. But the basic premise that Taylor was lured up there for some sort of celebration is still valid. It's the most likely scenario, in my view."

"But lured by whom, and to what end?"

"If we knew that, Riccardo, we could get this over with and I could go home to Trento."

Two hands dropped over Flavio's shoulders and they heard a feminine voice in English. "Have you and Rick solved the mystery?" The three men quickly slipped off their bar stools and stood facing Lori Shafer. She had gone from her more formal pantsuit to what Rick characterized as business casual, not a term he could translate easily, since in Italian it was an oxymoron.

"Lori," said Flavio, "I don't believe you have met Inspector Luca Albani."

She shook Luca's hand and switched into Italian. "*Un piacere, ispettore.*"

"Ah, you speak perfect Italian, Signora. I do not need to expose my wretched English. But I will allow you three to speak any language you wish, as I must, I'm afraid, return to the station. There are many details to attend to." He gave her a short bow and turned to Rick and Flavio. "Keep your minds working, gentlemen. We will speak later. You will excuse me?" He pulled out his wallet and Flavio waved it away.

"The beer is on me, Luca. Off to work you go."

"*Grazie*, Flavio. *A presto.*"

Another bow, and he was out the door. Rick moved over to give Lori the seat in the middle as the girl appeared behind the bar, took Luca's empty glass, and smiled at the new arrival. Lori settled into the middle place, but leaned slightly toward Flavio.

He reciprocated the lean. "*Cara*, what would you like?"

Her eyes moved from Rick's cognac to Flavio's beer. "*Birra*," she said to the girl, then settled back into English. "The inspector seems nice. I've met a few other Italian policemen with my consular work, and they've all been very pleasant with me."

"They have been charmed by you, Lori."

Flavio was getting back into his Casanova role. Rick wondered if Flavio was worse when Rick was around—showing off, so to speak, but returning to normal conversation when he was alone with the woman. He'd have to ask sometime, but not now in front of Lori. She was enjoying it.

"How is Cat doing, Lori? When I left her she seemed to have calmed down."

"Yes, Rick, she's much better." Her beer appeared and she took a long drink. "I made her some tea and we talked about movies, American TV, that kind of thing. I thought that was better than dwelling on what had just happened, or the decisions she still has to make about bringing her brother's body home."

"Your job is part therapist," Flavio said.

"Whatever helps," she answered, and then turned back to Rick. "She's looking forward to having dinner with you tonight, Rick."

Cat's done it again. He had no recollection of inviting her to dinner, though he probably should have. With all the confusion it hadn't entered his mind. Was this another way for Cat to avoid spending time with Lori?

"Oh, dear, Rick, from the look on your face I have the idea that she hasn't called you yet."

"Well, as a matter of fact—"

"Be surprised when she calls. She pushed me out so that she could go out and buy some food."

◇◇◇

He had acted appropriately surprised and pleased with the invitation, despite having looked forward to what was on the dinner menu at the hotel. He stopped at a wine shop to pick up a bottle and checked out the prosecco selections for the murder weapon. It wasn't there. After considering and rejecting the additional purchase of flowers he continued toward Cat's apartment.

Following the relative warmth of the day, a cold front was moving into the valley and with it a light snowfall. He remembered that in New Mexico some of the heaviest snowstorms followed unseasonably high winter temperatures. Perhaps that was also the way it worked in the Dolomites. Unlike people in the States, where weather was followed more closely than the stock market, Italians focused more on things over which they had some control. Or perhaps there was just less weather in Italy. Whatever it was, he'd become Italian about weather since moving to Rome.

He stopped in front of Bruno's shop and peered in at the merchandise. As it had been when he'd gone in with Luca, the store was almost deserted. One customer rummaged through merchandise at the table where the infamous hat had been discovered. At the cash register Bruno was checking out a customer who had purchased what looked to be a sweater or light coat. Even through thick glass and from a distance, Rick could see the tired look in Bruno's eyes. The previously sharp lines of his goatee were softened by light growth on the rest of his face, and his hair needed a comb. Business must be better than it looks; he's working too hard, Rick thought.

He carefully crossed the street, dodging a few cars, and stepped up onto the curb in front of Zia Mitzi's bakery. The lights were on, but he saw no one inside. As he walked toward Cat's door some movement caught his eye and he saw Mitzi's son, crouched down behind the counter, arranging the cakes behind the glass. There had been a space, likely occupied by a *torta* recently sold, that Vittorio Muller now filled by repositioning the five remaining cakes. Then he carefully placed decorative fruit and flowers between them. It was the classic penchant of Italian shopkeepers to make even the simplest displays elegant in their simplicity, something that always impressed Rick.

Rick walked to the door to Cat's building, rang the bell, shaking the snow off his hat while he waited.

A loud "Rick?" crackled from the small speaker.

"In the flesh, Cat."

The door buzzed and Rick pushed it open. Many times in Rome he'd been a guest for dinner at the apartment of some young woman. The aromas of sauces or simmering meat usually began to reach his senses as he began climbing the stairs, or if there was an elevator, they hit him when it opened on the floor. Then the hostess would throw open the door to welcome him, a stray bit of hair perhaps falling over her brow, a few light stains on her apron. It always marked the beginning of a wonderful evening.

When he reached her floor Cat was standing in the doorway. There were no aromas and no stained apron, but given the sweater and tight slacks, Rick was not disappointed. She kissed him on both cheeks, Italian style, though the lips lingered more than was typical for a friendly greeting. He wiped his boots on the doormat and dropped his coat and hat over a chair near the door.

"It ain't a fit night out for man nor beast," he said as he rubbed his hands together.

"Let me get you a cold drink to warm you up, Rick, if that makes sense."

"It does if it contains alcohol." He followed her into the kitchen where the small table was set for two.

"I have a bottle of prosecco in the refrigerator which we really have to drink. I don't know what I'm going to do with all of my brother's wine. Probably just give it to Daniele."

"I'll open the bottle if you get the glasses." He opened the refrigerator and found to his relief that it was a plain bottle, not of the decorative type used in the murder. And this was not the time to tell her about the murder weapon, if he ever would. He put the bottle on the counter, peeled off the foil around the top and unhooked the wire that held the cork in place. Then he carefully began pushing the top of the cork with his two thumbs, turned the bottle and pushed again, continuing until it popped, bouncing off the ceiling. Cat laughed and held out the glasses which he filled with the bubbling liquid. Nothing spilled.

"*A tua salute,*" said Rick as he touched his glass to hers.

She took a sip, keeping her eyes on his. "Rick, you're the only good thing that has come out of this trip for me."

"Cat, I really don't—"

"No, really, Rick. Apart from not being able to get through this without your help, I feel that we've really…well, let's leave it at that. Why don't we go into the other room? Our dining area tonight is not very elegant, but we don't have to stand around here while we have a drink. Bring the bottle, if you would."

Moving into the other room was fine with Rick, who was beginning to feel uncomfortable with the conversation. She led the way into the living room where she settled into one end of the sofa and motioned him to sit at the other. Rick put the bottle down on the floor and managed to sit, cross his boot over his leg, and lean back, all while keeping his glass steady.

"You seem to have recovered well from our little adventure this afternoon, Cat."

She grinned and took another drink from her glass. "It was an adventure, wasn't it? Did the police find the man?"

"No, he got onto a trail and his track was lost. They're still investigating."

"And they're still investigating Cam's murder."

"It's only been two days, Cat."

She rubbed the back of her neck with her hand, then took another drink of her prosecco. "I suppose so. I had a roommate at school who read murder mysteries all the time. That's all she did. If she were here we could ask her how long this should take. Do you read mysteries, Rick?"

"I've read a few." In fact he loved mysteries, but decided this wasn't the time to be talking about them with the sister of a murder victim. Light talk was what was in order now, but what? He picked up the bottle and poured her more wine without being asked. Then he topped off his own glass. "Have you been to Rome, Cat?"

"Years ago. I was in junior high and Cam was in high school. The required trip to the continent with my parents—London, Paris, Rome, Venice."

"The grand tour."

"I guess so. My father was constantly lecturing us on how important it was to be exposed to it all. Part of our education.

Unlike Cam, I was too young to appreciate it. It was on that trip that he caught the bug for Italy, as he used to say."

"Do you remember where you stayed in Rome?"

She closed her eyes tightly. "Hmm. I remember it was near the top of the Spanish Steps."

"The Hassler."

"That sounds right. I remember walking down the steps and getting in a carriage to take us around the city. The horse was cute. The rest of it was just looking at old stuff."

"There's a lot of old stuff in Rome."

"And I think we saw it all."

He decided this wasn't going anywhere. "What's for dinner? I must admit that all the excitement has given me an appetite."

She bounced to her feet, almost spilling her glass. "Me too. And I didn't even put out any peanuts." He almost said that she needed Maria around to remember such things, but decided against it. They walked into the kitchen, Rick still the keeper of the bottle, now less than half full.

Cat gestured for Rick to sit. "I went down to the deli and got anything that looked good and didn't require cooking. So I'm afraid everything will be cold. Like a picnic."

"Sounds fine to me. The wine will keep us warm." He took another swig of the prosecco, which was excellent. Cam Taylor, it seemed, had known his wines.

"They don't call it a deli, do they?"

"No, it would be a *salumaio*. But essentially the same thing."

"They don't have delis like this back home, Rick." She went to the small refrigerator and took out two trays, one in each hand, and placed them on the table. Each was wrapped in paper and tied with a string. She took a knife from one of the drawers, cut the string and removed the paper, revealing two cardboard trays of sliced meats, which she pushed to the middle of the table. "I don't know what they are, I just pointed and he sliced. Maybe you can tell me the names."

"Sure. This one here—"

"Wait a minute, Rick, let me get the rest." She drained her glass and placed it in front of Rick. While he dutifully filled it, she went back to the refrigerator and returned with two more trays that were again unwrapped and pushed into place. One was filled with various cheeses, the other held small bowls, each filled with a different item. She held up one finger and made a final run to the refrigerator, coming back with a larger bowl containing four thin artichokes in oil.

"I guess you didn't tell this guy there would be only two of us. Or have you invited the Italian army to join us?"

"I may have gotten a little carried away. Oh, one more thing." She went to the counter and found a long loaf of crusty bread. "I should slice this."

"No need, Cat, we'll just snap it off as we need it. That's what is meant when they talk about breaking bread with someone."

She pulled a few forks and spoons from a drawer, put them down on the trays, and sat across from Rick. "Okay, Rick, I'm ready for my vocabulary lesson. Not that I'll remember any of it." As if to make her point she took another pull of her prosecco. Rick picked up a fork to use as a pointer.

"Let's start with the *salumi*, the cold cuts. This is *prosciutto crudo*, cured ham, sliced thin, as you can see. Next, *bresaola*, cured beef that's a specialty of Lombardy. Then *speck*, a cured ham from the Alps—you'll love it—and, finally, a *cotto salami*. You can get it in the States." He moved to the bowls. "All right, here's pâté, no Italian word for it. Not sure what kind this is but I'm guessing some kind of game or fowl, like rabbit or duck. And this, with the shrimp in the gelatin on top, is *insalata russa*."

"Russian salad?"

"*Brava*, Cat. As you'll see when you get under the gelatin, it has a mixture of potatoes, carrots, peas, and a lot of mayonnaise. Next to it is a rice salad, with pieces of cheese and ham mixed through it, and here is *finocchio*, fennel, in oil. And, finally, in this bowl," he waved the fork with a flourish, "is *carciofi alla romana*, roman-style artichokes, cooked and served in oil. Probably not as good as you can get in Rome, but they look passable."

"Before you move on to the cheeses, Rick, we'd better open another bottle. There's one in the refrigerator."

Rick did as he was told, filling the glasses before returning to his chair and again picking up the fork. "All right. Your trusty *salumaio* has given us a good selection of cheese. This one, however, should really be over with the antipasto tray, *mozzarella di bufala*. If it's the real stuff, and only by tasting will we know, it has come from water buffalo near Naples. These other four are more desert cheeses. This one shaped like a log is *caprino*, a soft goat cheese. I think this next one is an *asiago*, which comes from around a town of the same name not too far from here. Here's some *gorgonzola*, Italy's blue cheese and a Milanese specialty. And this last one, I'm guessing, is a *pecorino*, hard goat cheese. But I'll have to taste it to be sure." He put down the fork and spread out his hands over the table. "We will not go hungry."

"I'll say," she giggled. "I'm full already. Please start."

Rick was glad to take the cue. He needed something in his stomach other than wine, and the food spread out before them was beckoning. He took the fork and transferred some of the sliced meats to his tray. Cat did the same while he waited.

"*Buon appetito*, Cat, and thank you for inviting me." He snapped off a chunk of bread and passed it to her.

"My pleasure, Rick, and *buon appetito*."

Several minutes of tasting and food discussion followed. Cat agreed that the *speck* was the best of the cold cuts, with the *bresaola* a close second. The Russian salad got higher points than the rice salad; the type of pâté could not be identified with precision; and the artichokes were acceptable, given the location of the cook. The decision was made to push back and take a breather before starting on the cheeses. In addition, at Rick's suggestion, they agreed to open a bottle of red wine to go with them. He was dispatched to the pantry to pick a bottle, and Cat disappeared into the back of the apartment.

Rick found a long shelf filled with bottles standing upright, making it easier to check labels. Again he looked for the holiday prosecco, but found only more bottles of the same one they were drinking. Reds and whites on the shelf were primarily from Lombardy; Cameron Taylor apparently had decided to stay close to Milan in his wine purchases. It would go along with his personality: learn local wines first and then branch out. All very organized. Rick decided on a Valcalepio, which, according to the label, came from the province of Bergamo, east of the Lombardian capital. He took it off the shelf and walked back into the kitchen where he was hit with an invisible wave of Cat's perfume.

"This one looks fine, Cat. It's red and it's liquid, so it should fit the bill with the cheese." He found a corkscrew in a drawer and popped open the bottle while she got two new glasses.

The cheese course conversation was more subdued; the wine was having its effect. After they had tried all five cheeses and were starting another round, Rick noticed that Cat's mood seemed to change slightly. She had just taken a long drink of the red wine when Rick noticed her staring at her glass. He waited.

"Rick, I was never a very good sister to Cam. He was right in wanting me to do better with myself, but I always tried to push him out of my life. I should have just accepted that he was better than I was and taken his advice."

Rick decided it would be better to let her talk. He cut a piece of *pecorino,* put it on his plate, and waited for her to continue.

"I wish he were here now to give me advice on how to get through this." She laughed while she pushed a tear from her eye with one finger. "That's funny. Even Cam would have laughed at that, and he didn't have much of a sense of humor."

"I'm sure you had some fun together as kids, Cat. Remember those times."

She took a deep breath and looked at the ceiling as she thought. "Yes, there were times when we were very young, before he got…well, you know. One time we locked Maria in her room when my parents were out, and ate cookies."

Rick popped the pecorino in his mouth. "I'll bet it was your idea."

"That I don't remember, but I'm sure it was Cam's. Mom and Dad thought he could do no wrong, but I knew better. This wine is good." She held out her glass to be filled. "A healthy body, but with just enough youth to give it some impertinence." She looked at Rick for a reaction. "That's the kind of thing Cam would say. I was never sure if he was serious or not."

"I hope he wasn't."

They ate some cheese and sipped more of the Valcalepio while they talked of wine, a topic about which both of them were interested but not fanatical. She talked about visiting the Napa Valley. He told her that the first vineyards in what would be the United States were planted in the Rio Grande valley. They agreed that prosecco was as good as any French champagne, but decided not to open another bottle.

Cat pushed her plate away and leaned back in the chair, wineglass in hand. After another sip she got to her feet, walked to the refrigerator and smiled back at him. "I have some desert for us, Rick."

He restrained himself and did not say what he was thinking. "Something light, I hope."

"Not too heavy. There's a wonderful bakery right here in the building. You passed it."

"I had a coffee there a couple days ago."

"Bruno from the ski shop recommended it, not that he needed to, since the smells from the ovens float up the air shaft into the kitchen. Cam never went in since he didn't like sweets."

"But you do. And you don't seem any the worse for your sweet tooth."

She giggled and posed as if she were on a fashion-house runway. "Do you think so?"

"Absolutely. So what is the desert?"

She opened the refrigerator and took out a small dish, which she placed on the table among the cheeses. Chocolate éclairs.

He stared at them. "Cat, I don't think I can do it. I love chocolate éclairs. Any other time I could eat both of them, but after that meal I just don't have the space."

"You know, Rick, I don't think I do either." She put them back in the refrigerator. "Room for coffee?"

"Coffee sounds like a good idea." He got to his feet and picked up his plate. "Let me help clean this up. Do you have some containers for what we didn't finish? There are at least a couple more good meals here." He glanced at Cat who was leaning against the counter. "Why, you can feed Lori tomorrow when she comes over."

That got another giggle. "Let's just put it all back on the same trays it came in."

They combined the leftovers on trays and she found room for them in the refrigerator. Rick remembered Cat's lack of coffee-making skills and began doing the needful in that department. Ten minutes later they were seated on the sofa in the living room, stirring small cups of hot, dark liquid.

"I'd put on some music, Rick, but this place doesn't have a sound system."

Rick blew on the coffee and took a small sip. "No need, Cat, we can listen to the snow."

Thick flakes, just visible from the lights of the room, were rapping against the picture window. It would be a long night for the street crews, and an early start for the men driving the snow-cats that groomed the trails. But a wonderful day for the skiers.

"It does make a nice sound, doesn't it?" She finished her coffee and put her cup and saucer on the table. "But we're cozy here inside." She snuggled closer to Rick and moved his arm so that it covered her shoulders.

He stretched to place his cup and saucer next to hers. "It appears that you have put today's danger out of your mind, Cat. I admire your resilience."

"I'm not sure how resilient my body is, Rick. Remember when I fell? That leg has been aching since I got back to the apartment."

"Has it? Perhaps we'd better get you to the *clinica* tomorrow."

"No, I don't think it's anything serious. But if you just massaged it, that will do the trick." She got out from under his arm, slipped out of her shoes, and flopped her right leg over his lap. "Right there is where it's sore."

Rick dutifully began to knead the designated muscles, but as he did, he could not keep a thought out of his mind.

I'd swear it was the other leg she fell on.

Chapter Twelve

Rick was waved past the policeman on duty and walked to the inspector's temporary office. The paper sign on the partially open door was slightly askew, so he carefully adjusted it before knocking. "*Buon giorno, ispettore.*"

Luca, in shirtsleeves, looked up from a stack of papers. "Riccardo, *buon giorno.* Come sit. I was just trying to organize my thoughts on this terrible crime, and you are the only other person who is aware of all that has happened. So you can be of great assistance. I just spoke with my public prosecutor, and she is no help at all. She wants everything in the case tied up with a nice bow, like a *torta* from Zia Mitzi's bakery, before she steps in. And she is pressing me to bake the cake."

Rick stripped off his coat and put it on a chair with his hat before taking a seat. "I was hoping you'd have it all solved by now."

"*Magari,*" answered Luca, the tips of his fingers touching. It was a word which could have various meanings, but Rick took it as "if only."

He rubbed his eyes and leaned back in the chair. "Luca, why don't I go over what we have, and you can tell me where I'm wrong? Starting with the suspects. The way I see it there are the big three and then some lesser names. The three first." He held up his thumb, Italian style, to start the count.

"The mayor. Grandi's motive is that his wife was fooling around with Taylor well before the divorce was final. And he doesn't have much of an alibi. He's anywhere and everywhere on the day of the murder." The index finger uncurled to join the thumb. "Melograno. Our real estate agent could have had an argument with Taylor about the loan. Perhaps the American was telling him he was inclined to recommend against it. And Melograno's whereabouts on the morning of the disappearance cannot be confirmed."

"Though if the barista's memory is correct, it can be confirmed for the time the body was dropped."

"That's true." Rick's hand was still in the air, and his middle finger joined the other two digits. "The third main suspect is Muller, since it was in his interest that Melograno not get the loan. As you observed after we talked to the man, if there's no banker there's no loan, or at least that's what Muller could have thought. And as he himself told us, he doesn't have much of an alibi for the day of the murder."

"Just like Grandi." Luca picked up a pencil and twirled it between his fingers.

"Just like the mayor, correct. Which brings us to the next level of suspects, or at least people who could have been involved. The former Signora Grandi, the volatile Gina Cortese, can top that list. Motive: she found out about other girlfriends after he'd told her she was the one and only. But she would need an accomplice, since she has an alibi, and with her size couldn't do it on her own anyway."

Luca tapped the table with the pencil. "Which brings up Bauer."

"Well, she and Bruno appeared to be very friendly the other night in the bar."

"We must find where Bauer spent the day on Saturday." He flipped open his notebook and used the pencil to write. "We will go see him this morning."

"That will work. I need to get new gloves after mine were ruined the other night."

"Perfect, we can catch two pigeons with one fava bean." He consulted his notes. "Next on the list is Spadacini, the electrician.

He could have been doing the dirty work for Muller along with his electrical jobs."

"And he is a suspect in the stabbing of Pittini."

Luca rubbed his eyes. "Ah, yes, Pittini. The poor man is still unconscious. Though after talking more with the men here at the station, I'm more open to the possibility that it was some jilted boyfriend or husband. The man apparently was quite a bounder. Unless you were the intended victim, of course."

Rick was trying to decide if Luca was making the *piccolo scherzo*, when the policeman continued.

"And when he realized he'd stabbed the wrong person, he went out and found himself a snowmobile."

"You aren't joking, are you Luca?"

"I wish I were, my American friend, but we have to consider that possibility."

"So I should be more careful."

Luca shrugged. "It wouldn't hurt. And now, Riccardo, who have we missed?"

"If Muller is involved in some way, we must include his wife and son. At the very least they could have known about it. I can't see Auntie Mitzi wielding a prosecco bottle or pushing the body from the gondola, but there may be some other way she was involved. The son, he could have done either or both. But it doesn't make sense that Taylor would have been up there with young Vittorio, even if there was someone else along."

Luca tapped his pencil. "There is another possibility that we have not yet considered."

Rick perked up. He had started to become frustrated that the case was going nowhere, as well as feeling claustrophobic in the windowless room.

"The man whose life you saved, Riccardo. He was, after all, on duty the night that the body was put on the gondola. He could have been somehow involved, and the knife attack was intended to keep him quiet."

"If it was, they succeeded."

"For the moment, at least. He could come back into consciousness at any time. So let's think about that possibility as we continue. Let's also focus on the vehicle that would have taken Taylor's body from the field to the base of the gondola. I don't want to try to ask for a search warrant from my prosecutor. She would want more evidence for the judge, but there may be ways to check the vehicles of our three main suspects by more informal means."

Rick smiled. "This could include me talking to Muller about his Jeep Cherokee?"

"Well, he was proud of it, and pleased that you showed interest. You could ask to see it."

"Sure, I can do that. What about Melograno? His car's in the shop."

"All businesses, including auto repair shops, need to be inspected from time to time by the authorities to protect consumers."

Rick grinned. "No doubt, Luca. But what about the mayor and his city Land Rover? You can't really pull him over to check his license and registration."

"We'll figure something out."

Rick got to his feet. "Let's figure it out somewhere else, this room is starting to close in on me again."

"Of course, Riccardo. The sergeant has checked on where our various suspects will be this morning, so we can make our rounds accordingly." He pushed his papers together in an attempt to create some semblance of order, but soon gave up. Instead he stood and picked up his jacket and hat from where they sat on another chair. "Why don't we go get a coffee and plan our next move? We can go to Mitzi's bakery and perhaps have something with the coffee."

"Fine with me, it's been a while since breakfast."

Luca was slipping on his coat. "I missed you this morning at breakfast. You must have been up very early."

"It's a habit." Rick pulled on his leather jacket and picked up his hat.

"Those raisin rolls they had were delicious, Riccardo, did you try them?"

"I had a chocolate éclair."

"Really? I didn't see any éclairs on the buffet table."

Rick opened the door for the inspector. "You just have to get up earlier, Luca."

◇◇◇

They were passing the chocolate shop when the muffled sound of the Lobo fight song came from Rick's pocket. He fumbled for a few seconds before fishing out his phone and checking the number. "Let me answer this, Luca, it shouldn't take long." The policeman gave him a "take your time" wave and strolled in the direction of the chocolate smell. Rick pressed a button and was about to give the usual greeting when the voice at the other end stopped him.

"Are you being careful?"

"Of course I am, Zio, why do you ask?" In fact Rick knew why: Luca's reports had made their way to his uncle's office in Rome.

"I wasn't concerned about the attack on the man. In fact I was pleased to see that your quick response may have saved his life. But this avalanche business, Riccardo, is something entirely different."

With his mother, Rick would have played down any danger, blamed it on a misunderstanding, assured her that there was nothing to be concerned about. He would not try that with his uncle, and not just because the professional policeman would have seen right through it. Their relationship since Rick's move to Rome had been devoid of artifice, unique in a country where subtlety and nuance was the norm in human interaction.

"Luca, I mean Inspector Albani, thought of the possibility that it was just a lost snowmobiler, but I know the guy was trying to get us. I could sense it. The only motive I can think of is that the murderer believes we are getting too close."

"So it was a warning. They know that both you and Albani are working on the case and they don't think much of Albani.

By getting rid of you, or scaring you off, the investigation is delayed or perhaps goes cold."

"I never thought of it that way, Zio. But if that's the case, they're underestimating Luca."

"From what I've heard about him, I would agree. A tad eccentric, perhaps, but highly competent. Are you getting close to finding who is responsible?"

"Luca and I were just going over it. I think we're closing in, but we can't seem to get the break we need. I hope we get one soon."

"The longer it goes, the colder the trail becomes, and so I hope you do. Riccardo, I have to go. I'll be anxious to hear all about it when you get back to Rome. I hope you're taking notes."

"It's all in my head, Zio. *A presto.*"

"*A presto*, Riccardo. *Fai bravo.*"

Rick closed his phone, glad that his uncle had finished by telling him to be good rather than to be careful. He looked around for Luca, and when he didn't see him, started walking toward the chocolate shop. Halfway there Luca came out of its door, a small sack in his hands. When he saw Rick, he quickly slipped it into his coat pocket.

"*La bella* Signora Taylor?"

"No, it was Commissario Fontana. You must try to keep my name out of your reports."

"That is not easy to do, my American friend. You keep getting yourself involved." He glanced up and tugged at the cap of his hat. It was not snowing, but the sky gave the impression it was going to try to sometime soon. "When you ski today, make a point of staying out of trouble. Then your uncle will have nothing to cause him any worry."

"I'll do my best, Luca."

The morning group of pensioners was sitting in silence today. They watched intently as a yellow front loader, its cab marked with the seal of the town, moved slowly around one end of the *piazza*. It was equipped with a deep bucket that dug into the small mountain of snow before backing up and raising its load to a waiting truck. The vehicle beeped when it was put in reverse, but another man, perhaps the driver of the parked truck, stood by to keep pedestrians out of harm's way. As Rick and Luca walked by the bench, the old men began to discuss how many runs it would take to get rid of the accumulated snow. Hands waved and voices raised, a clear indication that the snow removal was the most interesting event of recent days on the square.

"They'll be talking about that into next week," said Luca as they rounded the corner and started down Campiglio's main shopping street, which was beginning to come to life. Some shopkeepers were removing the locks that held their protective *saracinesche* to the sidewalk and rolling them up and out of sight with a metallic crash. Others brushed the sidewalk in front of their stores. All studied the sky, as if it would give a clue as to how business would be on this day.

Mitzi's bakery had been open since before dawn for the workers who needed a shot of coffee and something sweet before heading to their posts on the mountain. One man stood at the bar dressed in the heavy blue overalls of the corporation that ran all the trails and lifts. He watched Rick and Luca approach the bar, looked around as if to check who might be listening, and turned his attention to Luca.

"Are you the policeman?" The man's stubbled beard matched his baggy eyes, and his words had the guttural accent of the mountains.

Luca was shaking the snow from his hat. "I think you know the answer, Signore. Everyone in Campiglio seems to know who I am. And who are you?"

"I work with Guido Pittini. Have you discovered who stabbed him?" He kept his eyes on the inspector, as if Rick were invisible.

"If we had, I'm sure the word would already be around town. Do you have any theories?"

The man was about to speak when Mitzi came through the door behind the counter. He looked at her, gave Luca a hard stare, and threw down what was left in his cup. "No. No I don't." He walked quickly to the door and was gone.

"*Buon giorno, Ispettore*, Signor Montoya," said Mitzi as they all watched the man disappear from view. "I see you met Rino." She picked up the empty cup and placed it in the sink behind the counter.

"We were having a nice chat, Signora Muller. How are you this morning?"

"As well as can be expected with all the violence going on in Campiglio these days. But it doesn't appear to be having a negative effect on business. And what can I get for you gentlemen?"

"*Cappuccino* for me, please," answered Rick.

"*Lo stesso, per favore*. And while you're making them, we'll choose something to go with it."

While Rick and Luca perused the selection, Mitzi banged at the espresso machine. As was normal in bakeries, on top of the counter was a plastic case with a hinged front, allowing clients to get their own pastries. This one had a small heating element, so that each pastry felt like it had just come out of the oven. Rick took a paper napkin from the fanned stack next to it and immediately chose a chocolate-filled croissant. Luca took longer to decide, and perhaps thinking of the chocolates in his pocket, went with a plain brioche brushed with a thin, sugary glaze. When each took their first bite, Mitzi was bringing their *cappuccini* to saucers already in place. She placed a large sugar bowl between them and pushed its two spoon handles in their respective directions. After a sip of coffee, Rick was the first to speak.

"This is excellent, Signora. I expect that you supply the pastries for your husband's hotel?"

She wiped her hands on her apron and nodded. "I supply pastries, as well as bread, to several hotels and restaurants in Campiglio. It is the largest part of the business. My son is out delivering bread now." She crossed her arms across her ample chest and looked from one man to the other. "Do you really suspect my husband in this investigation?"

Luca choked slightly on his brioche but quickly regained his voice. "We are questioning everyone who could have had any connection with the murdered man, Signora. That is normal procedure in these cases."

"And you won't tell me who is suspect and who is not."

As she spoke, Rick studied her round face and decided there was more to Auntie Mitzi than her motherly smile and almond cookies. Perhaps she could be an effective mayor if she managed to beat Grandi, though if Flavio were to be believed, her victory was unlikely. "You know this town as well as anyone, Signora. Where do you think the inspector should be concentrating his efforts?"

She turned on the water in the small metal sink and began rinsing out the cups that were stacked there. "I am the wrong person to ask, Signor Montoya. As you know, I am a candidate for mayor, so I don't want to alienate any voters by giving their names to the police."

Rick could spot a clever answer when he heard one. Any attempt to assure her that whatever she said would be held in confidence was laughable in a town this size. Apparently Luca thought the same; there was no more talk of the murder as they finished their coffee. Rick insisted on paying and Luca did not protest. As she handed him his change, Mitzi thanked them and said: "If you're planning to talk to my husband again, you won't find him at the hotel today. He's in Pinzolo at the Hotel Miramonte. He owns it too."

Luca thanked her and glanced at Rick who was staring at the rows of cakes behind the glass. "Do you want to get something for your afternoon snack, Riccardo?"

"No, no, Luca. I was just…" He looked up at Mitzi's wooden smile. "Thank you, Signora. We will get some of your famous cookies on a future visit."

"Don't wait too long in the day, Signor Montoya, they sell out early."

He thanked her for the advice and they went from the enveloping warmth of the bakery to the crisp air of the street, buttoning their coats and adjusting their hats as they stood on the sidewalk.

"So, Riccardo, it appears that Signor Muller is in Pinzolo. Would you like to join me there this afternoon? You can talk to him about his car while I go to the mechanic to check on Melograno's car."

"I'm afraid I can't, Luca. I promised Cat I would take her skiing. But I promise to go see Muller this evening. And that way it won't appear connected to the investigation; I can show up at his hotel because I'm interested in his Jeep, and that's all."

"That's true. It won't be as contrived."

They checked the traffic in both directions, like school kids, before crossing the street to Bruno's store. According to the hours posted on the door, it had just opened, but there was one customer there already, a man trying on ski boots. He was being fitted by a woman who watched as the man clomped around the rug. Bruno stood at the cash register watching, but looked up when Rick and Luca came through the door. His expression stiffened, but quickly took on a rigid smile accompanied by a nod to Rick. If he'd wanted to hide, there was nowhere to go. He came out from behind the counter and shook hands with Rick. Luca had wandered to the sale table where he had previously found his beloved hat.

"*Salve*, Bruno."

"*Ciao*, Riccardo, *come stai?*"

"I'm well, thanks. I need some gloves."

Bauer looked relieved. "For skiing?"

"No, just a warm pair for walking around town. Maybe lined leather."

"Of course. I have—" He watched Luca fingering items on the sale table next to the shelf where gloves were on display.

"That's my friend Luca Albani," said Rick. "You sold him that hat a few days ago."

"Yes, of course. We sell a lot of hats, but I remember him. The policeman, correct?" He rubbed his goatee with the back of his hand.

"That's right, up from Trento investigating Cam Taylor's death."

The whole hand now massaged the goatee. "And Caterina, she is doing better after the tragedy? She seemed to be recovering when I saw her with you in the bar."

"She's coming along. I didn't know that you and Gina were seeing each other."

"You know Gina?"

"She didn't mention to you that we'd met?"

"Perhaps she did. Let me show you some gloves."

Bruno led the way to the gloves section where Luca was waiting with a pleasant smile and an outstretched hand. "Signor Bauer, I must thank you again for this hat. It is both warm and stylish." Bruno shook his hand and mumbled a response. "But please don't let me keep you from showing Riccardo some gloves. He's been walking around for days with his hands in his pockets."

It didn't take Rick long to find a pair in a color that somewhat matched the stained patina of his leather jacket. Bruno had moved behind the counter, snipping off the price tag, when Luca approached. "You're open every day in the winter, Signor Bauer?"

"Except for Monday mornings, Inspector. The ski season is when we make most of our money."

"I can understand that. You must take in considerably more outfitting skiers in the winter than hikers in the summer. And you are here all the time?"

"Most of the time." He handed the gloves to Rick. "I take an occasional break to ski, but I usually put in a ten-hour day."

"Weekends too? For example, last Saturday?"

Bauer took a deep breath, as if trying to remember. "The days tend to run together when you work all of them."

"I'm sure they do. That was the day Signor Taylor disappeared."

He tried to make his shrug appear casual. "I think I came in at the usual time, about nine, and was here until we closed. I left in the late afternoon for a while since I hadn't had lunch."

Rick silently watched the exchange, noting how Luca had shifted smoothly from innocent inquiries into what could only be described as an informal interrogation. Bauer knew what was going on, but seemed determined not to acknowledge it.

"A sandwich at a bar?"

"No, I went home. It is just a few blocks from here."

"Did you see Signor Taylor that morning, by any chance? He lived just across the street."

"No, I never saw him mornings."

"When was the last time you saw him?"

Again Bauer paused to think. "It must have been when he came in last week with his sister to rent her skis. I don't remember what day it was, but I can look it up if you wish."

"Don't bother, we can ask Signora Taylor." Luca looked around the store, which remained empty except for the one man, still clomping about, but now on his third pair of ski boots. "Riccardo, we should let Signor Bauer get back to his clients. Is business good, Signor Bauer?"

"It could be better, Inspector."

"Let's stand here in front of the store, Riccardo, where Bauer can see us." Luca adjusted his hat, a ritual Rick noticed each time they emerged into the open air. "He doesn't have much of an alibi. But the only motive I can think of is that he was annoyed with Taylor for being with Gina Cortese, which doesn't seem very strong."

Rick shrugged as he pulled on his new purchases. "People have killed for less." He held out one gloved hand, like a woman checking out her new manicure, then squeezed it into a fist before holding it up to his face to sniff the new leather. "Where to next?"

The inspector checked his watch. "We should be just in time to catch Gina Cortese between her classes. They told me she would be up here." He waved a finger toward the western side of the town.

They crossed back over the street and took the sidewalk past shops and apartment entrances until they reached an alley that led up to a set of scuffed wooden steps. At their top an open expanse of snow spread out where three ski trails ended and a four-seat chairlift picked up the skiers to take them back up to the top.

Among the kilometers of trails that cut through the forests on the three sides above Campiglio, the most difficult ones ended here. Thanks to a gentle final slope, one wide section at the end of the trails was filled with beginners, mostly children, taking their lessons. They were divided into small, chattering packs, each herded by an instructor. The kids had to learn to get up the hill before they could try to get down, so a short lift next to the line of trees served that purpose. Its cable had plastic discs dangling from the ends of poles that the operators patiently slipped between the legs of each small skier to take them up. Most kids mastered it immediately, riding the pole to the top before letting go, but along the way a few lost their balance and crumpled to the ground. They formed a line of wriggling snow-covered debris awaiting rescue.

Wearing a headband and goggles, Gina Cortese was easy to pick out from among the various instructors. Her diminutive charges, five in total, lined up behind her as she skied diagonally in wide arcs, urging them to imitate her exaggerated moves. Rick and Luca waited at the bottom of the run, their civilian clothes contrasting with that of the skiers around them. Gina reached the bottom, gave some final instructions to her class, and pushed herself toward the two men who were starting to stamp their feet to keep warm. She had spotted them on the way down, which was easy to do.

"You are waiting for me, I suppose?" She pushed her goggles to the top of her head.

"That is correct, Signora Cortese," Luca answered. "I had a couple more questions. You have the time now?"

"I do. My next lesson doesn't start for fifteen minutes. I imagine you want to ask me about Elio. He's got to be one of the suspects in this."

She gave the policeman a probing look, awaiting an answer. Rick was trying to remember who this Elio was, and from the initial expression on his face, so was Luca, who then responded. "Ah, your ex-husband. You believe the mayor should be a suspect in this crime?"

"If he's not involved directly, he has to know who did it. He knows everything that goes on in Campiglio. Even before he became mayor he had his nose into everybody's business."

"And what would be his motive?" asked Rick, wondering if she would mention her relationship with the dead man before her divorce from the mayor.

"Hell, I don't know. You're the detectives, you can figure something out. Cam was a banker, perhaps Elio had some financial deal that didn't work out. Nothing would surprise me."

Luca digested her comment. "Refresh my memory about last Saturday, Signora. You didn't see Signor Taylor that morning, if I remember correctly?"

Her expression tightened. "No. That's my busiest day of classes. You can check the ski school calendar. They start at ten and I came here immediately after breakfast."

"You have breakfast at home?"

"No, I always have it at Mitzi's. It's close to my morning lessons." She lifted her ski pole and pointed.

"Yes, we just came from there," said Luca. "Did Mitzi herself serve you?"

"I can't remember. Sometimes it's Mitzi, and sometimes Vittorio, her son. I don't know which it was that day. No, wait, it was Vittorio. I remember now since he was talking with Bruno when I got there."

"Bruno Bauer?" said Rick.

"Yes, his store is across the street. He told me the other night that you'd met."

"Yes, I know Bruno. In fact we just came from his store."

"You are covering the town well," Gina said, sliding her skis forward and back. "First Mitzi, then Bruno. You don't think that he could be involved, do you?" She looked at Luca.

"We went to his store since Riccardo needed new gloves." Backing up the inspector's statement, Rick held up his hands and flexed the fingers.

Gina leaned forward on her skis and stretched her back before turning to Rick. "Riccardo...It is Riccardo, isn't it?"

"That's right."

"Riccardo, every time I meet you I become upset. First when you two told me about Cam's disappearance. Then when you and Flavio saw me across the mountain. Even the other night, when I saw you with Cam's sister, it reminded me of his death. It's happening again. And now I have to worry about Bruno." She pulled her goggles down, either in annoyance to show she wanted the interview to finish, or to hide tears behind the tinted plastic lenses.

"Gina, I'm sorry it had to be this way. But I'm certain you want to find his murderer just as much as we do."

"Of course I do." She stared at the snow while taking the grips of her poles and jumping lightly in preparation for departure, but then looked at Rick. "There was an avalanche yesterday in which two Americans were almost buried. That wouldn't have been—"

"Cat Taylor and me. How did you hear about it?"

"This is a small town, Riccardo." She pushed on her poles and slid away toward a group of instructors.

◇◇◇

Upon reaching the top of the wooden stairs, Rick stamped his feet to bang off the accumulated snow and restart circulation. His cowboy boots were warm, but they were not intended to be worn while standing in snow for long periods. Luca appeared less affected by their trek.

"Well, Riccardo, what did you make of Signora Cortese on this occasion?" They stepped carefully down the stairs to the narrow street.

"She has her alibis, but that's nothing new. I was surprised when she mentioned seeing Bauer at Mitzi's bakery the morning of Taylor's disappearance."

Luca nodded as they walked. "He should have mentioned it himself. It confirms where he was at that time of the morning. She could be lying to protect him, but if she did, it wasn't very smart since I can ask Mitzi's son if he was there that morning."

"Unless Mitzi is in on it, and…" Rick waved his hand in front of his face as if he were clearing smoke. "No, never mind, that would make it all too complicated. My guess is that Bauer just forgot. And you noticed how she immediately tried to bring her ex-husband in as a suspect?"

"I did. Out of spite rather than anything concrete, I would guess. She just wants to make things difficult for him."

Rick recalled the seemingly friendly manner between the ex-couple in the bar, but said nothing to Luca.

They reached the main thoroughfare where workers were stringing a banner from light poles on opposite sides of the street. The few cars that were out at this time of day were stopped while ropes holding the canvas sign could be pulled taut and tied into place. Two men teetered at the tops of ladders while struggling with the ropes, and another man stood in the middle of the street directing them to slide it one way or another. When it was properly centered, the man on the ground gave a thumbs-up and waved on the cars.

"I didn't know that Campiglio was on the World Cup ski circuit," said Rick, reading the banner.

"Nor did I. Is that something important?"

"It's the best skiers in the world. It says it will take place on the trails that finish where we were talking with Gina. I trust they won't allow any children's lessons in that area when the professionals are hitting the finish line."

"I wouldn't think so." He checked his watch. "I'm afraid we won't find Signor Melograno in his office now. My sergeant called this morning and was told that the man had various appointments at properties around town. We could run into him, but I'll try to catch him this afternoon. I may have more questions for him after talking to the garage and seeing his vehicle."

"All those blood stains in the trunk?"

Luca looked sharply at Rick, and then his mouth formed a grin. "I keep forgetting your American sense of humor. Perhaps by the end of the week I will be used to it."

"At the end of the week I have to get back to Rome, Luca."

"Then we must solve this crime by then. But I am sensing a breakthrough. Perhaps it will come when I go to Pinzolo."

Rick wished he could be so optimistic. "I hope you're right, Luca. Where are you off to now?"

"I must return to the station for reports and to deal with my public prosecutor. It is not a part of the job that I prefer, but it must be done."

"I'll see you at lunch at the hotel."

"Probably not, I will get something near the station. You will be skiing this afternoon again with the lovely Signora Taylor, my friend?"

"That's right. But right now I thought I might go by Grandi's store. I have two nephews with birthdays coming up, and I saw some toys there. It won't hurt to deal with the mayor on something other than crime."

"Very true, Riccardo." He glanced at the sky, which was taking on a menacing gray tone. "Enjoy your skiing. And watch out for renegade snowmobiles."

◇◇◇

Rick studied the display in the window of Grandi's shop. In one corner an ornately carved *presepio*, complete with a thatched-roof manger, was surrounded by cows and sheep. Each figure, human and animal, had been painted in meticulous detail. The Montoya family nativity scene was from Naples, known for its religious carvings, but whoever carved this one could compete with the best of the Neapolitans. Rick pushed open the door and entered the shop, going from crisp cold air to the rich, warming smell of wood. The toy section was to the left, and he started walking to it when he heard the familiar deep voice of the mayor.

"Signor Montoya. And where is your assistant?"

Rick ignored Grandi's attempt at humor. "Inspector Albani is working at the station. I am not here regarding the investigation, Signor Grandi, unless there's something new which you need to pass to the inspector."

"No, no. I was hoping you brought some news. Can I help you find something?"

"Birthday gifts for my two nephews in America. One turns nine, the other ten."

"That should be easy. We have a number of toys for that age group." He led the way to the display of wooden cars and trucks. "We have these, or you might be interested in some kits, if they are into working with their hands." He pointed at some boxes stacked on a side shelf. "Or, you could get the two of them one big toy and they could play with it together." He noticed the frown on Rick's face, and added: "I see. That might not work. Separate gifts would be better."

Rick picked up one of the wooden cars and turned it in his hand. It was a Fiat 500, the traditional model rather than the new one. "I am without a car at the moment, Mr. Mayor, since I'm living in the center of Rome, but I'm thinking of buying something for weekends outside the city."

Grandi looked at the model in Rick's hand. "*Un Cinquecento?*"

"No, something larger, for the mountains. I'd like to drive up into the Apennines to hike, as I did in America. Are you happy with your Land Rover? A friend of mine had one and said that the shift is a little bit stiff."

"It does take some getting used to, but I'm fine with it. It's out in back, would you like to try it?"

This was going better than Rick had hoped. "I don't want to put you to any trouble."

"None at all, my assistant can cover the shop."

Though he was wearing a thin sweater, Grandi didn't bother to get a coat or hat, but given his size, he likely didn't feel the cold. As they walked out the door of the shop it hit Rick that if the Land Rover was used to transport the body, the man would not be so quick to show it. Someone could have driven it without the mayor's knowledge, but who would have an extra key? The Land Rover was parked just off the *piazza* in a space marked with the sign SINDACO. One of the perks of being mayor.

"This does not look anything like my friend's Land Rover," Rick said as he eyed the shiny chrome and sleek design. "His was kind of boxy. But a much older model than this one, of course."

"This is three years old, ordered by my predecessor. He should have waited until after the election so I could make the decision. Want to get in?" He opened the driver's side door.

"Sure." The interior was that of a luxury car, its dashboard futuristic, with a screen dominating the space between the front seats. Rick felt like he was sitting in a cockpit. He opened the door and climbed out. "Impressive. Lots of room in the back?"

"You mean the trunk? That's the best part."

Grandi walked behind and pulled a handle, causing half the rear panel to swing up while the other dropped down. Perfect for tailgating, was Rick's first thought. Or transporting bodies. The back seats had been laid flat, and the entire space was covered with a thick, soft blanket.

When he saw Rick studying the blanket, he said: "I often use it to transport my work," then stepped up and slammed the rear doors shut with a thump.

Rick thanked the mayor, made excuses about needing to return to the hotel, and promised to be back to pick out toys for his nephews. As he walked up the hill to the hotel, he thought about what he'd seen. The Land Rover, with four-wheel drive and snow tires, was perfect for transporting a body, no doubt about that. And Grandi was big enough to heave one in and out of it. If there had been any blood stains, the blanket covered them, but they could already have been cleaned anyway. However, the fact that the man had willingly shown off his vehicle should indicate that he had nothing to hide. Unless he merely wanted Rick to *think* he had nothing to hide. Bottom line: not much gained except to confirm that Grandi had the tools to pull off the murder. Add motive and lack of a good alibi, and the man continued to be a prime suspect. But how to prove it? The next logical step would be to get a warrant to search the Land Rover, though he wasn't sure if Luca wanted the political heat that would inevitably come with such scrutiny of the mayor. Rick passed the narrow street that led to the church, and for a moment entertained the idea of dropping in to say a prayer for guidance. It couldn't hurt. Instead, he continued up to the hotel.

Chapter Thirteen

Inspector Albani finished scanning the used car pages and put the copy of *Quattroruote* back on the table in front of him. Muller, he'd decided, subscribed to every Italian car magazine and wrote off the cost by sending the old issues to tables in his hotel lobbies. He checked his watch and looked around. This hotel, unlike the one in Campiglio, was all glass and metal, as modern as one could find in Italy. Curiously, the furniture looked like something out of an English drawing room: dark wood with large amounts of fringe and stuffing. Fortunately it was reasonably comfortable, given that he'd been waiting a long time for Muller to get out of his meeting. If indeed there was a meeting. He was about to reach for another car magazine when Muller appeared and walked quickly toward him. Once again, he was impeccably dressed. Luca started to get to his feet.

"Please stay seated, Inspector. I'll just sit over here." He chose the chair across from the policeman that kept him at the same eye level, despite his diminutive stature. "You've come down to Pinzolo just to see me? Must be something important."

"Actually, Signor Muller, I have something else to deal with in this lovely town, but your wife told me this morning that you would be here, so I thought I would drop by. I was hoping there might be something else you could have remembered that might have a bearing on this case. Or the attack on Pittini." He leaned forward and smiled broadly.

Muller looked at the policeman like he'd been asked the question in a foreign language. "Inspector, I answered all your questions the last time we met, and I thought I'd convinced you that not only do I know nothing about his murder, I barely knew the man himself. Should you not be talking with people who might have had some motive to see Taylor dead?"

Luca was going to bring up the point that Muller did indeed have a motive—to eliminate the funding source for his competitor in the purchase of the property. Instead he decided to follow the thread of the man's question. "And which people would that be?"

Muller took a few moments to answer. "I would imagine that Taylor's private life is the issue, Inspector," he said finally.

"Are you referring to his relationship with Mayor Grandi's former wife?"

"If she was indeed former when—" Muller put one hand over his mouth and held up the other. "I should not make such speculation. How do they say in the court? 'Strike that from the record?' Yes, that's it."

"So you think I should be talking to Grandi."

The shrug motion was shared by most of his small body. "Perhaps it would be better use of your time than talking with me. Or my wife."

It would be expected that Mitzi had called her husband to complain about being questioned, even if the questioners had bought coffee. "What about Pittini's attacker? Any new insights on who that might be?"

Muller may have been pleased to get away from talk of the murder, since his face went from derisive to thoughtful. "Well, I trust you have dropped any ideas that Gaetano was involved. He told me that he answered all your questions, so that should have satisfied any suspicions you may have had. And I can't afford to have my only electrician in prison." He grinned at the last comment, but Luca remained serious and quiet. "No, Inspector, I have no new ideas. You know, of course, that Pittini runs the gondola. Perhaps his attack was connected with Taylor's death. He did fall from the gondola, didn't he?"

Luca ignored the suggestion and rose from his seat. "I should let you get back to your meeting, Signor Muller. And I must be off to my next appointment. If you think of anything, you know where to reach me."

Muller got to his feet. "The American, he's not with you today? Has he left Campiglio?"

"Since he is on a ski holiday, he's doing some skiing this afternoon."

"I'm pleased to hear that."

They shook hands, and Muller watched the policeman walk through the door of the hotel before scuttling to the reception desk and picking up the phone.

◇◇◇

Dark clouds were forming around peaks far to the east, but too distant to be of any concern to the groups of people enjoying nearly perfect snow conditions. Among them were four skiers— one expert, two very competent, and one novice—who had just come off the lift. They stood in pairs. Rick and Cat watched as Flavio, standing close to Lori, gently pushed her body into the correct stance.

"I had a wonderful ski instructor at Vail," Cat said in Rick's ear. "He always just demonstrated himself the way I was supposed to lean on the skis."

"Flavio's a very hands-on kind of guy, Cat. He knows what he's doing."

"I can see that." She looked at the sky, now starting to cloud up. "How many more runs do you think we can get in?"

"It's slow-going with Lori, but we should manage a couple more. You don't mind taking it easy, do you?" He looked at Cat's expression, visible even with her goggles. "Cat?"

"We can take it easy, Rick. It's just that I was looking forward to some real skiing."

"The world can't always revolve around Catherine Taylor."

The comment did not please her. "You sound like my former husband."

He was rescued by his *telefonino*. He hurriedly fumbled with gloves and pocket zippers to fish it out. "I have to take this, Cat." He slid away from the group and opened his phone.

"Montoya."

"Rick, this is Mark Fries. I hope I'm not interrupting something."

Rick looked back at the group and saw that another skier had joined the trio. The man shook hands with Flavio and kissed Cat on the cheek. "No, Mark, not at all. What's up?"

"Well, I looked into that loan, the one that Cam was working on for the real estate developer?"

The new arrival pulled up his sunglasses. It was Bruno Bauer.

"Right. Melograno."

"Correct. The loan file showed Cam's thoroughness, with every *i* dotted and every *t* crossed. He was an excellent banker. He even used our investigator to be sure everything was legit with this Melograno fellow."

"Investigator?"

"Well, in addition to the standard credit checks, we occasionally look into people's backgrounds to be sure everything is on the up and up. Don't spread the word about that, if you don't mind."

"Of course, Mark. Did it turn up anything?"

"Apparently not. There was only the receipt from our investigator for services rendered, so apparently everything was fine. And, in fact, the loan was approved. Cam had signed off on it early last week. So I imagine that he was planning to give the man the good news in person."

Rick kept the phone to his ear while he closed his eyes, trying to understand the significance of the loan approval. To begin with, it shot down the scenario of Melograno going into a homicidal rage when he was told he would not get the loan. What had Taylor and Melograno talked about during their meeting in the developer's office on Thursday? Maybe Taylor just didn't like Melograno—no surprise there—and decided to keep him hanging for a few more days. And before he could give the man the good news, he got murdered. Rick was shaking his head when he looked over to see that Mary and John Smith had joined the group. Perhaps Gina Cortese would be the next to appear.

"But there is something else in the file that I found curious."

Rick returned his attention to the phone call. "What's that?"

"There's a message slip recording that Melograno called the office on Friday. Cam was already up skiing, as you know. The man asked about the loan and Cam's assistant told him it was approved. Shouldn't have done that, of course, but apparently Cam didn't leave any instructions to the contrary and—"

"So Melograno knew on Friday morning that he had the money."

"Yes, he did."

Rick thanked the banker, told him he would let him know if anything broke on the case, and ended the call. He kept the phone gripped in his hand while trying to make sense of what he'd heard, but nothing came. He was about to rejoin the group when he decided he should call Luca.

"Inspector Albani."

"Luca, Riccardo. I just had a call from the banker. Taylor's boss."

"And?"

Rick recounted Mark's message. When he was finished he thought the line had dropped. "Luca, are you there?"

"Yes, Riccardo, I'm still here. Just trying to figure out what this means for the case. Perhaps nothing. Do you recall our first meeting with Melograno on Monday, how he was secretive about his dealings with the bank? He may simply have decided that we didn't have any business knowing about his loan approval."

"Could be. But I would like to ask him about it."

"I would too, Riccardo. Are you still skiing? I can meet you in town in about a half hour."

"I'm still on the mountain, but I'll head down now. I'll see you outside Melograno's office."

As soon as he zipped the phone into his jacket another possibility hit him. If it was what really happened, he thought, then everything falls into place, including a strong motive. He considered calling Luca back, but decided it would be better to think it through a few times on the way down to be sure he had it all straight. Whatever his conclusion, he needed to get down fast.

◇◇◇

After taking Montoya's call, Luca got into the passenger side of the police vehicle waiting for him in front of the hotel and nodded to the driver. As the car moved through the streets of the town he thought about his conversation with Muller and how convenient it would be for the man if the mayor were involved in this crime. His wife's competition for the mayorship would be wiped out, and it wouldn't hurt to have his wife running the town. It was logical that he wanted to push the investigation in Grandi's direction, the only thing better for Muller would be to pull Melograno into the crime.

The policeman's thoughts moved from Muller's motives to his phone call from Riccardo. Did the new information from the bank help in any way at all?

The garage was in a section of Pinzolo designated for businesses necessary to the local economy but better located away from the eyes of the tourists. The plain, cement structure was wedged between a building supply warehouse and a lumberyard, all three sharing the same imposing line of high barbed-wire fencing. The police car drove through the fence gate and parked next to four cars lined up near the door to the building. Two of the cars had inventory tags hanging from their rear-view mirrors and pointed outward. The other two, which Luca guessed belonged to the mechanics, faced toward the building. He unwound himself from the seat, checked out a door marked "office," but walked through the wide opening instead. The temperature seemed to drop as he entered, and he pulled his hat down without thinking.

The garage was one large open space except for a glass-enclosed office to one side where a woman with thick glasses hunched in front of a computer screen. Or perhaps hunched over a space heater. Four bays lined the back wall, all but one with cars up on lifts. The one vehicle at floor level was the only

Mercedes in the shop, a late-model silver SUV, its open hood hiding the head of a man wearing insulated coveralls. He was the only one in the shop. Luca confirmed that the license plate was Melograno's before walking over and tapping on the rear fender of the Mercedes. The man extracted himself, stared at the policeman with a frown, and jerked a thumb toward the office.

"Talk to her to make an appointment."

Luca pulled out his identification. "Inspector Albani. I have a few questions. It won't take long." The mechanic rubbed his hands on a towel that had been covering the side of the car, though they did not appear to be very greasy, confirming what Melograno had said about an electrical problem. "We are investigating some stolen vehicles, including a Mercedes or two."

"Does this look like a chop shop, Inspector? I'm trying to figure out what's wrong with the alternator and I'm running late. But if you want to check it out, go right ahead." He stood back from the car as Luca peered at the VIN and made a flourish of writing the number down on his pad. Then he slowly circled the car, stopping at the rear where he looked at the mechanic and gestured toward the trunk. The man waved his hand, which the policeman took as permission to open it. The inside of the SUV looked like it had just come out of the showroom, or at least recently vacuumed, as the marks in the carpeting indicated. Luca carefully closed the trunk.

"I think I've seen all I need to see, so you can get back to your wiring. Has it been difficult to diagnose?"

"You might say that," the man answered, rubbing the stubble on his chin. "I've been at it since Thursday morning."

Luca had been going through the motions of making notes, but his eyes jerked up from his pad. "Thursday morning?"

The mechanic held up his hands defensively. "Yeah, I know, it should have taken less time, but this one has me stumped. I even got on the phone to Stuttgart. And let me tell you, the owner has been breaking my *coglioni* about it."

Luca wished the man good luck and stepped out into the relative warmth of the open air, pulling out his cell phone as he walked. His driver, who leaned against the car with a cigarette in his hand, called out. "There's no signal here, Inspector." He pointed to the mountain which rose steeply directly behind the building.

Luca walked back into the garage, pulling his coat collar around him, thankful for his warm hat. "Can I use your phone?" he called to the mechanic. The man pointed at a battered telephone in a niche near the door, and returned to his wires. As he dialed, Luca noticed that the woman in the office was still staring at her computer. The call was answered after three rings.

"Agenzia Immobiliare Melograno, how can I help you?"

The young voice sounded vaguely familiar. "This is Inspector Albani. I'd like to speak to Signor Melograno."

"Yes, Inspector, this is Alberto Zoff. I'm afraid he is not in the office at the moment."

Luca remembered that Zoff had tried to be very helpful when questioned about his boss' movements for Saturday, though it hadn't aided the investigation very much. "Is he expected back soon?"

"I think so, sir, but I can't be sure. Things have become very busy in the last few days. Signor Melograno is moving ahead quickly to get verbal commitments for the purchase of apartments in the new building. He's meeting with some possible buyers this afternoon."

"Are you referring to the project for the lot north of the city?"

"That's right, Inspector. And one of the prime apartments, which he had been holding back, is now for sale again."

"Perhaps I might be in the market."

"Really, Inspector?"

"No, Zoff, I was making the *piccolo scherzo*. I'm sure those apartments are outside of a policeman's financial reach." At least an honest policeman, he thought. Perhaps Zoff was thinking the same thing.

"Well, sir, if you know anyone in Trento who might be interested, you can have them contact me. Should I have Signor Melograno call you when he gets in?"

"No, I'll just drop in later." He glanced at the Mercedes. "By the way, Zoff, he told me that his car was in for repairs. How is he getting around?"

"Mostly he walks, Inspector, but I saw him driving a red vehicle."

"He rented a car?"

"I doubt it, sir. More likely is that someone lent it to him. There are many people in this town who owe Signor Melograno favors."

Rick exchanged greetings with the Smiths and Bruno before turning to Cat. "Sorry, but I have to get into town right away, something's come up."

"In the investigation, Rick? Was that the inspector on the phone?"

He looked around and saw that everyone had heard and were looking at him, awaiting an answer. "Let's just say there may be a break, Cat. Flavio, can you see that the ladies get another couple good runs before the end of the day?"

"Of course, Rick. Nothing would give me more pleasure."

"John and I will chaperone them, Rick," said Mary Smith, getting a laugh from all the others except Bauer.

Rick assumed that Bruno's English was not fluent enough to follow most of the exchange, but apparently he'd understood enough. "Riccardo," he said in Italian, "if you are in a hurry, why don't I go down with you? I really must get back to my store and I know a shortcut we can use."

"That would be great, Bruno." They said their good-byes and the group watched as the two skiers gained speed and disappeared over a rise.

"Rick is a very good skier," Lori said. "I've been working so hard to stay on my feet that I hadn't really watched him ski."

"He has come a long way," Flavio said. "You should have seen him before I began helping him out."

John Smith tapped his glove against his chest. "Perhaps you could give me a few pointers, Flavio."

"Well, John, let me look at your technique on the way down."
He looked at the captain's skis. "You certainly have good equipment, so that should help."

"Only the best from Bruno's shop. I love these skis."

Flavio pushed himself closer and checked them out. Suddenly he pulled down his goggles and adjusted the straps on his poles. "Please excuse me, Lori. John, if you would take care of the ladies, I must go."

Flavio ducked his head and began speeding down the slope.

The trail was one Rick had used a few times over the past days to get back to the base of the mountain, at least initially. When the terrain changed from wind-blown openness to forest, Bruno, who had been ahead since they'd left the group, veered to the right, a cloud of snow shooting from the back of his skis. He looked back, waving his ski pole to be sure Rick made the turn. This was the shortcut, marked by a wooded barrier and a sign, which Bruno had deftly skied around. Rick didn't bother reading the sign; he swooshed past it, keeping his eyes on Bruno.

Rick was impressed by the man's skill, but knew from Flavio that all children born in Campiglio had skis put on their feet as soon as they learned to walk. They were taught the languid style that he'd noticed the first time skiing with Flavio north of Santa Fe. It was a more fluid and elegant way of skiing than he'd seen with Americans. Even on snow, the importance of *bella figura* came through.

Dark clouds had slipped over them from the west, and a few flakes of snow showed up against the backdrop of the evergreen trees. They were now on a narrower and somewhat steeper track, so that Rick had to concentrate to avoid going into the trees while still keeping up with Bruno. The section had not been groomed, making it even trickier. As he made his turns he could see a fork in the trail about a hundred meters ahead. At the split he could just make out what looked to be a cliff, but the snow, now helped by wind, blurred his vision. He guessed they would be taking the left fork, the one his bearings told him would be a direct route to Campiglio. They were most of the way to the fork when Bruno swerved to a halt. Rick barely missed him as he skied by and stopped in the middle of the fork. Below him, after a small ledge, was a drop of about a hundred feet.

He looked up to get an indication as to which fork to take, but Bruno was adjusting his bindings. Just as well, Rick needed a few seconds to catch his breath after that last stretch. He leaned on his poles and looked at the precipice below. It reminded him of some of the cliffs he'd maneuvered under Sandia Peak east of Albuquerque, but his climbs and descents were never in the winter when snow and ice made it too dangerous. Out of habit he started to pick out a possible descent route, noting where there was vegetation or rock formations to offer a handhold.

As he peered down, Bruno slammed into him.

The blow caught Rick in the shoulder, causing him to flip toward the edge, landing on his side. Instinctively he rolled onto his stomach and spread out his body, getting as close to the ground as possible. One of his skis had popped off and lay a few feet from his head. The tip of the other, still on his boot, balanced over the ledge. The two ski poles were still looped around his wrists, but one was trapped under his body. He lifted his head and saw Bruno towering above him, his ski pole extending in Rick's direction.

"Jesus, Bruno, you could have killed me." He took his gloved hand out of its pole strap and reached up to grasp the extended lifeline. As he stretched his hand, Rick saw a strange smile on the man's face.

Bauer slapped Rick's arm with the pole and then drove it into his side like a spear. With his free hand, Rick grasped the pole, struggling to force it away from his body, but he felt himself slowly sliding toward the edge. He untangled his other hand from the strap of the pinned pole and raked the snow, hoping for a rock or bush buried underneath that he could grasp to stall his slide. His gloved fingers found a loose stone about the size of a softball. It's a weapon, Rick thought, as he stretched his fingers to grasp it.

Bruno saw what was happening and raised his other ski pole to strike. Rick cringed and braced for the blow, but instead of the pole coming down on his hand, Bruno's body pitched over him toward the cliff. Rick ducked and Bruno's shoulder crashed into the snow just beyond Rick's head. It was Bruno's turn to grasp at anything that would stop his fall, but he found nothing but loose snow and air. His heavy boots and skis pulled him into the abyss.

Rick crawled and slid to the edge and looked down to see Bruno's unconscious body about thirty feet down, caught on a rocky ledge. The position of his legs indicated that something had broken in the fall, but he appeared still to be alive. As Rick watched, a gust of wind drew snow from the rocks and sprinkled it on the man's upturned face. Rick took a deep breath and rolled back over.

"I guess I'm going to owe you big-time for this, Flavio."

"For the rest…of your…life." His friend was gasping after the exertion of his descent. "I won't let you forget it." After a few seconds his breaths came easier. "I thought he might take you down here. We used to ski this trail when I was a kid. When somebody took a dive off this cliff, they blocked it off."

Rick gathered his equipment and got to his feet. "How did you know Bruno was going to try something? I was rushing to get down to talk to Melograno with Luca. I didn't think Bruno was involved in this at all. To begin with, he didn't strike me as having the brains to pull it off."

"And you're right on the mark. It was John Smith's skis that tipped me off."

Rick looked up from examining the small, round tear in his ski coat made by Bruno's pole. "*Non capisco.*"

"Bruno rented John a beautiful pair of Kolmartz skis."

Rick shook his head. How could the guy be so stupid, or greedy, to rent out the dead man's skis? His mind flashed back to the investigation. Didn't Bruno have something of an alibi for the morning of the disappearance? And there was still something strange about Melograno in all this. They looked up to see two blue-clad members of the ski patrol descending the trail toward them.

"They must have seen me turn into this trail," Flavio said, leaning on his poles. "Let me talk to them and then I'll get you down to the hotel. Without any more accidents."

The toe of Rick's cowboy boot disappeared when he stepped out of the hotel door. In the lobby he'd seen the owner's teenage son pulling out a shovel and heard his grousing about fighting a losing battle. The kid was right, but it was a beautiful snowfall, and its powder would make Cat's final run of the day a pleasant one. His boots crunched in the snow as he walked down the hill to the station, past the churchyard, as he ran what just happened through his head. There was the phone call from the banker, after which Rick thought he had everything figured out. Unfortunately Bruno's attempt on his life knocked his theory into a cocked hat. Unable to help himself, Rick tried to think of an easy translation of "knocked into a cocked hat," but was unsuccessful.

At the police station the man at the desk said that Inspector Albani had not returned from Pinzolo, but then Rick remembered that they were to meet at Melograno's office. He thanked the sergeant and stepped back out into the snow. Two minutes later he was on the sidewalk opposite Melograno's building. No sign of Luca. As he began to cross, a Land Rover coming up the street stopped and the driver rolled down the passenger-side window.

"*Salve*, Montoya," the driver called. "Are you looking for Umberto?"

Rick grabbed his hat, which was about to blow off. "Yes, Signor Sindaco. I was on my way to his office."

"Get in," he shouted through the howling wind. "I can't hear you."

Rick opened the door and slipped in next to Grandi. The warmth from the heater hit him in the face and felt good. He returned to a normal voice. "It's getting rough out there. Yes, I'm on my way to Signor Melograno's office."

"He's not there, but I know where he is." He shifted into first gear and the Land Rover started to move up the hill. "I'm heading in that direction."

"But Signor Grandi, I—"

"Nonsense, it's not out of the way." He jerked his thumb toward the back of the SUV. "I was on my way to make some deliveries."

Rick looked back and saw that the rear seat had been laid flat, and the space was covered with carved figures on the same blanket he'd seen that morning. The wooden bears lay shoulder to shoulder, staring at the roof of the vehicle. "I hope you'll find good homes for all of them."

Grandi chuckled. The Land Rover moved steadily up the main street and out of the center of town where the space between the houses began to widen. After they passed under the gondola cables the trees began to line the road, now curving slowly left and right as it climbed. Rick thought about taking out his cell phone and calling Luca, but since it would be impossible to keep Grandi from hearing both sides of any conversation, rejected the idea. Melograno was likely at one of his rental properties, perhaps showing it to a potential client. When Grandi dropped him he could call Luca to tell him where he was. He would wait there until the policeman arrived.

They were approaching a stack of single-story vacation apartments. The mayor told Rick how they had been built during the term of his predecessor, but he was hoping to get more built in the space next to them. Every plot needed to be developed, he said, to help the local economy grow, though the available space was limited by government restrictions. It was a delicate balance between maintaining the mountain's integrity and allowing more construction, but Rick sensed which way Grandi leaned on the issue. They passed under the footbridge that connected mountain trails and ski lifts on the two sides of the road, and climbed past a hotel on the right. Rick remained silent as the mayor talked, thinking that they were on the same road Rick had taken with Luca to visit the old man. He hoped they weren't going all the way to Folgarida now.

They were not. Grandi downshifted, slowing the Land Rover before turning off the road to the right. He engaged the vehicle's four-wheel drive and started through the deep snow, which was getting deeper every minute as the wind swirled the flakes. Rick could make out ahead a Toyota parked in a wide field, facing toward them. Its red color was obscured by the snow accumulating on its roof. A man stood next to it holding down a large roll of paper spread on the hood. As they got closer he saw that it was Melograno. He wore a heavy coat but his head was uncovered, its thick hair flecked with white flakes. He looked up, and upon recognizing Grandi's car, smiled and waved a greeting. As Grandi slowed to a stop, Rick's phone rang.

"Please, take your call," the mayor said as he opened his door. "I have some business to take care of with Umberto." He closed the door and walked to Melograno.

Rick recognized the number. "Luca, I'm very glad you called."

"Where are you, Riccardo? I'm here at Melograno's office and didn't find either of you."

Rick quickly explained what had happened.

"I'll be there as soon as I can," Luca said. "Be careful."

Rick slipped the phone back into his coat and got out of the car. Melograno glared at him through hollow eyes. Rick was not smiling either. He now found himself in the middle of a deserted field with a man who could be involved in a crime. Bruno had, by his attempt on Rick's life, revealed himself as the murderer, but Melograno had to be involved. And having Grandi present, did that help or did it make it worse? There could be three men involved, and two of them were here in the snow with him. He hoped Luca would hurry.

"As I was saying, Umberto, Signor Montoya was looking for you, but I remembered you saying you were coming up here, so I gave him a ride." Grandi looked at the heavy paper Melograno was now rolling up. "Plans for the building?"

Melograno's eyes darted from one man to the other, but eventually rested on Rick. "Yes, the plans. This will finally be built. Nothing will stop it now."

"Your loan request has been approved, Signor Melograno?"

"What difference does it make to you?"

"It could have some bearing on the investigation."

"Investigation?" He spit the word out. "If it hadn't been for you, *Mister* Montoya, there would be no investigation. That buffoon from Trento could not investigate his way out of his own bathroom."

"Umberto," said Grandi in an overly soothing voice, "Signor Montoya has been doing his best to help."

Melograno slammed the roll down on the hood of the Toyota, causing snow to fly into the air and get picked up by the gusting wind. "Signor Montoya has been nothing but trouble. And he continues to be trouble." He walked to the rear door of the Toyota, opened it, and pulled out a long object from the seat. Rick took in a quick breath, but let it out slowly when he saw that it was a cardboard tube. Melograno pushed the rolled paper into the tube and tossed it on the seat. He left the door open and walked back to the front of the car, still staring at Rick, who was now positioned between the two men.

"Are you going to continue meddling, Montoya?"

Rick had to stall for time. He wasn't sure how this scene was going to play out, but wanted to have Luca there when it did. Better to keep the man talking. "I'm sure you want this crime solved as much as anyone, Signor Melograno. After all, Taylor was the person who got you the loan. You owe it to him."

The man's head turned slightly to one side but his eyes stayed on Rick. "So you know that the loan was approved."

"Well, I thought—"

"You see, Elio? He has been pushing his nose into my business." The mayor listened in silence "What kind of a town is Campiglio when some foreigner can snoop into the private affairs of one of its most prominent citizens? And one of your strongest supporters, Elio. Who knows what this so-called investigation could turn up?"

Rick looked at the mayor, whose face showed annoyance but also confusion. Was Grandi wondering which side to take?

Rick asked, "Does Mayor Grandi know what Taylor discovered when he was researching your loan, Signor Melograno?"

Grandi kept his perplexed look, but Melograno's face turned to rage.

"I knew it. I was right not to trust you Americans. Taylor told everything to his sister and now she has told you. Just as I feared." The wind whipped his unkempt hair as he backed up to the open door and reached inside. "You will not stop me now. And Elio does not want to risk his office because of the lies turned up by some nosy investigator."

"Umberto," said Grandi, his voice almost drowned out by the wind. "What does this mean?"

"It means, my friend, that I will have to finish what Bruno could not." He ducked into the backseat again, but this time his hands did not grasp a mailing tube. Instead he held a long, double-barreled shotgun, which he pointed directly at Rick's chest. Rick's eyes ran down the barrel to the top of the wooden stock as his mind flashed back to the three pheasants mounted in Melograno's office. "A lovely firearm, is it not, Signor Montoya? Its stock was lovingly carved and finished by our mayor here, a true artist in wood. I enjoy showing it to people, as Elio knows."

Rick kept his focus on the shotgun, but he could hear the mayor moving at his side.

"Unfortunately," Melograno continued, "it has a tendency to fire by accident. Elio will be able to confirm that too, should it happen now when I am showing it to you. Isn't that right, Elio?"

He glanced at Grandi while Rick's eyes darted between the gun and the man's face. Suddenly Melograno's eyes widened. As Rick's head turned instinctively toward the mayor, a large dark object flashed through the falling snow.

The wooden bear caught Melograno above the right eye with a sickening thud. The blow caused him to drop the shotgun, which disappeared into the snow with a dry thump. In an instant Rick was on his knees, pulling it from the white powder. He looked up to see the huge reeling body of Melograno, his face slowly changing from disbelief to anger. Rick didn't hesitate. He shoved the muzzle of the gun into the man's gut, getting the hoped-for effect. Melograno was doubled over in pain when the carved wooden stock crashed over the back of his head. His expression froze and he crumpled face-first into the snow.

Grandi crunched his way to the body. He stared down at the head wound, its dark blood mixing with the white snow starting to cover it. "Why didn't you shoot him? He was ready to kill you."

"I don't know much about shotguns. I could have hit one of us by accident." Rick noticed for the first time that his breath was forming small clouds of vapor before disappearing into the wind. He took his eyes off the man on the ground and looked at Grandi. "Melograno seemed quite sure you were going to back him when he aimed the gun at me."

The mayor took a heavy breath and let it out slowly. "Any politician needs supporters, Signor Montoya. Usually support comes with some strings attached, that's part of politics anywhere, including America." He kept his eyes on the body of Melograno. "But I would not go that far."

So, Rick thought, you're a sleazy politician, but just not that sleazy. Thank goodness for that. For the first time he loosened his grip on the shotgun. "And where did you learn such accuracy, Signor Sindaco? You were right on target with that bear."

"Years ago there was an ice football league in the region, if you can believe that. I played for the Campiglio team. Quarterback."

"You still have one hell of an arm."

Two police cars plowed to a stop behind them.

"So we both came to the same conclusion, but using slightly different evidence, am I right, Riccardo?"

Rick and Luca sat at opposite ends of the long table in the meeting room that had been the policeman's temporary office since arriving in Campiglio. Luca was again in his shirtsleeves, and had loosened his tie. A pencil turned in the fingers of one of his hands, but his eyes were on Rick.

"That appears to be the case, Luca." He leaned forward and tried to rub the fatigue from his eyes. "You heard from

his employee that Melograno had put one of the choice apartments in the building back on the market and concluded that
it had been held for Taylor. You decided that the bank would
not have allowed Taylor to have a personal interest in the loan,
so something must be amiss."

"Exactly. He was getting the apartment at a lower price, in
exchange for approving the loan."

"And now that Taylor was dead, he could sell it at full price."

The policeman shuffled his papers and held up a page from
the local newspaper. "Which would be about a quarter million
euros."

"Lots of money, but it wouldn't make sense, because if there
was a bribe to get the loan, it would have been paid before the
loan went through. I don't know much about bribes, but I would
assume they are taken up front, not on a promise to pay later"

"Especially when dealing with someone like Melograno."

"Exactly, Luca. There may have been a bribe earlier in the
process, to get the loan, but if a free or cut-rate apartment for
Taylor was in the works, there had to be something else."

"Blackmail."

"Exactly. I think when my banker friend looks deeper into the
loan file, we'll find that the investigator who checked on Melograno found something critical in the man's background. Serious
enough that if made public would have been devastating."

"He said as much before he pulled the gun on you in the
field."

"Yes he did." Rick leaned back in the chair. "So with Taylor
dead, Melograno thinks the blackmail information cannot be
exposed. And as a bonus, he can make more money from the
sale of Taylor's apartment."

Luca nodded. "Melograno lures Taylor up to the field in
Bauer's vehicle to celebrate the deal and bludgeons him to death
with a bottle of prosecco. Then he puts the body in the trunk
and gets Bauer, who owed him money, to dispose of it." The
pencil had moved to his writing hand and he used it to circle
the real estate ad in the newspaper. "It might have worked if

those kids hadn't strayed off the trails. The body could have been there for years."

Rick rubbed the back of his neck, fatigue setting in. "But then Melograno started to wonder if anyone else knew his secrets, and he logically thought of Cat, and by extension me."

"So the avalanche could well have been meant for both of you."

Rick preferred not to think about that.

"So you're done, Luca."

The inspector spread his hands over the papers and files. "Not quite. I have to tie all this up for the public prosecutor." He looked across at Rick. "And we can't forget the attack on Pittini. Which could really have been intended for you."

"Don't start that again, Luca."

"I can't rule it out. It was likely Bauer driving the snow-mobile. He very well could have been after you that night as well."

"If so, he's not a very good assassin with three unsuccessful tries. It's no wonder Melograno opted to take things into his own hands." Rick got to his feet and his eyes moved around the room. "But let's try to solve the stabbing somewhere else, preferably where I can get a coffee." He picked up his coat. "They really have to put a window in this room."

Chapter Fourteen

As the glass door closed behind them, Rick and Luca removed their hats and shook off the snow which had accumulated during the walk from the station. Rick slipped off his gloves and brushed his shoulders where the snow was already melting in the warmth of the bakery. Mitzi burst through the door behind the counter, rubbing her hands on her apron.

"Ah, Inspector Albani. And Signor Montoya. You have had a busy day. What can I get for you?" Her smile was more than normal for welcoming a customer into her shop.

"Word gets around quickly, Signora," Luca said. "A coffee for me, please. Riccardo?"

Rick nodded that he'd have the same. He moved slowly along the glass of the display case, admiring the cakes, cookies, and pastries. The glass shelves were full, and especially colorful, perhaps in preparation for the weekend visitors who would start arriving early the following afternoon.

"Shall we get something to go with the coffee, Riccardo? Perhaps some of Signora Muller's famous almond cookies."

Rick continued to study the gleaming case before looking up. "Huh? Oh, yes, the almond cookies. Absolutely."

Mitzi interrupted her coffee-making to pull a small plate from a stack against the wall, centering a paper napkin on it. As the two men watched, she used plastic tongs to transfer four cookies from their stack under the glass to the plate, then placed it on the counter between the two men. From her face, they knew she was dying to say something, and she finally succumbed.

"Umberto Melograno is not a nice man, but we didn't expect this."

Rick had never studied German, but could recognize *schadenfreude* when he heard it.

He took a bite of one of the cookies and decided that Flavio was right in singing their praises. Would they get stale on the train if he decided to take some back to Rome? He turned his thoughts back to Campiglio. "Are you planning to turn the business over to your son if you win the election, Signora?"

She was taken aback by the question. So was Luca, who looked at the woman's face as they waited for a reply. "Well, I hadn't really thought of it. Most people haven't given me much of a chance to win. But now, with…" She stopped in mid sentence before beginning again. "Vittorio has taken very well to working here, and in the long run I would love for him to take over. His baking skills are more than I could have hoped for with any employee. And I know he's changed." The last comment was directed at the policeman, a clear reference to the boy's earlier brushes with the authorities. "And Vittorio has returned to the faith, I'm proud to say. He goes to the church every day at this time." She pointed to the clock on the wall, as if to prove the boy's piety.

Rick took a second cookie and drained his coffee cup.

The door opened silently and Rick slipped inside, crossing himself as he surveyed the cold interior. It was larger than a typical country chapel but still consisted of one main room with a semicircular apse extended at the far end. The side walls wore a chalky white, except for a few places where the paint had been removed to reveal fragments of old decoration. Rick's eyes were drawn to the apse. Two pairs of stone columns flanked its opening, likely recycled from some ancient Roman building. Despite the dim lighting, the colorful figures on the ribbed ceiling of the apse, perhaps recently restored, showed a vibrancy that contrasted with the drabness of the rest of the church. That was the idea, to have the worshippers kneel in awe at the sight of Christ looking down on them in all his majesty. Rick could make out other figures, saints for sure, likely including San Vigilio himself, who had given his name to the sanctuary. The only furniture in the church, besides the altar, were four rows of rustic wooden pews. In one of them sat Vittorio Muller, head bowed in prayer.

Rick's boots clicked softly on the stone floor. The seated man did not react to the sound, nor did he appear to notice when Rick slipped in next to him. His hands were clasped and he leaned forward, elbows on the back of the next pew. He kept his gaze on the row of robed figures above him, but his eyes were dull, almost lifeless. After they had been sitting together for almost two minutes, the young man slowly turned his head toward Rick.

"You're the American," he finally said. "With the policeman."

"Yes."

Vittorio's tired eyes searched Rick's face, then he slowly nodded and returned his attention to the altar. After a slow sigh, he spoke. "You know, don't you?"

"Yes, Vittorio. And I understand why you did it."

There was no attempt to wipe the tear that crept down his cheek. "Fiametta should not have died." The voice was hoarse and firm. "I'll go, I knew I would have to eventually." He turned around, understanding what was going on. Luca and a uniformed policeman stood in the back of the church, just inside the door. "Not here. It would not be right." He stood, touched his chest to form a cross, and walked to the side door.

Rick turned back and held up a hand to Luca.

When he emerged into the graveyard, the scene was what Rick expected. Heavy snow had begun to cover the smaller headstones on the ground, and the wind was pushing gray drifts against the stone walls. Luca and the other policeman stood back patiently, collars turned up to protect themselves from the icy wind. They watched Vittorio, who knelt in the snow before the girl's grave, one hand touching the photograph on the stone slab before him. After moving his lips silently he rose to his feet, adjusted the plastic flowers in the metal vase, and walked slowly toward the policemen.

Rick began to follow him, but something made him stop and turn his eyes up toward the side of the church. The day was losing light, and the storm was gaining strength, but he could still see them. As they had done for centuries, and would be doing for centuries to come, the skeletons performed their dance of death.

Rick poked through the bread basket and found a piece of crusty *pane rustico*. "I thought that the encounter with Vittorio was going to take away my appetite, but I'm *affamato*. Though I can't stop feeling sorry for the kid."

"So will a judge," said Flavio. "I know Luca is obliged to tell us that people can't just go around stabbing other people, but if there ever was a justification for violence, Vittorio had it. Fiametta, the girl he loves, gets involved with a married man who then gets her pregnant, forces her into an abortion, and abandons her. What man would not want revenge?"

"He will, at the very most, get a minimum sentence," Luca said. "I may not have the highest opinion of my public prosecutor, but she will look at all the aspects of this case." He swirled the wine in his glass. "You are correct, Flavio, we police must frown on stabbing, no matter what the motive. But at least Vittorio had the right man, and it wasn't Riccardo."

"One more attempt on Rick's life wouldn't matter. He's used to it by now."

"If my mother finds out about all this, I *will* have to fear for my life."

"Your uncle will not tell his sister, Riccardo?"

"Fortunately not, Luca." He chewed on the bread without enthusiasm. "How did Bruno get caught up in this?"

"It was the store, Rick," answered Flavio. "Melograno had lent him the money to do the renovations. But business was not good, as everyone in town knew. So my guess is he was having trouble paying off the loan. Umberto was in a perfect position to extract a big favor from the guy. He could have put Bruno out of business if he wanted."

"We did notice that," said Luca. "Not many customers in the place." He saw Flavio looking toward Lori's empty table. "Flavio, your *consolesa* is not dining with you tonight? Is it because you prefer the company of Riccardo and me?"

Rick chuckled. "Hardly, Luca. She is having dinner with Signora Taylor. I invited Cat to join us here at the hotel, but she declined, said she needed to take care of some final details with Lori."

"I don't get it," said Flavio, shaking his head. "Cat Taylor looked for any excuse to avoid spending time with Lori, and now she chooses to have dinner with her."

Luca swished his wine and leaned back in his chair. "Gentlemen, I am reminded of my Aunt Giulia."

Rick and Flavio exchanged glances, and Flavio heaved a sigh.

"Giulia," Luca went on, "is married to my mother's brother, and is the mother of my cousin Federico who is several years younger than I. They live in a small town about two hours south of Rome. I've only been there once. When Federico was growing up, at family events Aunt Giulia never wasted an opportunity to extol the pious virtues of her son. He was going to be a priest, and a smart one too. No doubt about it, he was destined for the priesthood and he would not be just some parish priest. Something in the curia, perhaps even a red hat someday. I remember Federico as being a quiet kid who sat in the corner by himself at family gatherings. I assumed he was pondering the life of saints or preparing future homilies. When he finished the *liceo*, he went off to seminary in Rome."

Rick picked up the wine bottle and refreshed the other two glasses before filling his own.

"*Grazie* Riccardo." Luca took a sip and continued. "Or so we thought he had."

"I think I can see this coming," Flavio said.

Luca held up a hand. "About that time, I was working on a case in the Borgo, near the Vatican, and was in a nightclub trying to track down a shady character. I didn't find the guy, but I did run into my cousin Federico. He was in there with a friend and their two female companions. Let's just say he wasn't trying to convert anyone that night."

"That's a fascinating story, but—"

"The story isn't done, Riccardo. We met for coffee the next morning and he told me that he was glad I'd seen him at the nightclub. It had forced him to come to terms with himself, to stop living a lie. He had dropped out of the seminary and was studying accounting, which was his true calling. That weekend he would go home and tell his parents the truth."

Luca drank some wine while Rick and Flavio watched, sensing that the story was still not finished. They were correct.

"Aunt Giulia has never spoken to me again. At every family gathering since then, whether a wedding, funeral, or christening, she avoids me as if I have some dread disease. She talks to everyone else, but not to me. I've come now to accept it."

Luca spread his hands to indicate he was done. Rick and Flavio looked at each other and then back at the policeman, who was savoring another drink from his glass.

"Don't you see? Signora Taylor is my Aunt Giulia."

"That could be it," Rick finally said. "She didn't like her brother very much, but the one part of him she was able to admire was his business ethics. Then it turns out he was a blackmailing scoundrel, but instead of blaming her brother, she takes it out on you for discovering his sins. She doesn't want to be around you."

Luca hesitated, glancing at Flavio before answering. "Or, Riccardo, she doesn't want to be around *us*. You were as much involved in this investigation as I."

Flavio laughed. "That's great, you find her brother's murderer and that's the thanks you get. But as strange as Luca's aunt story was, it does make a certain sense." He picked up his wineglass. "Let's forget the vagaries of the Taylor family, drink to the successful end of Luca's investigations, and change the subject to what is on the menu."

After the toast, Flavio held the floor, and Rick was glad that he did. The analysis of Cat's behavior rang true. He was the messenger and he was getting the blame.

"This exquisite Valpolicella," Flavio was saying, "from the hills north of Verona, will be the perfect accompaniment to one of the specialty dishes of the Trentino region." He paused for dramatic effect. "*Pizzoccheri*."

At that moment the waitress arrived with a large platter, and with her serving fork and spoon began dishing out a pasta which looked different from anything Rick had ever seen. Had Flavio timed this?

"…made with buckwheat flour, thus the brownish coloring, tossed in butter with, as you can see, a bit of chard, slices of potato, and very importantly, soft *casera* cheese. Look how nicely the cheese has melted. And we shall add some grated cheese to enhance the taste. I prefer *grana padana* on this dish, but this *parmigiano reggiano* will certainly do no harm. It never does."

The girl served the three and departed. Discussion of the investigation or anything else came to a temporary halt as they lifted their forks.

Chapter Fifteen

"You did not see her again?"

Commissario Piero Fontana looked across the starched, white tablecloth over tortoiseshell half-glasses. The glasses, Rick had decided, were a major concession for his uncle, a man who prided himself on cheating Father Time. At first it was only for reading. Now he used them in restaurants, not just for the menu but to better enjoy the visual as well as the gustatory aspects of a good meal. Naturally, his glasses were the height of fashion, which in this case meant traditional. As was his suit this day, a double-breasted charcoal gray to go with an off-white shirt and dark blue print tie.

"She left for Milan the next morning, without saying good-bye, but three days later called from Malpensa. I was on the train back to Rome. My guess is she was in the first-class lounge and had just downed a couple of glasses of prosecco while waiting for her flight."

The policeman looked at his glass. "Prosecco? How ironic."

Rick shook his head. "I never thought of that. Anyway, she thanked me and apologized for the way she'd slipped out of Campiglio. Then what you'd expect: look me up when you're in the States, that kind of thing.

"Without much conviction."

Rick shrugged and took a drink of wine.

"And you didn't invite her to Rome?"

"I did not."

Uncle Piero nodded and rubbed his chin, a sure sign that another question was coming. "Did she drive to Milan? That wouldn't seem like something she would take on, even under normal circumstances."

Rick smiled. "Only you would think of that small detail, Zio. No, her brother's car was actually owned by the bank, and they later sent someone to get it. She was driven back by Daniele Lotti."

"Ah. The landlord of the holiday apartment."

"Ah indeed."

The commissario tilted his head as he looked at his nephew. "Riccardo, you should take up this Taylor woman's invitation to look her up in America. You could visit her and also drop in on someone else you know well. Erica is still there, is she not?" He paused, enjoying himself. "Has it occurred to you that the two of you could run into each other sometime?"

"It's a big country, Zio. I think I'm safe."

The second course appeared. It was a cold day for Rome, so they both had chosen a substantial pasta dish to start, *penne all' arrabbiata.* The spicy tomato sauce was tame by New Mexico standards, but this was Rome, not Albuquerque. For the first time in their collective memory, both men also chose the same dish for their *secondo. Carpaccio* was as far from a thick steak that a diner could go and still have a meat dish: raw beef sliced paper thin, covered by equally thin shreds of *parmigiano reggiano,* and then very lightly drizzled with olive oil. After a second mutual "*buon appetito*," they pushed the meat onto their forks and savored its pure taste. It was a few moments before conversation resumed.

"Your friend Flavio. Does he ever come to Rome? I would like to meet him. Not just to thank him for saving the life of my favorite nephew, but he also sounds like a fine young man."

"He's promised to get to Rome, but I suspect he will be finding more reasons to do business in Milano these days. He and the vice consul hit it off quite well."

They took more bites of the *carpaccio* and sipped the dark *vino rosso*.

"So this man Muller, he will now build his hotel on the fated land?"

"It's up in the air. The sale was made, but with all the publicity, some environmental groups have noticed its location and decided the land should remain in its natural state. Between legal cases and public pressure, they have blocked the construction. Flavio tells me it could be tied up in litigation for years."

"A case held up in the Italian legal system for that long?" the policeman deadpanned. "I would be shocked." He speared some beef with his fork, wrapped it around a sliver of cheese with the help of his knife, and pushed it around the oil. "And about your mayor friend, has the election taken place?"

"He won in a landslide. Taking down a murderer, it appears, never hurts in an election campaign. And his business is booming, thanks to all the news stories. He displays the bear he used on Melograno in a place of honor in his shop window, and he can't carve copies fast enough to meet the demand."

"You didn't get one?"

"No, but I got a couple of wooden cars for Susana's two boys. Pricey but nice."

The commissario smiled. "Nothing is too good for one's nephews. *Il carpaccio*? You enjoyed it?"

Rick's plate was already bare. "Excellent. I must have it again sometime."

His uncle looked at his wineglass as if searching for something in its darkness. "Riccardo, as you know well, I have always regretted that you did not go into police work. You have the mind, and the patience, to become one of the best." He saw that Rick was about to speak and held up his hand, a glint of gold cuff link peeking out from the coat sleeve. "But this time, I was fearful of your safety. I never would have forgiven myself should some harm have come to you."

Rick watched his uncle drain his glass. It was a different side to a man who was always relaxed when around his nephew but now carefully chose his words. Or had he rehearsed them beforehand? The mood passed quickly.

"And now, my dear Riccardo, what is on your calendar? Some visiting monolingual dignitary to accompany around Rome perhaps? Or one of those international seminars?"

"There are a few professional conferences in the north that I may be working. Nothing firm yet."

"Nothing in southern Italy? Your work never seems to send you there."

"With the Mafia and the Camorra? Much too dangerous, Zio."

Author's Note

While the characters and story of this book are completely fictitious, the town of Campiglio is not, though its full name on the map and in Italy tourism books is Madonna di Campiglio. It is one of numerous delightful ski towns scattered around the Italian Alps, but a special one for my family since we spent many pleasant days there. I have tried to portray the town with reasonable accuracy, but for plot logistics have taken some liberties with locations and other specifics. For example, the two-gondola cable system featured in the first chapter was long ago replaced with efficient multiple cars. Also, while the town has a magical main square, the businesses put on it, and on other streets, may not correspond with reality.

The hotel in which the book's characters are lodged is modeled on an establishment that was always our base in Madonna di Campiglio, the Hotel Erika. It is named for its founder, a special woman who passed away too young, but whose work has been carried on by her family. Besides offering a warm and welcoming atmosphere, the Hotel Erika has a menu for its guests that is as good as you will find anywhere in the Dolomites.

One of the delights of traveling around Italy is stumbling on some amazing work of art or architecture not found in the standard guide books. The tenth-century church of San Vigilio, whose frescoes and interior are described on these pages, was one of them for us. Its *Dansa Macabra*, painted in 1539 by Simone Baschenis, is considered a masterpiece, and if you see it in person, or even bring it up on your computer screen, you will agree. (You can see photographs of the church on my website, www. davidpwagnerauthor.com.) Please note, however, that I have taken one major liberty with the church of San Vigilio, in that I moved it to Campiglio from somewhere else. In reality it is located in the town of Pinzolo, about a dozen kilometers down the valley from Madonna di Campiglio, reached by a winding and scenic road.

Trento, where Rick's buddy Flavio lives, is the capital of Trentino-Alto Adige, one of Italy's autonomous regions, where German is an official language with Italian. It is most famous outside of Italy as the site of the Council of Trent which met off and on between 1545 and 1563. Trento is a city worth visiting, not just to see the cathedral where the council took place, but to take in the rest of its medieval historical center, including the ancient Castello del Buonconsiglio, a fascinating museum.

The Dolomites do not draw foreign visitors in the same numbers as other Italian regions, which is unfortunate. It is hard to match the combination of breathtaking alpine scenery, interesting history, and the charm of towns like Madonna di Campiglio which sparkle like gems among the valleys and peaks. And there's also the food, of course.

Besides my wonderful wife, who constantly gave me support and suggestions with this book, I would like to thank my son Max for lending his expertise on heavy machinery, Jeeps, and firearms. I hope I have written accurately. Also a thank you to Roman Rede, who shared his experience as a firefighter to set me straight on the fine art of carrying dead weight. And *tante grazie* to my good friend in Rome, Guido Garavoglia, for checking details about things Italian that may have become fuzzy in my memory. Finally, *un abrazo* with deep gratitude to Bill Oglesby for his help and encouragement throughout the writing process.

To receive a free catalog of Poisoned Pen Press titles, please contact us in one of the following ways:

Phone: 1-800-421-3976
Facsimile: 1-480-949-1707
Email: info@poisonedpenpress.com
Website: www.poisonedpenpress.com

Poisoned Pen Press
6962 E. First Ave. Ste 103
Scottsdale, AZ 85251